How to Grow Feelings like Flowers

Jey Withane

Published by Jey Withane, 2024.

HOW TO GROW FEELINGS LIKE FLOWERS

First edition. December 5, 2024.

Copyright © 2024 Jey Withane.

ISBN: 979-8230405764

Written by Jey Withane.

Table of Contents

To

everyone who has a heart that meows

and is the reason they get up in the morning sometimes.

Chapter One – Find yourself an empty flower bed (don't be sad that it's so empty)

. . . .

This was the first time Mr Hendrikson hit me.

It wasn't his fault.

He had always been one of my favourite clients. Partly because he was one of my first and had stuck with me even as I had stopped working on the streets and started taking the big checks. Partly because his parents had once come from Poland, just like me, and although he spoke an English free of the accent which lay on my own tongue, I found comfort in the few words he would sometimes let slip when he thought no one was listening. He was a good man. Although he was a few centuries old, he knew how to navigate through the dangerously colourful and shiny waves of modern fashion and how to never embarrass me with attempted youth slang. He would hold doors open for me and offer me his arm, he would pull and push my chair to seat me, and he would always order the cab for me the next morning when it was time for him to return to his family. He also never spoke badly of his wife, which many of my clients did - some to impress me, some because their opinions about their wives were the reason why they saw me in the first place – and which I appreciated. Recently, though, he had stopped talking about his wife, and thus, I knew that it wasn't his fault that he hit me.

It had only been a single swing, too, back of hand meeting rouge of cheek, wham! - like the band -, like that, almost suddenly.

Staring at him, I pressed my fingers down on the telephone's plunger, its reaction a dead tooting sound. "Okay," I breathed.

"Okay," he nodded.

"Sorry."

"It's ... okay." He had backed off and averted his gaze, pinching the bridge of his nose. He was red in the face, the fact that he had come running all the way from the bathroom to keep me from calling the room service had left him breathless. I had told him multiple times to go on a diet but he never listened.

I straightened up. "I think it's best if I go now."

His hand dropped, and he looked at me. "What? No. Antoni, this was a mistake. I'm sorry, it won't happen again. Don't–,"

"It's all right, Mr Hendrikson, it was my fault." I insisted, calmly, "I should've listened. But I still think it's best if I jam now. You are not well, and there is no reason to pretend this didn't happen."

Mr Hendrikson was stressed. This wasn't the first time I noticed that something about him had changed. Maybe it was the way his glance would so often jump to the door of whichever restaurant we were in, maybe it was the way he would loosen his cravat whenever he could, breathing heavily, gasping for air, maybe it was the way he would pull me closer after sex and just hold me, silently crying into the skin between my shoulder blades. Something at home wasn't going quite right, and I wasn't going to blame him for lashing out at me. He was just stressed. It wasn't his fault. And yet I stuck to my words.

"I'm going. Would you hand me my trousers, please."

"Don't. Please," he whispered.

I only extended my hand. "My trousers. Or I'll leave this room in my bathrobe, screaming, and you will wish I had called the room service instead after all. Your choice."

I am sure you are all familiar with generic hotel rooms, so just imagine Mr Hendrikson standing in the small passage between the foot of the bed and the wall, thus standing between me and the exit. So when he came even closer again, I couldn't just leave. Instead, I moved backwards against the wall, cocking up my chin in the hope to look more confident.

"Antoni. Antoni, my boy. Please," he urged me, reaching out to grab my shoulders, his face turning redder with every word. No, don't worry, not out of anger, though. On the contrary. Tears were forming in his eyes. Pathetic, really. "Please."

I sighed. "For fuck's sake, Mr Hendrikson, let go of me." I pushed him away and climbed over the bed instead, collecting my clothes and the toys I had left here and there, all while Mr Hendrikson started sobbing. Like white background noise. Or a mosquito. Quite annoying.

Once dressed – more or less and not even counting my shoes yet, which I decided could wait until I was down by the lobby – I wanted to make my way to the exit, but Mr Hendrikson came running – wheezing and stumbling like the walrus he was – to catch me in the narrow corridor before the door.

"Antoni," he sobbed, falling to his knees and clutching my legs. "Antoni, please, stay with me. I beg you. Don't you love me at least a little? Don't you pity your old Mr Hendrikson? It won't ever happen again, I promise." He repeated it, over and over again, weeping now like in an Italian telenovela. I rolled my eyes.

"I warn you, Mr Hendrikson. Let go of me. It's in the fucking contract you fucking signed. If you hit me, I get to take the money and fuck off. So let go of me, or I'll pin your name to the blackboard, and you'll never see me again."

He howled out my name. "Antoni!"

I gently smacked him with a pink dildo.

. . . .

I was rarely outside on the streets that late at night anymore.

Back in Poland, I had gone out to clubs and bars at least twice a week, as most young people do, but finding myself all alone in London and without friends caused me to give this habit up rather soon. Of course, I had attempted to go to all those famous pubs, drinking until my eyes turned blue and making friends with strangers while dancing in the streets like the songs tell you to do, but nothing felt quite as real as it should. It turned out that everything can be romanticised, even London's nightlife. So now I was either at work or asleep during this time of the day when only neon signs and flickering street lights still pretended to be serving the public.

Not that I pitied the fact that I didn't have to walk the streets anymore.

I did not live in a particularly kind neighbourhood. My apartment wasn't in a pretty house with a garden, or a penthouse, or even in a small-yet-romantic-under-the-roof situation. It was on the eleventh floor of one of those grey, square buildings that had shot out of the ground after the war, as though the city had had an erection at the prospect of not being bombed down anymore. You know, the ones that had meant to give entire families shelter and safety but were now riddled with criminality and disease-infected syringes. Even drug dealers preferred not to work here.

The small mile I had to walk from the bus station to my building always made me think of reconsidering my New Year's resolutions and working out again. Because even with the shoulder pads in my jacket, no one would ever look at the twig of a person I was and think: Oh, look at him, he sure looks hard to mug. Especially not when I didn't have time to change and was still wearing glistening plateau shoes, shiny plastic trousers and a wig that even Tina Turner would find a little too massive. I sighed. Luckily for me, I had long stopped being scared for my own life.

My hand drove into the wig and tore it off; it had started raining, and I could not have it getting wet. Letting it disappear into my bag, I drew my jacket over my head and cursed Mr Hendrikson for hitting me. Everything would've been so much easier if we could've just fucked and slept and taken the cab the next morning in broad daylight like we usually did. Stupid rain. Stupid Mr Hendrikson.

Stupid Mrs Hendrikson for stressing her husband. Stupid England and its shitty weather. Stupid-...

"Huh. Hello?"

A person was standing in front of the building.

Their face was turned towards the pouring sky, their arms extended to the sides. They were swaying, slowly, softly as though dancing to a blues song only they could hear, and perhaps, if it had been a little less dark, I would have seen the peaceful smile on their lips. Unfortunately, upon hearing my voice, they startled. Their eyes shot towards me. Their body tensed.

I stared back at them, taken aback by their existence as much as by their undeniable yet foreign and almost inexplicable beauty. "Hi." I breathed.

"What is it?" they asked. Their voice was surprisingly low and sturdy for their elegant, almost delicate body frame.

"I, um–..." What had they been doing? Who were they? Not that I knew everyone in my neighbourhood, far from it, but there was something almost inhumane, something extraterrestrial about their appearance, about their long, black clothes, about their slim, fairy-like build, about the sharpness of their facial features. I blinked. What had they been asking? "Oh. Um, hi. I live here." I said, mildly distracted now by the way they took in the sight of me, the way their head moved along with their eyes, like a cat would do it, and the way the rest of them was completely still. No swaying still. And no answer. I cleared my throat. "D'you need help? Did you lock yourself out or something?"

Their gaze moved back to my face. Then away. What it was now directed at, I could not fathom.

"Wait," I said, smiling hastily to reassure them that I could help, and taking a step closer towards the building, I started rummaging through my bag. "Wait, wait, wait, give me a second, let me find my–,"

Keys. The person was holding up theirs. Their expression was perfectly blank; no amusement or mockery about having guessed what I was looking for was to be found in it.

"Oh." I cleared my throat. "Um." I motioned towards them and their keys. Their hands were covered in white bandages. "Shibby. Good. Um. Well. Then, uh." It felt incredibly difficult to grasp proper thoughts right now. "Mind opening me?"

Silence. Their eyes were still directed at the darkness around us. Had they heard me? Were they waiting for something? I did not dare move. Eventually, though, they nodded.

"Thanks." I breathed as they went to open the door for me. "Are you sure you want to stay in the rain?"

"I'm not made of sugar," they replied in a mumble.

"I wouldn't have been able to guess." To be fair, I didn't try to be sarcastic, just flirtatious, but somehow, my voice had failed me, and I had spoken it with such sincere solemnity that you'd think I had just confessed a truth to my local priest.

But the person hardly even reacted to what I said, merely raised a single eyebrow, which might have just as well been meant for the door they were busy unlocking.

I felt my breath hitching. No, of course. Such an old joke, saying someone was as sweet as sugar, why would they laugh at that? What an embarrassment I was, gosh. I took a breath, but instead of simply mocking myself for having made such a joke – a cheap joke which, by the way, I had already made many, many times so you'd think it would roll smoothly off my lips – I gibbered out the most tremendous and non-explanatory line of babbled vocals I had ever witnessed: "I mean sweet because-, because rain is like water so sugar is-, ah, hng. I–, What–, I meant to say is-, falignsk-, uh. Hm." What? What the fuck had that been? I stared at them, hoping for a reaction. A laugh. A smile. A bloody glance which would at least tell me they didn't think me completely crazy! But no. They did not look at me. Maybe for the better, because I was turning bright pink, I could feel it on my cheeks, and with my last breath, I pushed out: "Just insert a pun with sweet, for fuck's sake!"

A pause. The hand the person had on the door handle stilled. More silence. Then they blinked, pursed their lips, and glanced at me.

I almost lost my balance.

A moment later, their expression was blank again, and they shook their head, looking back into the darkness. "Insert a pun with thank you, then."

Oh. My lips parted. But not even I was sure anymore if I wanted to say something or if I just needed air. And before I could analyse myself further, they pushed the door open. So I stepped through it. I felt strangely heavy, and I was sure the blush was still vivid on my cheeks.

When the door was slowly falling closed behind me, and I had already hit the button for the elevator, I turned back around. "Hey?"

Through the ajar door, I could see how they turned their head. I only saw their profile and their gaze fixed on something outside, but it was enough to see how, once again, a single eyebrow was raised. "You sure everything's all right?" I asked. Perhaps they had been beaten up at home or something. They looked young. Younger than me. And even if they had avoided looking at me as I had pushed myself past them, and I was almost certain that they had flinched away when our arms had brushed against each other, I was not going to let a kid stand in the rain only because it had abusive parents at home. "You sure you don't want to come in, too? That piss weather isn't going to get any better soon, you know." I continued, even without receiving a reaction, leaning to the side to keep my eyes on theirs as the door slowly continued swinging closed. "I mean, I've got no food at home, but a shower and a couch, it's definitely enough for a night, so if you want–,"

The door fell closed.

. . . .

"Honey?"

"Yes?"

"Can I take the bubbly wine too?"

A pause. "The champagne?!" Airy laughter. "But we're having pizza!"

I took the champagne out of the fridge anyway, bringing it back to the living room. "No one says you can't have pizza and some class at the same time." I smiled, leaning against the door frame with my shoulder and trying to pop the bottle open while Liza Minnelli answered me with her beautiful: Maybe This Time.

Meanwhile, Lenny, who was seated on the couch, fought with the pizza, which apparently had a quite stubborn crust and refused to yield to his knife and weak arms. Consequently, when the champagne popped, my "Ah," of wonder, was an "Ah!" of surprise pain for him.

"Oh, honey." I sighed and walked over to him. "Give me your hand, let me see."

"It's nothing," he stammered, holding out his hand anyway and looking in the far opposite direction. It was indeed nothing, hardly even bleeding, but I knew Lenny, and I knew his pain tolerance, so I brought his finger to my mouth and gave it a little kiss.

I adored Lenny. His real name was Leonard Rudolf Maria Kensington III, but he would flinch hearing this name, and I knew it was because he shared it with his father. A man who, albeit blessing his son with an allowance of many hundreds of pounds a month, did not have much kindness left for him. I was well aware that I was playing his late mother's replacement most of the time. But honestly? Spreading a bit of kindness here and there had never hurt anybody.

And if you squint your eyes, the difference between a finger and a dick isn't that big either.

"Better?" I asked.

Lenny had turned pink and nodded, his blond curls jumping up and down frantically.

"Good. So, what are we listening to tonight? Except *Cabaret*. For the seventh time this month. Boy, how do you even deal?"

Lenny shrugged shyly. "Do you mind?"

"No." I laughed. "Everything that makes you happy makes me happy, too." And while, yes, this was a work phrase of mine, I genuinely meant it. Albeit being ridden with anxiety so bad that it had taken him six months to get a real full sentence out in my presence, Lenny was a sweet young man. He did not leave his apartment much, worked from his desk – that wasn't pushed against a window but a wall because he had once watched a bird crash against his bedroom window and it had traumatised him à vie – and spent all his money on new music records. Most of them were musicals to which we would then listen, arm in arm, head against head, sometimes lying, sometimes sitting, sometimes dancing.

"I do have the Footloose album now, though. If you want?" He sounded timid about his suggestion.

"I'd love to. But don't stress about *Cabaret*. Let's listen to the end while we have our pizza, yes?"

"Yes. And the–, the bubbly wine."

I laughed.

The best thing about this meal really was the champagne, but even if I had never quite gotten around to loving what they called fast food here, I ate the pizza with great pleasure. After all, I hadn't eaten anything since Mr Hendrikson and I had left the restaurant last night. Lenny must've noticed how hungry I had been by the way I slung down the food, because when there was nothing left on our porcelain plates but a single piece of crust, he asked if I was satisfied now.

"Satisfied's not the word I'd go with, but, yes, thank you, I feel much better."

Lenny chuckled airily, reaching out for the plates to busy himself with stacking them and making sure no forks and knives escaped from his clumsy hands. "You're always so vulgar."

I took all of it from him and stood up to bring it back to the kitchen. "Oh, shush, I know you like it."

He glanced at me, and I managed to catch his eyes. They were a beautiful set of bright blue eyes, which unfortunately rarely ever stayed still. Ceaselessly they were always jumping from one spot to the next, chasing noises that came from outside those walls, hunting long-faded memories and searching for thoughts that perhaps should not exist in the first place. Today he held my gaze for almost five seconds, before turning away, flustered.

"C'mon," I smirked, "save all this blushing for other parts of your body, yes?"

"Can we not?" he asked, a little too hastily, a little too loudly, a little too urgently to make it sound anything but panicked.

I frowned, tilting my head to the side as I waited for an explanation.

"Tonight?" was what I got. "Can we not ... tonight? Please?"

I blinked. And this little request had taken up so much courage? A fond chuckle escaped me. "Oh, honey." I set the plates back down on the couch table and reached out to take his face into my hands. "You know that you don't have to ask me that."

He avoided my eyes now.

My fingers moved under his chin, but not to make him look at me. What was the point of forcing him? "Yes," I whispered, simply pressing a kiss to his forehead instead, "yes, we can not tonight."

HOW TO GROW FEELINGS LIKE FLOWERS

His always-fumbling hands let go of each other to find their way to me, to my shirt, to my back, holding me as he slowly buried his face into my stomach.

I remembered when George Langston had first talked about him to me. 'He's an odd one, ' he had said, and because my English had still been very broken then, I had asked what 'odd' meant. 'A weird one, y'know?' had been the answer. 'Someone who's not normal in his head, can't really talk and act like a man, is a bit brain-dead, get what I mean?'. I had laughed back then, and wondered why a crazy-rich father would hire his brain-dead son someone to fuck. I had wondered this for six and a half months whenever I was ordered into his apartment, and then, one day, out of boredom, I had asked Lenny about the huge shelves of records in his living room, and his eyes had lit up. What had been a dull and never quite catchable grey-blue had suddenly turned into the oceans of Greece and the Summer sky over Prague. For the first time, I saw him come alive. Words flooded me like waterfalls as his hands danced so vividly through the air that even the Bolshoi ballerinas would have been jealous of it. Record after record, he picked his favourite songs and showed me the scenes and lines he loved them for, hour after hour, he dared to smile and joke more and more, and day after day, it would take him less and less time to warm up to me. So much so that one day, at the end of our first year together, my phone rang, and when I picked up, it was neither George Langston nor Leonard Rudolf Maria Kensington II, but Lenny himself. Asking if I wanted to see *The Little Shop of Horrors* with him in the West End.

"I'm sorry, he mumbled into my shirt.

"It's all right," I replied because I had long learned that sometimes, telling someone that there was nothing to apologise for did not mean that to them there was no reason to do it anyway. "Can you help me out of my trousers anyway, please?"

There was a moment of silence, then Lenny nodded and pulled back. In his eyes, I saw tears glistening and wondered if I would have cried with him now if I hadn't forgotten how to. My fingers played with his golden locks while he worked the buttons of my jeans open, slipped under their hem, pushed it down. A laugh was to be heard. "What is that?!" he exclaimed, loudly.

"My underwear, of course." I grinned.

"There's a giant cat eye looking at me!"

"Well, yeah! It's the *Eye of the Tiger*. Rawr."

Seeing my playful feline-claw-gesture, Lenny burst into laughter, hiding his face behind his hands. I felt terribly proud that my plan had worked out so well.

After taking off my trousers properly, I went to find the record Lenny had spoken of before dinner and put it on, apologising to Joel Grey for interrupting him so brusquely. Footloose started playing, and – after startling at the sudden volume – I turned back around and brought the pizza plates to the kitchen. When I returned, Lenny was promptly giggling again when he saw the eye-of-the-tiger slip coming towards him.

"I'm glad the sight of my cock brings you so much joy today," I smirked and tackled him down onto the couch. Between me singing the song and my fingers viciously attacking his sides, Lenny was quickly reduced to giggles. Especially the 'rising up' line got to him.

Squeaking with struggle and laughter, he yelped: "Help, someone help me, I'm being sung to by a horrible singer!"

It went on like this until we were a few songs into the Footloose soundtrack, and we had exhausted all puns there were to make about tigers and eyes and things rising. By then, Lenny was the one lying on me, having caught and defeated my treacherous hands, and his head lay on the couch next to mine, so close that his blond curls were falling into my face. I could feel his heavy breath moving his chest against mine, and I wondered if he was doing it on purpose so that it fit the beat of the currently playing song. His eyes were closed, his lips slightly parted, and the beautiful pink hue on his cheeks spoke of the few moments of unrestrained fun his mind had allowed himself to have for once. He looked exhausted and yet more handsome than ever. Carefully, I freed my hand from his slumber-loosened grip and moved it to his back, running my fingers up and down his spine in a gentle caress.

I had almost fallen asleep, too, when Lenny let out a little sigh and shifted in my arms. He rolled off me and down onto the couch between the fluffy backrest and me. I let him do so and then carefully turned, wrapping myself around him, partly because I knew he liked that, partly because the couch was long but not wide, and I really didn't want to fall down from it. I kept right; as soon as everyone was settled, Lenny let out another little sigh of happiness, wiggled his butt against me to close the distance between our bodies, then searched for my hand, linking our fingers when he found it. Imagine if all you needed to be perfectly content was a pair of arms holding you when you sleep. Imagine how simple life could be. I nuzzled his hair, smiling, because at least for Lenny, this was his reality.

. . . .

The next time I woke up, the night had left us, yet the day was not quite there, either. Unfriendly, cold and grey light came in through the windows, making the room look far bigger than it did at night. The lamps we had turned on last night were still burning, and I really, really, really needed to pee.

I tried to be quiet as I got up, but when I came back from the bathroom, Lenny had turned around, watching me with a drowsy smile on his lips. I smiled back and winked at him, emptying my champagne glass from last night.

"What time is it?"

"4 or 5 o'clock, I think."

His glance jumped to the great window, to the desk with the record player, to me, to the champagne, down to the slip with the cat eye on it, then back to me. "Do you have to leave already?"

"Not if you will still have me for a bit."

He shyly opened his arms, and I willingly settled into them, lying down with my back against his stomach. His hand went all around me until his fingers could tuck themselves between the side of my chest and the couch. That was how close he wanted to have me. I smiled.

"Hey, honey?"

"Hmm?"

"Why was there bubbly wine in the fridge?" Lenny usually never had alcohol at home, one of the reasons why I had been so eager to pop the champagne yesterday. And now that the taste was lingering on my lips again, I remembered why everyone was so after it. "Did you buy it? You know that if you want to drown your sorrows in alcohol, there are far cheaper ways, right?"

Silence.

"Lenny?"

He shook his head, I could feel his nose brushing against the back of my neck. "I know, yes."

"So?"

More silence.

"I mean you don't have to answer me, but–,"

"It was my birthday."

This time, it was I who fell silent.

"Yesterday. It was my birthday yesterday; my father was here and brought me cake and champagne."

"Oh." I hadn't known. Not that I was ever informed about my clients' lives in detail like that, although usually when I knew about someone's birthday it was because I was specially booked for the occasion, but somehow I was surprised Lenny hadn't told me. "Happy belated birthday ,then, honey."

"Thank you." He did not sound thankful, and I turned my head to look at him, but because he held me so closely, I could hardly even see his face.

Carefully, I thus attempted a joke. "And you ate the whole cake by yourself? Without me?"

"I lied."

"You ... lied about the cake?"

"No. I lied about my father being here. It's not true. He sent it all via mail, so I took the champagne and told the postman to have fun with the cake."

I blinked. "Wow." That didn't sound much like him if I were being honest, and yet I found myself believing this story. When it came to his father, Lenny was a different person sometimes. "You must've been m-,"

"He didn't even call. I bet he forgot. I bet it was his secretary who sent it to me." Some people push others away when they are angry or hurt. Lenny only pulled me closer, as though trying to disappear in the warmth beneath my shirt.

I gave up trying to look into his face and instead brushed my fingers over his arm. "It's okay," I whispered, trying to comfort him, "you don't need him. He already did his job. He planted you in the earth, and now you're growing all by yourself. You should be proud of yourself for making it through another year without him. Only strong flowers get this far without their gardeners."

Lenny did not reply to this once again, but his silence felt softer now. His lips moved against the back of my neck, yet not in soundless words. Kisses. Very soft ones, plenty of them, timidly and clumsily placed to my skin, slow and few at first, then more and more.

Feeling warmth spreading through me, I closed my eyes. "I'll write this day down on my calendar, and next year, I'll be here," I promised in a whisper when Lenny's hand emerged from underneath me and started wandering across my torso. "I'll bring you champagne and cake myself, and we'll have a party together. All right?"

"All right," he breathed, and for a moment, the kisses paused. "Antoni?"

"Yes?"

"Remember when I asked if we could not do it tonight?"

"Of course?" It felt a little unfair to be reminded of it right after having been teased with kisses, but if the promise of no sex still stood, I was not going to insist.

However, as it turned out, Lenny was going in a totally different direction. "Can we? Maybe? Please?"

"Please." I nodded and looked over my shoulder at him, but before I could say more, lips were crashing onto mine, surprisingly hungry in their motions, considering that we had had a whole pizza only a few hours ago. My hand found his, and together, they slid behind the eye of the tiger.

• • • •

When the great churches of London rang at noon, I was bidding Lenny goodbye. He was wearing the slip now, but apart from that, nothing else, and if I hadn't been so terribly selfish and man-body-lusting, I would've probably told him that I was worried he'd catch a cold like this.

"There is a party, you know," he said as I was putting on my shoes. "On Friday, in two weeks." He looked shy telling me this, and the fact that I frowned with confusion didn't help. "For–, for my birthday? You said–, You said next year you'd give a party for me. There–, I'm just saying that–, that there is going to be a party. For me. By me. With colleagues from work and, uh, friends. Here."

"Ah. Oh. Well." I smiled. "How nice. Good on you, honey. I hope you enjoy yourself."

Lenny scrunched up his nose. "Would you like to come?"

If this had been any other client, I would've taken it as a joke and laughed it off. But this was Lenny, and his face was red and his fingers fumbling so nervously now that I feared he would accidentally break them any second. So I was very careful when I replied: "I would love to. But you know your father. If he hears about me being there, he'll-... He wouldn't appreciate that."

Lenny nodded, hastily. "No. Right. What was I thinking? I know, I know." He even tried a laugh, but the sound was so dead that even I felt something like sadness upon hearing it.

I sighed. "Oh, honey." I closed the distance between us and cupped his face, this time with the intent to have him look at me. "Let me see your beautiful eyes. Can you see mine too? Can you see that they're not lying when I say that I'd be there for the party if it were only a matter between the two of us? Can you see that I'm being absolutely honest when I say that I enjoyed our date today? Can you see that I really, really like you and that I really, really believe you'll have lots of fun at the party without me?"

His fingers were curling into the front of my raincoat, helplessly holding on. I could see his lips forming a: 'How?', but he never voiced it. Instead, he pursed his lips and nodded.

I kissed him. "You can call me after the party if you want. I'll stay close to my phone. All right?"

He nodded.

"How old did you turn, anyway?"

"Twenty-one," he smiled, shyly.

"Such a baby you are."

He chuckled with me, even if there was a pout on his lips. I kissed them again. The pout was still there. Another kiss. Pout still there.

Another two kisses. A smile. "Why?" he laughed a bit, "How old are you?"

"Twenty-three next month."

He chuckled a little louder. "You're dumb. Calling me a baby."

"Hey, have you checked yourself in the mirror recently? No one's more babe than you are." I kissed his lips a last time, letting it linger, then pulled back. "I'll see you next week, then? Same time, same place?"

He nodded again.

He watched me leave down the corridor for so long that even as I reached the very end of it and was about to turn the corner, he had still not closed the door.

. . . .

"Minush!" I called into my apartment, "Minush, *my love, I'm home.*"

Minush came hobbling over to me, the bell around her neck tinkling joyfully. Before I could even fully close the door, she was purring and rubbing herself against my legs.

"Yes, *my love,* I missed you, too." I crouched down and ruffled her fur. "You'll have to bear with me, though, I didn't buy us food yet. I need to shower and change first, you know how people are. They see someone like me at night, and they hoot at me. They see me in broad daylight and think their society is under attack."

Minush did not seem to mind.

"*Good, good.*" I got up and brought my bag to the couch, then went to open the window. My apartment was about as big as Lenny's living room, the kitchen was the bedroom was the living room was the entrance hall, all stuffed into a single room with a single window offering air when you needed it. I was pretty sure someone had once died here, and they had never bothered to fully clean the place out because whenever you left the window closed for longer than a day, it would start smelling like rotten flesh.

HOW TO GROW FEELINGS LIKE FLOWERS

The bathroom – crammed into 2x2m² – was the only part of the apartment that was separated by a door, which, to be honest, I considered a masterpiece and a prime example of architectural failure; the door opened to the inside. Now try opening a one-metre wide door in a two-metre wide room when half of that room was shower-toilet-sink. Stupid. Just saying. Also, the light was broken, but that was my own fault and not really a problem. I didn't need to see myself while showering, and at least it kept me from re-enacting dramatic staring-into-the-bathroom-mirror scenes from those movies that used far too much meaningful colour coding. You know which ones.

Once showered, not smelling like Lenny anymore, and dressed in what the fashion industry had optimistically named 'tracksuit' but which I was more realistic about and called 'pyjama', I fell down on my couch with a long sigh. Minush chirped at me and came to settle down on my chest, immediately starting to knead my neck. "Are you baking bread, *my love*?"

She blinked at me.

"Or is that your way of telling me I should go buy bread?"

Another slow blink.

"All right, all right, no need to pressure me." But I didn't move. Instead, I reached behind me and searched my bag for the white envelope Lenny had given me. My clients usually gave it to me at the beginning of our dates, because I found it ruined the mood to be given it at the end. However, Lenny was the only client whose envelopes I didn't check before entering his place. I trusted him. And today, it proved right to do so. "Fucking hell, Minush. He gave me 50 pounds more than the contract says." I took out the 350 pounds and stared at them. That was a huge sum of money. My fingers ran over the big notes, then picked out the five smaller 10-pound bills. "*Looks like we're going to feast tonight, my love.*"

Minush rubbed her head against the money, and I chuckled, putting the big bills back into the envelope.

In the store, I stood in front of the cat food for about twenty minutes. For myself, I had only gotten a few cans of ravioli and a bottle of orange juice. I decided that should be enough for the next two weeks and that Minush needed some quality food much more than I did anyway. However, how do you buy quality food if you don't actually plan on eating any of the choices before you? How could I be sure that the expensive stuff was what Minush preferred? So I stood there, tapping my lips and rolling from my heels to the balls of my feet, back and forth, back and forth, trying to decide.

"But Moooooooooom," a kid's cry jolted me out of my thoughts.

"Shh, I already bought you chewing gum yesterday, I told you not to eat it all at once." the mother hissed back and as I turned around and caught her eyes, she gave me an apologetic look. Her hair was completely tousled out of her ponytail, her tights had a massive rip in them, and sweat was glistening on her forehead.

"But Mom, pleeeaaaase! Just one!"

"Now, will you stop screaming?" Her grip was firm on her son's arm, tugging on it as she dragged him to the next aisle. For a long moment, I looked at where they had been standing, wondering why parents brought their kids to go shopping in the first place if it was so stressful. But then again, I also usually wondered why people generally brought kids into their lives. That already seemed unnecessarily stressful. I sighed and shook my head, grabbed about two dozen cans of cat food and then made my way to the checkout.

Something I missed about my hometown was that everyone knew each other. When you stood in line at the supermarket, you could converse and joke and pass the time rather than counting the number of items the person before you had put on the counter. Though then again, you also stood in line for a much longer time because the cashier would ask every single individual about their day, their husband, their pets, their job, and possibly their neighbours too. Going shopping used to be a whole day-consuming adventure, and back then it would annoy me that you had to go through several interviews and the entire town's gossip before being allowed to bring your milk home to have your cereals, but now, as I stood in the line and counted – 7 items: chips, carrots, flour, sugar, kale, orange juice and spinach – I longed for the familiarity and slowness of a small town's daily life.

"Sir?"

I blinked. "Oh. I'm sorry. What did you say?"

"That makes 18 pounds and 70 pence, Sir."

"Right. Yes. Sorry." I dug my hands into my jeans pockets and drew out two of the 10-pound notes. I hesitated. I looked over my shoulder at the mother with her son, who had stopped crying but was now red in the face and sulked with his arms crossed. One of her hands was on his head in something that looked like a loving attempt to make him feel better, the other was holding her basket. There was not much in it, and yet she seemed barely to have the strength to lift it properly.

"Sir?" the cashier asked me again.

"Yes, sorry. Can you also give me three of your chewing gums there?"

"Sure." He handed them to me, but I shook my head.

"Give them to the lady with the child over there, yes? When it's their turn."

The cashier blinked, then hastily nodded. "Of–, of course. Yes, Sir, if you wish. Is that all?"

"Yes, thank you." I gave him the 20 pounds and then stuffed everything into my bag, not looking back.

. . . .

"Antoniii…" the door to my building sighed when I pushed it open.

"Hello, Door."

"Hiii."

With a foot, I held it open as I fumbled with my keys to search for the one that would open my letter box. "They still haven't fixed your hinges, huh?"

"Nooo." the door sighed as I took my foot away.

"Well, don't worry, Door. I'm sure they haven't forgotten about you."

"Thank yooouu." It was still slowly falling closed, and before it clicked shut, it snapped out a last: "Look up."

Confused, I frowned – I had received no letters whatsoever, as always – and did as it told me to do. "Looking up? Looking up where?" My gaze went up, and I startled.

There stood that person from last night again. Motionless, their eyes fixed on me, only one doubtful eyebrow raised. So I had not been hallucinating; their eyes really were pitch black, like holes into which you'd fall if you looked at them for too long.

Was it not good, then, that they tore their gaze away so soon?

"I'm not crazy." I spluttered, lifting a finger, "I'm–, I'm not crazy. I was just kidding, I wasn't really talking to the door. I swear."

The person lifted their other eyebrow, their eyes on the keys in my hand.

"I–, I mean, why would I do that, right? Ha. Just fooling around. Silly me. Ha-ha!"

It did not show whether they believed me or not, nor did it show whether they were amused or confused. They seemed to be taking everything in without judging it, and yet looking as though they judged it more than enough. "Right," they said, eventually, and continued down the last flight of stairs to the exit.

The daylight made the blackness of their leather jacket shimmer blue and gave their lips a delicate pink colour, and as they passed me, a scent of eucalyptus met me. I smiled without knowing why.

Their entire appearance spoke of a well-polished shell, which held something crumbling, breaking and dying captive within itself, and yet they carried themselves with that certain kind of toughness which only existed to hide something beautiful. How could they be full if their expression was so terribly blank? Even their gaze seemed empty.

"Oh." Their gaze. They were looking at me. I almost gasped.

"What is it?" they asked, over their shoulder, obviously puzzled about why I was looking at them for so long.

I quickly averted my gaze, only to find something very odd: They wore no shoes. "Aren't you going to be cold?" I asked, surprised.

Their hand was already on the door handle as they paused. Their gaze wandered down to their bare feet. With a completely blank face, they took in this information, then looked back up at me. "Yes." they answered, toneless, and then left.

"Bye, Leeeeev," the door sighed as it fell closed.

• • • •

Upstairs, I told Minush about the incident as I put the contents of two cans of cat food onto a plate for her and the contents of two cans of ravioli onto a plate for me. If you squinted your eyes, it looked a bit like we were sharing a meal.

"Anyway. I think their name is Lev, or Leev, or something like that. It's a weird name, but why would Door lie, right?"

Minush did not reply; she was busy feasting. Then again, she was a cat, so what would she have answered?

My phone rang.

"No."

It rang again.

"Nooo."

It rang again, more angrily.

"Come ooon, I just sat down for lunch." For a moment, I thought it had given up. But it hadn't. So I got up from the kitchen floor and lazily shuffled into the hallway. "Yes, hello?" I asked.

A gasp, a click, and from inside the phone, it tooted at me.

I groaned, hung up, and went back to Minush, sitting down with her again. "So what was I saying? Ah, yes. I think that even if Lev, or Leev, is a weird name, Door has no reason to–..."

The phone rang again.

"Oh fuck off you fucking devil box! I'm not getting up, fuck you, no!"

Minush looked at me with wide eyes. I shrugged.

"Sorry. No cursing during lunch, I know, I know. But still. Do they always have to call during lunchtime?"

The phone rang and rang and rang, and then there was a click, and the answering machine took over. "Hello, Antoni, my dear." It was my mother. "*I've been trying to reach you for three days now. Could you call back soon, please?*" I let out a gasp, jumped to my feet and ran back to the phone. "*I miss your v–,*"

"*Mama?*"

"*Antoni! I thought I had missed you again.*"

"*Hello, Mama. No, no, I'm here. I've got a day off work today.*"

"*Today?*"

"*Yes. I was just–... I was just cooking.*"

"*Ah, are you eating well, my son?*"

"*Yes, I'm making sure to eat.*"

"*I'm proud. You have a day off from work today?*"

"*Yes, no work today.*"

"*Ah, you must have worked well. They must be proud of you.*"

"*Yes, Mama, they're proud of me. I made a lot of money this week already.*"

"*Ah, my son, you're making me proud, too. And you're eating well, yes?*"

"*Yes, Mama. I'm–,*" I looked down at the plate of ravioli in my hand. "*I'm eating right now.*"

"*And have you finally found yourself a girl, my son? A beautiful girl you can bring home?*" I looked at Minush, joyfully devouring her plate of meat.

"*Yes.*"

"*How is she? Is she beautiful?*"

"*She's–... She's always there for me. She's my beating heart.*"

"*So you're not lonely, son? You're not lonely anymore?*"

I looked at the couch where I had thrown all my glittery-shimmery work clothes on. "*I'm not alone, no.*"

"*And are you happy?*"

I looked out the window, which was still wide open, and watched the blanket of shaded grey clouds pass by. "*Yes, Mama. I'm not sad anymore.*"

There was a moment of silence, and I wasn't sure who was causing it. Then I heard her voice again. "*We miss you a lot, Antoni.*"

I nodded, even though she could not see it. I never lied to my mother, but sometimes it was simply impossible to speak the truth. There had once been a time when each of her calls had caused my throat to close up and my hands to tremble. Now I felt strangely calm. Empty.

"*It's Pia's birthday next week.*"

"*I know. I got her something pretty. It should arrive soon.*"

"*Oh, she'll be happy to hear that, Antoni.*"

"*Don't tell her, though. It's a surprise. I hope it doesn't get lost because of some lazy postman, though.*"

"*I won't ask what it is, then. But you say it is pretty?*"

I laughed a bit. "*Yes, Mama. Very pretty.*"

"*It must've been expensive. Antoni, you don't forget to feed yourself just to give your sister a pretty present, do you?!*"

This time, I laughed out loud. "*Mama!*"

"*Okay, okay. I'm your mother, Antoni. I worry about you. You must not be mad at me for it.*" Even she sounded amused now.

I chuckled and shook my head. "*I love you, Mama. I promise I'm fine, though. Are you okay, too? How is–...*" I bit my lower lip, looking out the window again. "*How's the sink? Did you fix it?*"

My mother, too, seemed to take a moment to reply. "*The plumber stopped by, yes. We–... Your money helped.*"

I nodded. Minush had finished eating and was now stretching herself. "*I'll send more next week. But I–... I have to go now, Mama.*"

My mother's voice was very quiet when she finally answered me. "*We're so very proud of you, Antoni.*"

I closed my eyes and nodded.

She hung up.

For a long moment, I stood there, the plate in one hand, the phone in the other, pressing the hearer against my head until its tooting became a melody too ugly for me to listen to Eventually, I set both, plate and phone, down on the small table and went to bed. Minush joined me, and together, we watched the birds fly outside the window until night fell.

• • • •

I was by the phone before I was fully awake. "Hello?" I asked. It had woken me up, though I could not remember it ringing. "Hello?"

Silence. A click. Tooting.

"Oh, for fuck's sake." I sighed and hung up, too. I looked around. The window was still wide open, and icy autumn air was filling my room. The plate of ravioli still stood next to the telephone, too. Minush, having been woken up with me, was licking herself clean on the bed. I scratched my head. What time was it? Before I could go to check the alarm clock on my nightstand, though, the phone rang again. This time, I picked up immediately. "Listen, I don't know who you are, but I'd greatly appreciate it if you didn't call me only to hang up all the time."

"I apologise," a man's voice replied.

I blinked in surprise. "How can I help?"

There was a great moment of silence, and I feared he'd hang up again. But he was just struggling with what he wanted to say. "Is this-... M–, my name is Richard Leaflet a–, and I–... Am I–, I'm sorry I'm bothering you, but a–, um, ah, am I talking to ... Horny Pokorny?"

"Yes, sweetie, you are." I chuckled, picking up a cold ravioli and stuffing it into my mouth. "It's 300 a night, 200 for a dinner, 100 for a party. How can I help?"

Toot, toot, toot.

Chapter Two – Find yourself some seeds (don't worry that they're so fragile)

. . . .

"I am not saying I defend her. I am not saying I would do it like her. I am not saying that it is not brutally inhumane what she is doing. I am just asking: What do they expect? What do they think is going to happen if they let themselves die? Will it help them? Will it help their wives and children? Will it help their future? What are they expecting?!"

Resigned, I removed my tongue from Mrs Potter's clit. "Am I working with you or against you here?" I asked.

She looked down at me. "Oh, no, no, you go, boy, you're doing just fine." And she patted my head approvingly with the hand that wasn't holding her wine glass.

I sighed and went back between her legs.

Mrs Potter had once been in a leading position of her political party, and because her father and her father's father had been political leaders too, she was a born orator. Unfortunately, she had married early and a man who did not think highly of women who orated, so he put her in his kitchen and made her vacuum the house whenever she started talking a bit too much. Mrs Potter's wet dream was, therefore, standing in front of a crowd and ranting about her opinions that no one bothered listening to anymore. Hearing her own voice brought her to climax better than anything I could do. Still, she borrowed me at least once a month, ironically paying me to listen to her with her late father's money. He had earned it with his speeches, she now spent it with hers.

. . . .

"How much do I owe you?"

HOW TO GROW FEELINGS LIKE FLOWERS

The best thing about Mrs Potter was that she lived just down the street, and when I was away over the weekend, which happened relatively often, she would check on Minush once a day.

"100, please."

"Just 100? But the last time, you wanted 200."

"But I still owe you for keeping care of Minush and buying all that cat food for that time when I was stuck in the mountains for a week, remember?"

Mrs Potter waved me off. "Of course, of course, I haven't forgotten about that, but that wasn't a whole 100 pounds' worth, that little bit of caring for your cat. I hardly spent more than twenty, and you know I love cats so much. Harold never-..."

"Please, Mrs Potter." I placed my hands over hers, looking her reassuringly in the eyes. "It's a friendly turn for your kindness, yes? Please accept it."

Mrs Potter freed one of her hands only to wave me off some more, looking all flustered now, though. "Oh, boy, you know how to make a lady feel special."

We – that is, she – talked for another little half hour before I finally made it out the door. She promised to stop by every day at eleven – "A steady routine is very important for cats, you know." – and then bid me goodbye, waving her handkerchief as she watched me walk down the street. A street which led from those narrow and small one-family worker houses to the high buildings of social housing projects by just a turn. If it hadn't smelled like shit and burned plastic all over the place, it would have been a pretty romantic end of the scene, too, considering that the sun was setting in the far distant horizon, colouring the sky purple.

"Antoniiii..."

"Shut up. You embarrassed me. I don't want to talk to you anymore."

"Minush, my love?"

Minush came hobbling over to me, chirping and looking curious.

"We have to pack now; Baker invited me to his beach house again," I said, running my hand over Minush's silky back. "Mrs Potter is going to come and care for you while I'm gone. Is that okay with you?" Minush did not reply, but she was rubbing herself against me and purring, so I counted it as a yes. And why wouldn't she be excited about that news? After all, Mrs Potter was always spoiling her with treats. "We're living quite the same kind of life, do you know that, Minush? We're letting other people pay for our food in return for letting them pet us, then we purr and groom ourselves, and sleep a lot. It's not a bad life, you know. I think we're a little bit lucky to be living it."

Mr C. Baker, who wanted to be addressed as such but who probably had a very different name, had a lot of secrets and a house by the sea. He always wore expensive suits and his hair open and in a colossal, fluffy afro, which I called 'hip' once and then never again because Baker said that that was racist, and I believed him. Why he always brought me with him on his vacation, where he sought nothing but silence and solitude, I did not know and was not allowed to ask, but I never complained. He was a proper and terribly intelligent man who, despite probably being worth millions of pounds, still cooked and cleaned everything by himself, and because of that, his hands were rough and skilled. I loved feeling them run down my body as much as watching them prepare our dinner. There was something poetic about the way he moved them.

It was already autumn, so we did not go swimming in the sea like we had last time, a few weeks prior. Instead, over those next four days, we would sit on a blanket in the dunes, a cup of tea in our hands, and watch the sun dye the sky. As it set. As it rose. As it wandered so peacefully, unaware of how its movement affected us in such a tremendous way, us, those tiny creatures, so very far away.

HOW TO GROW FEELINGS LIKE FLOWERS

Sometimes, we would say nothing for hours, scarcely acknowledging each other's presence. Sometimes, he would eventually push me into the sand, gently, and let his hands travel over me, blessing my skin with touches so soft and intentional that it felt like I was becoming one of those colours above us, melting into being an infinitely temporary, temporarily infinite hue.

"Mr C. Baker?"

It was Monday, our last day here, and I had spent the night alone in our bed. He must've been awake all night. Now he was leaning over the wooden balustrade that surrounded the small house, watching the waves' attempts to conquer the land before them, the water glistening in the forenoon sun. Upon hearing my voice, he turned, looking at me with patient yet perfectly silent eyes.

"I wondered if we could go into town today. I wish to send a few postcards and perhaps a parcel. If that is all right with you. It's my sister's birthday soon."

Baker gave it a nod and a smile, and I returned it gratefully.

We had not gone into the small fisherman's town often, but I knew that he never held my hand there and preferred it when I did not wear any of my flashy clothes. I had no trouble conforming to that, considering that none of the clothes he provided for me instead were ever of cheap, embarrassing quality. On the contrary. Sometimes, it was even a little scary just how perfectly they suited me, hugging my frame as though tailored specifically for me.

"Would you want some ice cream?" Baker asked.

It was always a surprise to hear him speak, let alone address me first, so I took a second to reply. "N-, No thank you, Mr C. Baker.

"Do you mind if I permit myself a scoop?"

"Uh, no, of course. Please, go ahead."

It must've been quite the sight, this giant of a man licking his strawberry ice cream as he followed the twig of a boy through this old, melancholic village. In a way, I minded it as much as I didn't mind. You see, I adored being stared at as I walked down the streets of a crowded city, I adored dancing on pub counters and house party tables, I adored wearing all of the colours and all of the metallic details at once or dressing myself up as the great stars of forgotten times only to draw gazes towards me and my impeccable ten-inch-heels strut. Being watched in this fishing town was no different. I loved the attention. However, I hated that I got it for all the wrong reasons.

A grown-ass man licking his ice cream waffle to keep his hands from getting all sticky – how emasculating, right? I sighed. The mere thought annoyed me. The mere idea of people thinking themselves superior without ever having questioned their beliefs annoyed me. And thus, their gazes annoyed me.

Baker let me buy three postcards, one for George Langston, one for Karolina, one for my family, and we filled their square backs with words at the tables inside the post office. There was the ever-same silent, peaceful expression resting on Baker's face, with this tinge of beautiful melancholy that I would watch slip off his face only when he fell asleep. Only then would he look happy. Perhaps that was why he never allowed himself to sleep much. Perhaps he did not think he deserved to be happy.

He, too, was writing two postcards home. On the first, he wrote quite a lot, his neat handwriting seemingly unfazed by the lack of space. On the second day, he drew a few pictures, like a sun, waves, and a little hut. I did not dare look for long, as reading his letters came close to asking unwanted questions, but I assumed the second one was for a child and wondered if perhaps it was his own. He quite looked like a father, Mr C. Baker. Young, perhaps in his mid-thirties, who was quite the age to have a child, whose reading comprehension was reduced to little drawings. Handsome but without making you stop and drop all you were doing just to look at his face. And wise, but without giving it the heaviness of a professor or a grandfather. Not that my own father was either of those three things and therefore less of a father, but I pushed the thought aside.

"I think I'm done writing," I said instead, smiling up at Baker.

He returned the smile and gave it a nod. "You spoke of a parcel?"

"Oh, yes. For my sister. I hope shipping it will not be too expensive, though."

Baker merely got to his feet and went to queue up. There was only one counter open right now, manned by a woman who wore a thick, white wool sweater and very red lipstick. Somehow this mix of provincial style and aggressive modernity united in a single person had me smirk.

Only one man stood in line before us.

"How old will she turn?"

"Who? My sister?"

Baker nodded. He was not even looking at me. His gaze was on the post office woman.

"Seventeen."

"That is young."

"It is. Pia's the youngest, the hatchling of the family. She's a very lovely person, though; we used to be very close. I miss her."

"And you are the oldest?"

"Yes. Why, does it show?"

Baker was not one to always show his appreciation of my jokes, – the few I made in his presence. I had learned to adapt to my clients, to become what pleased them most without them asking for it out loud, sometimes even without them knowing that it was what pleased them most, - but today Baker was smiling.

"Next, please?" the post office woman called.

His hand was on my shoulder as he gently moved me to the counter.

"Two stamps for inside the UK and three outside." the woman hummed as she glanced at the addresses on the postcards. Her fingers worked fast, detaching the required stamps, putting them on the postcards, letting them slide away into a great red box which was probably where all postcards went. "Anything else?"

Baker looked at me.

"A package to Poland, please. If that's possible."

"We cannot ship food," the woman replied.

I blinked. "It's not food."

"May I see?"

I glanced up at Baker, whose smile had disappeared but whose expression seemed as serene as always. So I fumbled in my bags and pulled out a dark blue and flat plastic box, along with an envelope, which, albeit small, was bulky because it was filled with a large number of pound notes. Never had any of the post office workers in London asked me about what I was sending home, so there was this strange tingle of doubt and anxiety lingering in my chest now.

"What is inside here?"

I opened the plastic box, turned it, and presented the breathtakingly beautiful set of jewellery to the woman. A bracelet surrounded by a necklace and accompanied by earrings lay, neatly placed, on a little pillow inside the box. They were all in shining white gold, the chains were ivy-like plants intertwining, and each had a single ruby-stoned flower added to them as a delicate detail. The first time I had seen this set, I had felt my knees growing weak, and perhaps the post office woman felt quite similarly because she took a moment before talking again.

"Who is supposed to receive this?"

"My family. It's–, it's a birthday present for my sister. She–, she loves jewellery, y–... And she's been wishing for a fitting set like this for many years now, I–..."

"So it is supposed to be sent to Poland, yes?"

The interruption made my throat feel dry. "Yes." I breathed, and it almost sounded like a question.

"And what is in the envelope?"

I felt cold shivers run down my spine. But before I could speak, Baker's hand landed heavily on my shoulder.

I looked up at him, but his eyes were on the post office woman, even as he gently pushed me aside, moving closer to the counter and holding out a small card for the woman to take. He was propping his elbow on the counter and leaning far in, almost as though forcing me out of the scene by hiding me behind his largeness. "Curtis B. Johnson, Miss, here is my card. Read it carefully, you might recognise the label."

Her eyes widened. "Oh, Mr Johnson, I did not realise–..."

"Perfectly fine, Miss." Baker was smiling, almost charmingly, and I realised I had never seen him look so ... noticeable. It was as though he had grown in size, as though his presence took up much more space now. "This is Tony Pokorny, his first record will appear next year, and this here is his contract money. As you see, everything is perfectly legal."

The woman's hand was hastily driving through her hair as though to make it look less flat, and she nodded, short-breathed. "Of course, of course. I did not doubt that." Her eyes were jumping back and forth between Baker and me. "I apologise, Mr–..."

"Pokorny."

"Mr Pokorny. We will of course ship this to your family. Would you wish it to be shipped via aeroplane so it arrives before the end of the week?"

"I–... Sure."

She nodded, and with clumsy, hasty hands, she now worked twice as fast to get our postcards and parcels sent off, tossing us little smiles from time to time. I stared at her the entire time, not entirely sure how to react to any of that. Only after Baker paid and moved me to the exit with his large hand on my back did I consider casting her a friendly smile. But I didn't dare turn back. I felt strange, tensed and relieved at the same time. I didn't dare look at Baker.

Foolish. I'd been foolish for trying to send home thousands of pounds without trying to conceal it. Had I lived in illegality for so long that I didn't feel its threat anymore?

My family told me often they missed me and wished me back in their midst. But surely not at this price, surely they didn't want me to be escorted back to Poland by the hands of law. And it wasn't just the fear of them learning how I had earned my money, how often I had lied to them, it was also the fear of no longer being able to do so.

After we'd walked for a while towards the beach, Baker spoke again: "That was a very expensive present for a seventeen-year-old."

I closed my eyes, feeling those words drawing a puff of air from me. "She loves jewellery..." I repeated in a whisper, and with the thoughts, the feelings dissipated as well.

"She must be very proud of you."

"Proud?" I looked at him, finally.

"To have a brother who works so hard to give her a nice present. Who goes so far away despite missing his family, just to help them out. Who is so eager to protect them," Baker went on, and my eyes widened. "This world is a cruel one, Antoni, and some laws need to be respected to keep everyone safe, but other laws have long lost their meaning and sense. Breaking them does not mean you are a moral criminal. Sometimes it is more important to respect life than to respect the law."

We had both stopped walking. I was still looking at Baker, but it was only he who had fully turned to face me. I was still facing the direction in which we had walked, as though turning to him was too much like turning back, and seeing the danger of my mistakes. I lived in constant danger, and I had forgotten about it. Now I denied it.

I took a breath and turned towards him. "Curtis B. Johnson. Is that your real name?"

"Sometimes," he replied. "When it is necessary."

"Was it necessary now?"

Baker raised his eyebrows. "Do you want to be deported back home?"

I shook my head.

"Then yes. It was necessary."

The walls of the house were of stone and washed white, from the outside and the inside, which gave the house a very friendly and bright appearance, making the dark wood of the furniture inside look elegant and classic instead of dirty and old. Except for the large sheep rug serving to make it a little more homely in here, there was hardly any unnecessary furniture. Only seashells had been put on the window sills as decoration, and I liked it. There was something very simplistic about the look of it all, even the way pieces of water-crafted wood knotted onto a string then hung up from the ceiling like curtains were used to divide the different areas of the house; one curtain in front of the open bathroom, one curtain in front of the almost-always open entrance door, and one curtain in front of the bed, on which I was currently lying. The house had probably once been a boathouse, as it was of only one floor and relatively narrow compared to its length, the ceiling low. I liked it. It was very comfortable, and there was something about the smallness of the space that muffled sounds in quite a strange, almost mysterious way. Words – and gasps and moans for that matter – seemed much louder and clearer there, but without any echo or sharpness. One of my favourite things to do was to run my finger along the wall, mimicking the sound of the waves outside. First the tip, then the pad, then the length, and finally the palm, starting quietly, becoming louder, ebbing away. Sometimes, I would do it for many, many minutes, disappearing into this sound, until in the end, my fingers felt both raw and inexplicably soft.

Today there was another sound joining the imitation of waves. It was the snip, snip, snip of a knife going through carrots in the kitchen. For many a moment, I had listened to the dinner preparation, noticing how Baker seemed to be moving to the motion of the waves, too.

With the pad of my middle finger, I drew circles on the pad of my thumb, feeling how soft they were and gazing out of the window, mindlessly. Clouds were covering the sky, and I knew that we would not watch the sunset tonight. Perhaps it was for the better, as this meant we would not stay here for too long. Baker did not like driving when it was dark outside. Eventually, I dropped my hand to my chest and sighed. It was not a sigh of resignation or boredom. On the contrary. Being here was as much of a treat for me as being cared for by Mrs Potter was for Minush. It was always calm and quiet with Baker, and time moved slowly, allowing your thoughts to regain the peace they needed to not run in circles. It was a sigh of contentment. And with the same contentment, I sat up. The smell of the soup Baker was making had started filling the hut, and I decided to set the table.

When I rose to my feet, I felt both heavy and light. Heavy, the way you do after a nap, even though I hadn't slept. And light, because there was nothing here to pack my chest with emotions. Perhaps that was why so many people who lived in the city were always so exhausted. Because they never had the chance to just listen to the waves and look at smooth, white walls.

"Your hair," Baker noted as he cast me a glance after I joined him in the kitchen, drying clean dishes and putting them into their respective cupboards.

"Hmm?" My hand moved to my hair, feeling how awkwardly tousled it was. I chuckled. "Untamable curls." I ran my fingers through them, attempting to *coiff* them into place, but Baker shook his head.

"Leave it. I like it like that."

I looked at him again, then nodded and turned back to drying the dishes, feeling warm.

After setting the table, I sat on the bench behind Baker, listening to the boiling of the water, the rushing of the waves, and the snip snip snip of Baker cutting some herbs for the soup. Sometimes, his feet would brush against the ground as he moved to reach for something, and that added to the concert of whispered instruments.

My own feet were bare, so were my calves. I had rolled up the legs of my trousers as Baker didn't like them dirty or ripped. They were his trousers, too. Well, mine, but he had bought them, a style to his liking. The same went for the perfume he made me wear. Neither was my style, but I never complained. Didn't dare to argue.

"Can I do anything else to help?"

He declined.

"Stir the soup? Sweep the floor? Iron your shirts?"

But Baker still did not look up from his herbs, continuing to cut them peacefully and without giving me more than a shake of his head.

Thus, in silence, I looked at him from the side, his pale lips and broad nose, his ever-kind eyes. He had his ears pierced but never wore any jewellery, and his neck was usually hidden behind a turtleneck. His shoulders were as broad as his arms were strong, defined and noticeable but not muscled in an overly ambitious way; it appeared rather natural, as though he had simply grown this way. And his hands. Well, his hands.

I sighed. Then, slowly, I slipped between him and the kitchen counter, looking up at him.

He looked down at me, smiling with silent amusement and curiosity. "I cannot work like this, Antoni." he said and although there was some scolding tone in his voice, it was soft anyway, almost fond.

"I want to help."

Baker raised his eyebrows, ever so slightly tilting his head to the side, but did not look like he planned on answering. Nor did he plan on arguing or asking why I seemed to want to. He already knew; he had saved my ass today and I wanted to return the favour. Perhaps that was the only thing that gave me the courage to be stubborn just now. "You are already very helpful, Antoni."

Our gazes were firmly locked until I broke mine away. I couldn't argue with him, I just couldn't. However, just because Baker didn't want help didn't mean he was opposed to helping me.

I turned around, my back against him now, before me the counter. I reached for the knife Baker had worked with, as well as the parsley. "Teach me," I murmured.

Hesitation. Then I felt Baker move closer against me, his warmth engulfing my shoulders as his hands came to rest over mine, closing around them before tightening the grip with gentle pressure as the knife, snip, snip, snip, went through the parsley. Even with my unskilled fingers between him and his work, his hands worked with precision and beauty. Each cut was like the motion of a wave, not crashing down with rough force but rolling against the cutting board with intention, and each time he pushed the knife down with this serene kind of firmness, his body pressed against mine, and I felt my lungs pushing out breaths, too.

• • • •

Because the Night was playing on the car radio.

I hummed along quietly, remembering how we would dance to it in the clubs of the cities nearby, how we would sometimes drive for hours in the hope of finding an open bar at two A.M. on a Tuesday night, emptying bottle after bottle before even reaching the flickering signs and crowded streets, and how we would sing the lyrics without ever knowing what the words actually said, enjoying them just as much anyway. I wondered if Karolina would like my postcard.

"You're not from here, Mr C. Baker, are you?"

"Are you being racist again?" he asked back, keeping his eyes on the road.

"No. Just curious." And after a moment of bashful silence, I added: "Your accent sounds different."

He smiled but said nothing. I was not surprised about that.

"Did you have a nice time?" Baker asked when Patti's voice had faded away, a new song was starting to play on the radio, and he turned the car onto my street.

"Very much so, Mr C. Baker. I always enjoy being by the beach with you. Thank you for inviting me."

He gave it a nod.

"And you? Did you enjoy your vacation?"

He cast me a glance, looking amused. "Of course," he smiled. "I enjoy being by the beach with you, too."

I smiled back, looking down at my hands, feeling shy. Of course, I knew that no one paid 12 hundred pounds and very expensive smelling perfume to hang out with someone they did not like, but it was still nice to hear those words out loud. Especially coming from Baker.

"Antoni."

"Yes, Mr C. Baker?"

I looked at him. His face had lost all smile and beauty. Tensed, he nodded out the window, and I followed his gaze. A gasp escaped me.

My building was burning. People were standing in the streets, staring up at the flames that came out of the windows of the upper floors, and the just fallen night was burning in orange. I felt the air getting stuck in my throat, a single thought crossing my mind.

"Minush!"

I pushed the car door open and jumped out before Baker even had the time to fully come to a halt, then ran closer to the crowd. Some of them were crying.

"Minush!" I screamed. "Minush! I'm sorry, excuse me, has anyone–, have you seen a black cat? H–, Her name is Minush, she's very small, have you–, Please? Anyone? Minush!"

"Antoni!"

I turned and saw Mrs Potter come running towards me, panic written all over her face. "Where's Minush?" I asked, my voice cracking with fear. And this time, it was real fear, not the cheap replica I had taught myself to feel months ago.

She shook her head. "I've just heard of this, it must've started less than an hour ago. I went to check on her this morning."

At eleven, just like she had promised. My throat felt drier with every new breath I sucked in, as I kept turning around myself, chasing the shadows of everything that looked like a cat. None of it was Minush, and my throat burned. "Minush!" I cried once more, but the sound was drowned by the fire brigade arriving, their alarm blaring away all sounds and the blue flickering light of their car announcing the end of the orange flickering light of the fire. But why did they only come now? How much longer until they were to put an end to all this? I stared at the building, frantically trying to count the floors and wondering if ours had already been reached by the flames, but my eyes failed to stay still, and I miscounted again and again until I could not take it anymore. I pushed myself past Mrs Potter and through the crowd to the building, fumbling and fumbling with my keys before I finally managed to push them into the keyhole. I turned them. Nothing happened. The door remained closed.

"No," the door winced as I shook it. "No, no, no."

Panic overcame me. "Fucking hell, Door!" I yelled, "Let me in! Minush is in there! I need to save her! Door!"

"No, no, no," I pushed out with each of my attempts to forcefully crash it open with my shoulder.

"Door!"

"No!"

A hand was put on my shoulder, and I clutched onto the door handle. "Antoni, come away from here; you'll hurt yourself."

"I don't care, my cat is inside, my Minush is inside, I need to get her, she'll die, she'll die if I don't get her." Nothing in my apartment was of any particular worth, everything could be replaced with as little as the money I had made over this weekend. But what were a couch and a few glittery shoes compared to your only and best friend? "Please. Please let me in." I begged one last time, but the door refused, and the arms that wrapped around me were strong. My fingers failed to hold onto the door, which then let out a last: "Trust!" as it snapped from my grip.

With horror, I watched the firefighters pass us as Baker dragged me backwards, and helplessly, I had to watch them open the door as though it had never been locked in the first place. They were never going to get there in time. The fire had reached floor number eleven long ago, and they would not have hesitated to save a cat if people were still inside. It was too late. The realisation drew all air from my lungs, and if it hadn't been for Baker's arms holding me, I think I would've fallen to my knees. Instead, he turned me around, letting me bury myself in his chest.

I was not crying, as I had long since unlearned how to cry, but every piece, every inch of me was burning with pain so vivid that it felt like I was dying in the fire, too.

"Excuse me? Antoni?"

"Yes?" Baker answered for me when I did not let go of him. Whoever this was, it did not matter now. Nothing mattered anymore. At least, I thought so. "Oh." A small pause. "Antoni?"

I shook my head.

"Antoni, there is someone for you."

My breath hitched, the way it does when not all hope has been lost, and I looked up.

There stood Lev, covered in soot from head to toe, and with their thick leather jacket wrapped tightly around them. Avoiding my eyes, they opened it carefully and revealed the tiniest cat sitting in their arms. "Think I found something," they mumbled, and I missed all of it because a loud cry of joy escaped me.

"Minush!"

We fell into each other's arms. Thrilled to see me, Minush had immediately fought to come over to me, and as soon as Lev loosened the grip on her, she had jumped into my hands. Standing on her hind legs, she put her paws on my shoulder and rubbed her head against mine, purring as loudly as I was repeating her name again and again. Likely, I was mostly just feeling relieved, but I like to think that for once, at this very moment, I was capable of being at least a little bit happy.

"What a hero," Baker said. He had let go of me and was now gladly watching me being reunited with my cat.

Lev only shrugged. They had crossed their arms and seemed neither pleased nor proud nor impatient. They mostly seemed bored, their gaze glassy and distant as it rested on Minush.

"You should thank your hero, Antoni." Baker reminded me and momentarily distracted me from Minush's purring, making me remember that, indeed, I should show some gratitude. And hell, that was easy.

"Thank you so much." I breathed, taking a step towards Lev and clutching Minush against my chest. "Thank you, thank you, thank you. He is right. Anything and everything you want as a reward, I'll get it for you."

"It's cool," they said, simply.

"No, please." I insisted. "Just say whatever's on your mind, right here and now, no matter what it is, and you'll have it, gift-wrapped with a cherry on top."

Their expression – if there had really been one – faded into nothingness. Then they rolled their eyes up and over to the burning building. "Gift wrapped," they repeated.

"Yes." I breathed, then went back to nuzzling Minush because her little paw had been placed on my cheek to demand my attention back.

Baker was smiling, and if I had been more attentive, I might have noticed that he had grown in size again, like earlier that day when he had talked to the post office woman. "You should let the paramedics take a look at you," he said to Lev. "By the look of you, you might've burnt yourself. Did you get close to the fire?"

"Nah, I'm fine."

"You do look pretty burnt, though," I added, mindlessly reaching out for their face to get some soot on my finger to show them.

They leaned backwards immediately.

I drew my hand back. "Sorry."

They just looked back at Minush, stuffed their hands firmly into their pockets. "Just make sure to give her lots of water these next couple of days."

"I will. Fuck, I'm so glad she's okay. How did you find her?"

They shrugged. "The way you find a cat."

"On trees?" I grinned, but it wasn't returned.

Instead, they looked up at Baker, to Minush, then back to the burning building. "Anyway. I shall now," they mumbled. "I'm starving, and they'll need a couple of hours to get that doused. So." They gave it a single-minded wave, then turned on their heels. Bare heels.

"But if you're hungry!" I called. "I can invite you to dinner!" I had already eaten with Baker, and this only about three hours ago, but what did that matter? I'd eat a thousand meals again if that was how I could repay them.

But Lev neither seemed impressed by the suggestion nor enthused. Their gaze was fixed on the grey horizon of buildings before them.

"As fancy as your stomach demands, I've got enough money on me," I added, keen to convince them to say yes.

"Nah," they shrugged. "Thanks."

I leapt forward and grabbed their arm. "Please! There must be something I can do! I just-,"

"I know one thing." they interrupted me, stiffly, suddenly, their face turning tense and pale as they forcefully tried not to look at me.

I blinked. "Yes?"

"Let go of me. Now."

"I-..."

From the side, I could see their jaws clenching, the muscles underneath their jacket seemingly bulking, then our eyes met and their dark gaze burnt itself into mine. "It's cool." they hissed, pushing the words out forcedly, then freed themselves and left.

I stood speechless. Confused. Helpless.

"A friend of yours?" Baker asked as he so often did, not trying to address the problem at hand but distracting from it instead.

"Not how I'd call it, no," I mumbled.

"Well, they did save your cat."

I looked back at Lev, who was halfway down the street now. Lev? Leev? We had never introduced ourselves to each other, had we? I frowned. "Mr C. Baker?"

"Yes?"

"I don't-... I never told them I had a cat."

Chapter Three – Plant your seeds, but give them room to grow (don't bury them too deep)

· · · ·

Introduction:

First, you will see them introduce themselves to you.

Studies say that it takes less than ten minutes for you to know whether you could see yourself married to someone or not. Newer studies say it takes less than five minutes to know whether you could see yourself falling in love with that person. I say it takes less than a minute to know whether you want to fuck them or not.

Our species has come to terms with proper and formal introductions. Handshakes. Bows. Tongues pulled out at each other. All cultures have their own way, all a bit different, all a bit quirky to people who do not belong, but we have it all in common: We introduce ourselves. And we all say that the first impression counts the most. So we squeeze our palms together, trying to assert dominance. So we bend our backs as low as we can, trying to imply respect. So we brush our tongues before meeting someone new, making sure it's not sickly yellow. Kidding. I don't actually know about that last one.

A hell of a lot of effort into introducing ourselves. Yet we seem to be perfectly incapable of noticing and considering that all that is not being introduced to us is of far greater importance.

Yes, yes, I see that you put brand-new cuffs into your sleeves, well done. Yes, yes, I see that you had a haircut worth about a hundred pounds last week, congratulations. Yes, yes, your shoes are shiny, your voice loud, your shoulders broad and pulled back with confidence. I am very proud of you. But you know what 'yes, yes' means where I come from? Lick my ass. And do you know why that's so funny to me? Because at the end of the day, that's exactly what I will want you to do.

Lick my fucking ass.

And for that, I don't need your gold credit card or your skill of spitting perfectly good wine back into your glass. For that, I only need to see the way you wave for the waiter. The way you look at people across the room. The way you comb your fingers through your hair or fidget with your napkin while telling a story. The way you hesitate on your way to the bathroom, and how your face lights up when you come back and see me for the first time all over again.

I don't give a fuck about the introduction you are trying to force onto me. What I want is the introduction I draw from your lips when we first kiss. And trust me, sometimes I do need less than a minute to get there.

• • • •

"Harold, darling, I'm back."

"I've already had dinner now, though."

"That's fine. I will have to reheat everything for our friend Antoni here, anyway."

It was only then that Mr Potter's eyes fell on me. He was seated on the sofa of what I assumed was their living and dining room, reading a newspaper, and the return of his wife had apparently been no reason for him to look up from that. Only upon realising that the tone in which he usually addressed his wife was no longer private, he made himself presentable, which, honestly, made him even less likeable than this enormous beast of a moustache on his face.

"Good evening?"

I was glad I was wearing the black turtleneck sweater under this suit jacket Baker had given me this morning, or else this scrutiny of a gaze would have probably pierced through me twice as spitefully.

"Good evening, Mr Potter, Sir," I said, crossing the room to offer him my hand.

Mr Potter, being perhaps an unpleasant creature but also the kind of man who puts a lot of effort into appearing proper and educated, rose to his feet and took it. "And who are you?" he asked, shaking my hand with purposeful dominance.

"Antoni Pokorny, Sir. I'm-, I'm a friend of your wife."

Our handshake stuttered. Mr Potter's eyes locked with mine.

"He's the boy with the cat, darling." Mrs Potter explained, "He lives in the burning building down the road."

Slowly, Mr Potter detached his eyes from me to look at Minush in Mrs Potter's arms. "Well. Lived," he said and - praise the Lord - finally let go of my hand. "Henrietta, dear, may I talk to you for a moment?"

There was a beat of dead, drowning silence before Mrs Potter reacted. "Of course. Yes, of course. Antoni, my boy, why don't you make yourself feel at home? Take off your shoes, there are slippers in the cabinet by the door, and make little Minush and yourself a nice glass of milk from the kitchen, hm? I'll be right back." She had handed me Minush and was now following her husband, who was, although politely, impatiently holding the door open to what I knew was the washing room.

I did not know what to say, so I just nodded and smiled, trying not to look too awkward. But just as the door was about to close, I did remember something. "Oh, Mrs Potter?"

She hurriedly turned to look back at me. "Yes, my boy?"

"Could I use your phone, please?"

"Of course, of course. It's-,"

"Henrietta."

"Just a second, darling. It's at the entrance, right next to the cabinet with the slippers. And, ah, take yourself some! The floor is cold. I'll be right back, okay?"

"Yes. Thank you."

The door flung closed, and I was left alone in the living room. Well, almost alone. Minush let out a little, curious chirp.

"*No, I don't understand the* Straights *either.* Making it look like two men loving each other is the end of polite society, only to then have their husbands treat their wives as though she's a piece of spunk that needs to be scratched off the bedroom walls." I sighed. *"Let's call George Langston. We'll be better off there."*

I sat by the wall telephone in the entrance hall and dialled his number. It rang empty. From the room next door, I could hear that Mr and Mrs Potter were arguing, and it made my throat feel stiff and achy. So after a moment, I dialled again.

"Hello, at the Pokornys, who's speaking?"

"Laura? Is that you? It's me, Antoni."

"Tolek!" my sister exclaimed. She sounded happy. *"Tolek, hi! How are you?"*

Smiling, I closed my eyes and leaned against the wall. *"I'm fine,"* I said, and for once, it did not entirely feel like a lie. Fuck. She sounded so very happy. *"And you? How are you? How is Milosz?"*

My sister gasped. *"Mama did not tell you, did she?! I told her not to tell anyone!"* But the vibrant joy of her tone did not disappear, not even as her voice, a little muffled, as though the phone was pressed against her chest now, called for our mother. *"Mama! Did you tell Antoni?! Mama!"*

"Wait, wait, wait." I laughed, having no idea what was happening. *"Laura? Laura, are you still th–,"*

"Yes?"

"Laura?"

"Tolek?"

"Yes. What is going on? What did Mama tell me?"

My sister's laugh chimed through the rustling of the phone so beautifully that even Minush had started sniffing the device curiously. "*I'm pregnant, Tolek!*"

I was glad that she was telling me this over the phone because, for a split second, my entire face slipped into an expression of shock. "*What?!*"

"*I'm pregnant! I'm carrying a tiny human inside myself! I'm going to have a baby! With Milosz! I'm going to be a Mama, Tolek! Can you believe it?*"

"*Oh my God.*" I breathed, and then - I could literally feel Laura's excitement tugging on the corners of my lips and pulling them into a broad smile - let out a laugh, too. "*Oh my God, Laura! You're going to be a Mama!*"

"*Yes!*" she exclaimed, and her laugh filled me with something that, albeit not happiness, came very close to it. "*And you will be her godfather.*"

"*What? Me?! But Laura-, Wait. Her? Do you already know it's a girl?*"

"*Of course I know; a mother knows these things.*"

"*Of course.*" I grinned and then thought of something else. "*But Laura, how long have you known you're-... The wedding's only in March!*"

Laura laughed some more, and I could almost see it before my eyes, the way her long blonde hair would fall over her shoulders as she tilted her head back, her entire body in visual harmony with this sound. Oh, she was going to be a beautiful mother, my beloved sister. "*I did not know you were so conservative, my dearest brother.*"

"*I'm not.*" I huffed, amused, and slightly feeling like I was caught lying. "*But what did Mama say? Is she not... You know. To hear that?*"

"*Oh, Tolek.*"

"*What?! Don't you remember when you were caught kissing this boy once? They made you pray seventeen Marias for it.*"

"That was when I was sixteen, Antoni. I'm twenty-one now, and Milosz is my fiancé. We're still going to be wed before the baby comes, and Mama is very happy. She's already started knitting tiny socks and tiny hats. Don't worry." There was emphasis in her voice now, but the happiness still danced in it.

"Fine. You win." And because I couldn't kiss my sister now, I pressed one to Minush's head instead.

For a moment, it was silent, and I wished it wouldn't be because it made me hear the fight Mr and Mrs Potter were having. But then Laura did go on, and I longed for silence instead. *"I think she's just happy that there's a chance that Papa will still be able to meet the baby."*

I opened my eyes. *"Why would you say that."* It wasn't a question.

"I'm sorry."

I pushed myself off the wall and let Minush down. *"Don't say things like that, Laura. It's bad luck."*

"Antoni..."

"I've got to go now. Tell Mama I'll call tomorrow morning, and that she needs to be there. It's important."

"Important? Did something happen?"

"I can't explain right now. Just tell her I'll call again, will you?"

Laura agreed, and I hung up. It was perfectly silent within me. No anger, no sadness, no hurt. No happiness. I looked at the door to the washing room.

"Sorry?" I knocked and opened the door, not looking inside yet. I could hear Mr Potter sigh.

"Come in, my boy." Mrs Potter said anyway, and somehow she seemed even less confident than usual: Her eyes were not exactly red, but there was something puffy and unnerved about her nevertheless, an expression of helplessness. "What is it?"

I glanced at her, giving her a brief smile, then turned my attention towards Mr Potter. "I'm sorry I'm an inconvenience, Sir, but I've called my friends and by tomorrow I'll be gone. It's only for tonight, and considering that you're neither the one cooking nor the one making the beds or cleaning, I think you will hardly notice my presence."

"Excuse me?" Mr Potter blinked.

"It's all right. As for the cat, I'll make sure she won't go into the upper rooms but stay with me, so there is no need to worry about that either." I held out my arm for Mrs Potter to take it. "Mrs Potter, you haven't had dinner yet, have you? Would you wish to come to the kitchen with me?"

Mrs Potter was looking just as taken aback as Mr Potter was, but quicker than him, she managed to free herself from it. Brushing over her skirt, she gave her husband a last glance, then followed me outside.

For the rest of the night, the mood was light and cheerful. We did not speak of her and her husband's fight, and simply enjoyed the meal she had cooked earlier that day. She told me about when she had seen the flames in my building and how panicked she had been. I told her about my weekend, leaving out the smut and the incident at the post office, and she confessed that she hadn't been by the sea in almost twenty years. I asked her about that last time, and she asked if Baker was a 'professional or a private companion', and we both found ourselves a little flustered while answering. Eventually, after dinner, just as the conversation about the new underground and bus lines was starting to bore me, Mrs Potter's thoughts were dragged back to her husband after all.

"I have to make Harold his good night tea now," she sighed, looking at the kitchen clock. "Are you very tired, or can you wait another fifteen minutes?"

"Both." I chuckled. "How about I make you your teas, and you go get yourself bed-ready? And then we see each other here again in fifteen minutes?"

"Oh, but my boy. You'll see me in quite an inappropriate state, I'll be embarrassed." Mrs Potter laughed. I shushed her, insisting that I had seen her in far more inappropriate states. She agreed to tell me how her husband liked his tea, and I promptly went to make it.

. . . .

I thought I would find Mr Potter in the living room, but instead, I had to carry the tea all the way up to their shared bedroom – a path I knew uncomfortably well. Knocking on the door, I took a breath. "Excuse me, Mr Potter, Sir?"

The rustling of newspapers was to be heard. "Yes?"

I held the tea through the ajar door into the room. "Your wife has taken the night off from her wifely duties. Would you like your tea anyway?"

Mr Potter cleared his throat, and more rustling could be heard. "Come on in." He was sitting in his bed, the comforter neatly pulled over his legs, the night lamp on, the window next to him tipped open, and the newspaper I had heard was folded over his lap. For a man in pyjamas, he dripped with confidence. Nevertheless, there was no doubt that my presence made him at least slightly uncomfortable. "Thank you."

"I hope you'll like it. I was not born in England, you see, so I'm not an expert when it comes to tea." It was a joke, but Mr Potter showed no sign of amusement. He was not even looking at me. So, after a moment of hesitation, I turned to leave.

"How did you and Henrietta meet?"

I paused, neither out of fear nor out of confusion, but because I wondered if this was a question of which the answer mattered, or of which the reason why it was asked was what you had to pay attention to. "We met in the supermarket line." I said, honest, "She asked me about the cat food I was buying."

Mr Potter was frowning, and for a long moment, neither of us moved or said anything. Eventually, he sighed and looked down at his tea again. I kept my eyes on him, though, and after another moment in which he did not actively dismiss me, I closed the door behind us.

"Why did you two fight? Earlier on?"

Because of you, was the obvious answer. But in Mr Potter's eyes, I could read that he knew that I knew that it was the obvious answer. Too obvious. He sighed. "She's not happy with me anymore. She hasn't been in a long time, but today, she finally said it out loud."

I lowered my gaze. Oh, Mrs Potter. Quietly, I moved to her bed and sat down on it, facing Mr Potter.

"She always wanted a cat," he said.

"She does a great job caring for Minush."

He nodded. "The first time I met her, it was in this bar. A dance bar. Everyone in our neighbourhood would go there every first Saturday of the month, and so many of us met our first girlfriends and boyfriends there. I was very shy, so I never danced with any of the girls. Just stood by the side. One night, my friend dared me to go talk to this dazzling girl, who looked so much smarter and so much more confident than I did. I summoned all my courage, approached her, but realised quickly I did not know what to say, so I stuttered and stuttered and stuttered. It was a mess. When I had turned completely red, that's when she stopped me and told me to ask her what her favourite animal was. I did, and she told me it was cats." He huffed out a soundless laugh. "I thought she was going to make a joke, or a pun, or recite one of those horrible Christmas cracker jokes. But nothing. She just told me her favourite animal. And that's when I knew I wanted to marry her."

I was smiling at him from across the room. The story made no sense to me, but the way his finger was now caressing the rim of his teacup told me it did to him. And that was all that mattered.

"I always wanted to make her happy. And now she isn't. I don't know where it went wrong."

I hummed.

"I've never hit her, I've never cheated on her, I've never denied her any of her monetary wishes, but when she looks at me..."

Bringing one leg to my chest, I rested my chin on my knee and hummed again. "Perhaps it is not a matter of what you don't do, but a matter of what you do do."

"Like letting her have a cat."

I snorted. "No, Mr Potter. Like letting her be herself."

He looked at me, and I was strangely reminded of Pia, my youngest sister, when she had done something wrong and was now begging with her big blue eyes for forgiveness. "How do you know my wife so well?"

"But I don't." I shrugged, wondering if knowing the colour of her labia could be considered 'knowing her well.' Probably not. "I just enjoy her as a person and let her be herself."

Mr Potter said nothing more. He caressed his teacup so longingly that I wondered if it would help him if the teacup started caressing him back.

"I think I'll go now."

"I know who you are," he said, fast, before I even had the chance to get to my feet. I blinked. "Or at least I thought I knew who you were until you walked through that door."

Not entirely sure which door he meant, I just sat and waited.

"She m-... Henrietta sometimes speaks your name. In her sleep."

My eyes grew wide, and my lips formed an 'oh.'

"She's always been a vivid dreamer, babbling in her sleep like the woman she is. But she never moaned another man's name."

Well, that was awkward. I opened my mouth to reply, but Mr Potter did not let me.

"Until very recently. And you're not even a man. You're a boy." He huffed. "When I heard her moan your name, I thought that the day I'd meet you, I'd face a man, an Adonis of a man, young, sure, but grown. And each night when I heard her say your name, I imagined the moment I'd step up to face you and punch you and carry her back home over the threshold like the day we got married. She would never have a reason to think of another man ever again." He motioned towards me, his voice had risen in volume, but had not turned angry. "And–, and then you stand there, tell me your name, and I think–, I think I must've misunderstood something. This is the man with whom my wife is supposed to be cheating on me? This boy?! You could be our son!"

I stared at him, not entirely sure whether to be offended or amused, but entirely unimpressed. "Thanks," I said.

He sighed. "I'm sorry."

I ran my hand through my hair, still not entirely sure how I was supposed to feel, but professional enough to know how to react. "Are you really? Sorry? Or are you disappointed that it takes as little as me to make your wife cheat on you? Because, yes, you're perfectly right. I'm nothing special, hardly handsome and hardly a grown man. But it's also not me that your wife is lusting after, and you know that. You like to imagine that I was this Adonis of a man because that would make it so much easier to put the blame on me, while now, you're forced to face the truth: It's not my fault. I'm not your competition. Your wife simply has a problem with you. End of story." I shrugged and got to my feet. "You know, I'd never cheat on the person I love. Because I believe that when you love someone, you trust them, and that if you trust someone, then you don't lie to them. Then you're not afraid of communication. But your kind? You're always scared of communication. Of talking to the person you love about how you truly feel. It makes me wonder how much you really love them." My steps were light as I made my way across the room to take the teacup from Mr Potter, and I extended my hand, gave him a practised smile. "All the people I sleep with when they can't stand their own partners anymore, do you know what they have in common? They have forgotten who they are, and just for a night, I'm allowing them to remember."

Mr Potter said nothing, and I knew that my hovering over him surely did not help with how small he probably felt now. "How can I help her remember? I feel like I don't know my wife at all," he whispered.

I chuckled. "Get to know her, then."

. . . .

"*Mama?*"

"*Antoni, is that you? Laura told me you would call now, so I waited by the phone. How are you?*"

I smiled. "*I'm fine, Mama. A little tired.*"

"*Did you not sleep well?*"

"*Yes, I did, but it was a short night.*" Six hours to be precise, which, for someone who liked to sleep twelve full hours without interruption, was the very definition of a short night. But I could not help it. As soon as the sun had started peeking into the living room, I was itchy with anticipation to be out of there. As ironic as it sounds, I simply wasn't used to sleeping at other people's places. Not like this. Not while being so little in control. Helpless, or rather, worse, in need of help. "*How are you?*"

"*I'm well, my son, but what did you need to tell me? Laura said You sounded very serious. Are you doing well?*"

"*Yes, Mama, everyone is doing well. It's not very serious. There was a fire in my building, and it might take a few days until they can tell us if we can move back in. But it's all right, I did not have anything important inside the apartment, and I've got friends who are letting me stay at theirs. I just wanted you to know so you don't call me and worry because I'm not picking up.*" There was only silence on the other side of the line. "*Mama?*"

"*Yes, Antoni, I hear you.*"

"*Oh. Okay. Good. So ... yes. I'm doing okay, I'm just going to be without a phone for a couple of days. You don't worry, okay?*"

"*Okay.*"

I frowned. For someone who worried about the amount of vegetables I consumed in a week, I found that my mother was strangely quiet now. "*Mama, is everything all right?*"

"*Yes, my son. You say I should not worry, so I don't worry. You know how to take care of yourself, so I must trust you. But promise me to call us as soon as you can, yes?*"

I blinked. Was this really my mother? "*Um. Yes. Sure. Of course.*"

"*Very well. Thank you for your call, Antoni. We love you a lot. Take care of yourself!*"

"*Thank you, I will. Have a nice week. I love you, too.*"

"*And don't forget to eat!*"

I laughed. Well. Perhaps this was my mother, after all.

Minush was climbing up my leg, so I picked her up. "I know," I whispered, "but we can't go back to bed now. We need to find George Langston." I glanced up the stairs to the bedrooms, hoping my phone call had not woken up the Potters. For just a moment, I wondered if I could risk going upstairs and take a shower—but no. I'd be able to shower as soon as I was with George Langston, for now, Baker's perfume would have to do. I put on my shoes. "I promise that we'll go to sleep early tonight. Now hop on; we shouldn't stay here for too long."

Minush did as I told her, climbing onto my shoulders and lying there like a long loaf of black bread, and together we made our way out.

· · · ·

London lay still under the grey light of those early morning hours, and I felt oddly alone, as though swallowed by the many events of yesterday and yet standing far apart from those memories. Not even twenty-four hours had passed since I had nearly been caught because of jewellery in a box, yet it felt like those memories belonged to a whole different life. A whole different me. Had I changed? My hand moved to my chest, as though feeling for a heartbeat. No. Everything was as quiet and motionless as always. Not even anxiety resided there anymore.

I didn't worry about my apartment being gone. Of course, I wouldn't mind if it turned out that it had been left untouched by the fire, but even if everything inside had gone up in flames, I would be all right. I'd manage. If anything, I was worried for all the other people in the building. Living here in this neighbourhood didn't exactly give you the 'upper class' title, and I doubted that any of them had a job like mine that could temporarily lodge them in a fancy hotel. I had been on the streets before, I knew I could manage, but what about the rest of them? The children who had just lost all their toys? The students who had lost their books? The old people who had lost memories older than my entire life?

I felt nauseous.

"Maybe we should stop by a *McDonald's Hamburgers* first and grab something to eat before we go to Georgie, hm? What do you think?" Perhaps I just needed something in my stomach.

• • • •

Turned out I didn't. So, as I sat in one of the restaurant's booths, watching the businessmen and women hurry past the big shop window, only half-heartedly munching on my fries, lost in my own thoughts. What was Lev doing? How had they known Minush was my cat? I never let her out of the apartment, nor had I ever talked to someone about her. Was Lev perhaps a friend of a friend, and I simply didn't recognise them? At least that would explain why they knew my name. However, it did not answer how they were doing right now, and if yesterday they had found a place to eat, wash and sleep. I hoped they had, though. And I hoped that the next time I'd see them, they would let me thank them properly. If only I knew more about them. It would make it so much easier to find a good gift for them.

My gaze jumped down to Minush. "Ugh, no, don't eat that."

Minush angrily chirped at me when I dragged her away from the something she had found on the ground.

"You're disgusting, Minush."

She tried to strike at me.

"Bitch." I gasped and stuffed her under my arm as I got up. "*Here I am, caring for you, and you try to claw my pretty face out! That's how you show gratitude?!*"

Minush wiggled in my grip, but I did not let her go. The Lord knew where she'd run off.

As I eventually had to stuff her into my backpack, I wondered if my trying to hold Lev's hand was about the same as Minush clawing at me. But then again, I really hadn't meant to hurt them.

• • • •

"Antoni? What-,"

"Hi, George. Been a while, hasn't it? May I come in?" And I pushed myself past George Langston into his apartment. The thick stench of windows having been closed for too long crept into my nose immediately, and I covered my nose with the back of my hand. To my displeasure, yet not surprise, it was as messy and dirty as it had always been. Clothes lay on the carpeted floor, pizza boxes were stacked on top of each other in the corners of those heavy-wallpapered walls, fallen-over wine and champagne glasses and bottles could be found on various tables and dressers, some even on the piano, and while the curtains were drawn close and the lights turned off, I was almost sure that the little packs of something on the sofa weren't filled with flour.

"Antoni, what are you doing here?"

"My house burned down, and I need a place to stay. I called you yesterday but–,"

"I was busy…"

"… but you didn't pick up, so I thought I might as well come see you personally. It is not like we don't both know that you never leave your apartment before noon." I turned to look at him again. "Aren't you happy to see me?"

George Langston sighed.

"Too bad. I thought you'd at least be happy to see me alive."

"I'm hella happy to see you alive, but–,"

"But not in your apartment? How sad, because look who I brought." I had set down the bag with Minush on the ground and was now opening it carefully. Minush peered her head out of the bag and glanced around, naturally curious as she was. "We'll need some extra water for her, please."

George Langston's eyes widened. "What?! You still have the pussy?!" he exclaimed, the volume of his voice scaring Minush back into the bag. He crossed the room and reached into it, pulling Minush out by the scruff, then cradled her like a baby in his arms. "How you've grown! Such a beautiful pussy you are." He petted her despite Minush's offended attempts to free herself from his grip. "I really didn't think you'd keep her alive for so long."

"Of course you didn't. Not everyone manages to keep the women in his life around. Or alive for that matter."

"Now you're being unfair, you know very well that it wasn't me who killed Loretta."

"Not with your own hands, no. Now. Don't you owe me a pound or something?"

"A dollar. It was a dollar per year that you keep her alive. So I guess two dollars?"

"Only two dollars?" That was nothing. You could hardly buy yourself a coffee with that. I shrugged. "Fine. Money is money."

George Langston laughed heartily. "Ah, I'm glad to see that nothing changed with you."

I rolled my eyes. "Glad to see nothing changed with you either, Georgie." I patted his exposed stomach – a very round beer belly that had been there ever since I could remember – and then took off my coat, laying it over the sofa's backrest.

Upon seeing what I was wearing, George Langston was visibly amused and snickered out a: "What is that outfit? Did Mr C. Baker give those to you?"

"You guessed?"

"Well. Yee, you do look exactly like him. Slightly outdated but incredibly fashionable."

I had to admit, there was only a difference in size between the typical black turtleneck and long elephant trousers Baker was usually wearing and the ones on me at this very moment. I disliked this look greatly. It was so plain and serious, drew all the attention to my face and hair. But it was the only clothes I had with me, and at least they would keep me warm and safe, whether day or night. "Well, at least Mr C. Baker is a decent man. It's not like everyone can be walking around like the Ancient Greeks all day."

George Langston looked down at the towel around his hips – the only thing he was wearing – and grimaced. "Ah, you see–..."

But he did not have to say much more. There was a rustling from one of the backrooms, and both Minush's and my ears twitched towards it.

"Antoni..." George Langston immediately said, warily, setting down Minush on the sofa, then raising a warning finger at me.

HOW TO GROW FEELINGS LIKE FLOWERS

"You can't be serious!" I exclaimed, shaking my head and turning to follow the noise. "Is that why you don't pick up the phone anymore?" The kitchen was empty. "Is that what you call being busy?" The bathroom was empty. "Because you–, Oh for Christ's sake, George! He's a child!" The bedroom wasn't empty.

On the bed sat a boy with the appearance of an angel, small-framed and delicate, and the blush on his cheeks made him look painfully vulnerable. "Hi," he said, awkwardly, breathless.

"Georgie!" I sighed, exasperated, "How old are y–, How old is he, George? You're a fucking paedophile, do you have no shame?"

"He's eighteen, I promise." George Langston whimpered, having hurried to follow me, "Tell him, Ismail, tell him you're eighteen."

"I'm eighteen." the boy smiled, and although he did not seem to be lying, he still looked terribly out of place on this giant king-size bed with the meaningful dark red bedsheets.

"And you're ancient, Georgie. Be ashamed of yourself."

George Langston did look ashamed of himself, but he was still trying to defend himself. "He liked it. He's the one who flirted with me, I swear, I'm innocent in this scenario."

"Fuck you, Georgie, you haven't been innocent since 1954."

"Whoa, are you really that old?" Ismail asked, sounding genuinely amazed and genuinely not meaning to be rude, and somehow I couldn't help but instantly grow a little fond of him.

"He's even older." I therefore replied, looking at the boy. "See that fluffy hair of his? It's a toupee. Wanna see what happens when you tug on it?" I took a step towards George Langston, who immediately backed away, raising both hands.

"I warn you."

"Come here, just a little tug."

"Don't come closer! Take your hands away! No–,"

"What, are you scared you'll actually feel old next to him?!"

"No-, Antoni, no, I warn you..!"

"Oh. So you're Antoni?" Ismail's voice cut through our little fight.

My attack on George Langston interrupted, both of us paused, blinking with surprise. After a brief moment of wondering what Ismail could mean, I turned to look at him. "Am I famous now, or what?"

"No!" Ismail laughed, then suddenly looked apologetic and hastily shook his head. "I mean, at least I don't think so." Behind me, George Langston sighed. "But Mr Langston tried to call you this morning, repeatedly. He said the fire brigade had been where you live, and he worried something might have happened to you."

For a long, long second, I stared at Ismail, then I turned to face George Langston, who, after some hesitation, returned my gaze. He gave me a tiny, apologetic shrug.

· · · ·

"This is wrong," I mumbled.

The pub was dark. The wood of the furniture was almost black, the leather on the sofas dark green, the stench in the air was a mix between weed, stark beer and dried sweat - which to me had always been kind of the same smell anyway - and the drinks served a little too fast and a little too plentiful. We were sitting in the very back of it, in a booth so dimly lit they had set up a candle for us despite it being only four in the afternoon, George Langston and I on one side, Ismail on the other, facing us.

"This is just so wrong."

"He's eighteen." George Langston grumbled, repeating this for the dozenth time now. "Now, please, this lovely drink I paid for."

Glaring at George Langston with my eyes on Ismail, I picked up my cocktail and sipped it spitefully. "I will not sleep with him in the same bed."

"Lucky us, then, since literally no one invited you into my bed in the first place."

"I did. Just now. Did you not listen?"

Ismail grinned, George Langston sighed.

"Come on, Georgie. Have a heart."

"A heart? On my momma's grave, that's rich from you."

I turned in my seat to look at him, unimpressed by that statement. "Really? You go that low? Now?! My apartment has probably gone up in flames, and hotels usually don't allow pets. What else do you want me to do? Go back to Louisanne?"

"No! No, of course n–," He sighed again, a little more exasperated and a little more urgent now, fully turning towards me, too. "Antoni, of course, I don't want you to go back to Louisanne. You know that. Don't say those things. But–... For Christ's sake, usually people ask for a sofa, not the entire bed."

"Half of the bed."

"Third of a bed."

"Half of a bed. I don't do sofas anymore. I did that last night and it gave me headaches. I can't have that. I've got work tomorrow and you know how hard it is to cum when you've got a head bigger than-..." I shot Ismail a glance. "Children are present, you know what I'm saying." A vague hand motion was to explain the rest. "No sofas."

George Langston tried not to look amused. "Your house burnt down, and you're still going to work?"

I nodded, returning the amusement without being able to quite help it. "It was scheduled weeks in advance, and you know how our Queen Virgin doesn't like it when you cancel out on her."

"The Queen Virgin?!" George Langston asked in astonishment. "I wasn't aware she's still in London."

I nodded. "Comes and goes, as always."

"As always, yes," he laughed.

"This reminds me of something I meant to ask you, though. Do you know a certain, ah, what was his name again, a certain Richard Leaf? He's been trying to reach me multiple times but seems a bit ... shy."

George Langston waved it off. "Yes, yes, Richard Leaflet. Nice young man, queer as a three dollar bill, on a good way to be a successful bankster and all that."

"So it was you who gave him my number? Because he kept calling and then hanging up again. I was starting to wonder if perhaps it was a prank."

"No, no, yes, yes. It was me. You'll like him, I had a good chit-chat with him in one of those fancy bars where everything is black and white, you know the type. It seems like it'll be a one-time thing for him, though."

"That's fine. I was just puzzled. Thank you. Do you have his number, too? Because with the building burning down and all that..."

George Langston nodded reassuringly, sipping his beer. "I'll arrange it for you. Next week?"

"Not tonight?"

"Tonight?!" He laughed. "And I thought you were so desperate to have my sofa. Wait, is this you needing the money, or you needing some stress relief?"

Clicking my tongue, I smacked George Langston's arm. "I just don't like letting people wait. What if he decides to go somewhere else?"

For an inexplicable reason, this made George Langston laugh even more.

"What?"

"Don't worry, he won't. I'll ask him for Friday."

Sceptically, I narrowed my eyes but said nothing more about it. To me, the main topic had been settled. Now I only needed the official 'okay'. "So. Tomorrow and on Thursday I'm away, and on

Friday the fire brigade people will tell us whether we move back into the building or not. If we can't, I'll have to look for a new apartment anyway, but other than that, it would only be for tonight and for a place to wash my stuff, shower and feed Minush. Yes?"

I thought George Langston would need another moment to prove to me how much he was hesitating, but instead, he nodded immediately, as though he never really needed convincing anyway. "Yes."

We looked at each other. His small, glistening eyes took in the sight of me, and I could but feel like coming home. Oh, Georgie, I thought, who would I be without your fat ass and your even fatter heart? The slight orange note in his tan so familiar with the sun that it had turned brown and leathery, the clean-shaven cologne-stinking cheeks, the flashing white teeth of a smile either inexistent or overly broad, the bolo ties in his brightly coloured shirts. And of course, the toupee, which looked like it had been glued to his head in the sixties and had never been taken off since. All of this, the entire vastness of this ugliness, it all made me believe that as long as I could look at it, nothing would ever be able to harm me.

"As long as you make me your dumplings." George Langston added.

"Dumplings? Oh." I laughed. "Yes, I'll cook for you, Georgie. I'll also clean up this mess of an apartment. For free."

"Don't lie like that. Nothing's ever been free with you, Pokorny." He gave me an amicable smirk.

"What can I say? Money makes the world go round."

"Something has to," he replied with a shrug.

For just a moment, my thoughts went to Lenny, to his beautiful apartment, to his records, to his warmth, to his bed. Would he let me share it with him without negotiation, pretence or otherwise? I pushed the thought aside. "Compared to my usual demands, half of a bed can almost be counted as 'free', wouldn't you say? Not even the whole bed, just half of it. But not just a third eith–..."

Our eyes grew wide as we simultaneously remembered something.

Ismail.

We turned to the boy. "Oh."

"Dear God." George Langston sighed.

Ismail had fallen asleep with his head on the table.

I reached out for Ismail's half-finished whisky glass, tipping it towards me to look inside. "Remember when half of a drink could knock you out like this?"

"Barely." George Langston replied. "But be nice to him, Antoni, he had a long night."

Clicking my tongue, I set the glass back down and gave George Langston a reprimanding glare. "Gross. You're really an abomination, do you know that?"

I received a nod. "But!" He raised a finger. A lot of pressure was put on this hopeful finger's upcoming argument. "You did not seem to mind when you were his age."

· · · ·

In the end, when we received our bill, it turned out that Little Ismail had had more than just one whiskey in the course of the two hours we had spent in that pub. I felt a little bad for not having supervised him better, but George Langston reminded me that at least like this, he would not notice that he was sleeping on the sofa.

Back at home – it was early night by now – the first thing I thus did was take off his shoes while George Langston was carefully tucking a blanket around his small frame, making sure it would not slip off him in the middle of the night. That was what I meant when people asked me how I could possibly be friends with someone like George Langston, how I could call him caring without then urged to wash my mouth with soap; yes, George Langston would never think about giving you a blanket, he would not even consider the fact that you might get cold in the night, but if you asked him for one, he would go great lengths to make sure it was the warmest, most comfiest blanket in the world. It was a different kind of caring that people couldn't seem to understand, and sometimes I wondered if the root of it was perhaps their definition of politeness. Because it wasn't proper to ask for help. Strange how so many preferred to suffer rather than express their needs. Ha.

Minush followed George Langston into the kitchen to be fed and watered, and finally, finding myself vis-à-vis with all the mess in this apartment, I decided to tidy up a bit. I knew this apartment so well, it was as though I was cleaning up my own home. The pizza boxes went into plastic bags, the wine glasses went into the kitchen sink, and in little time, the surfaces of various sticky and dusty pieces of furniture were like new again.

Eventually, my gaze fell on Little Ismail. He really deserved better than this, didn't he? "Oh." I noticed that he was still wearing his jewellery. My mother had often told me not to wear rings and necklaces to bed because they could choke you or cut off your circulation, and while I knew that those warnings were probably directed at a very young version of me, I could not help but worry about Little Ismail's air-and-blood situation. So I kneeled next to him, carefully feeling for the opening of the necklace behind his neck, then clicking it open and taking it off.

The pendant in my palm, I looked at it. It was made of black stone with silver lines and patterns carved into it, and it was slightly shaped like the body of a woman.

"Are you going to steal it?"

I startled a bit, looking at the heavy-lidded eyes that had just opened. He did not seem alarmed or upset. "No." I therefore smiled. "I was just taking it off so it won't hurt you."

Little Ismail nodded, seeming rather all right with that answer. His hand appeared from underneath the blanket to reach out for it anyway. "Please don't take Him from me. I need His charms to protect me."

"Of-... Of course. I'm sorry." I put the necklace into his palm, and his fingers loosely closed around it. "Charms?"

He smiled. "The words of the Prophet, woven into this necklace like charms. See?"

But all I could see were lines and fine adornments. Beautiful, but nonsensical to me. I nodded anyway.

"When I was little, I never slept well. My grandmother said that's because, in my sleep, I was probably forgetting about Allaah, and it let bad dreams in. So she gave me this necklace and said it would protect me so that the eyes of Allaah never fail to watch over me." He looked so peaceful as he said this, tying the necklace close again before lying back down. It made me smile.

"Is Allaah your God?"

Little Ismail nodded. "He is everyone's God."

I laughed quietly. "Don't let my grandmother hear that."

Little Ismail, too, had to grin at that, the sleepiness written all over his face. "But your God is our God is everyone's God, too. We only call Him differently because our human tongues scramble for words. But our hearts? Our hearts know that it's all the same God."

I said nothing to that, my eyes losing focus as they rested on the necklace's pendant.

"What is it?" he asked. "You don't believe in God?"

I shrugged. I felt like no matter what I would say, whether it was agreeing to what he said or saying what I believed, it all felt like being dishonest. "I think I once did. If I still do, then he has long left me, though." For a moment, I wanted to say more, tell him of my grandmother, my education, the last five years in London and how they had robbed me of every emotion possible, including what had once perhaps been faith. And Little Ismail looked as though he was ready to listen. As though he knew that no matter how light I was, there was one last grain of weight within me I had never dared to free myself of. In the end, I only shrugged again, and he smiled. "And hey, aren't you supposed to stay away from alcohol?" I asked, poking his chest with my finger. "Are you sure He'll protect you with all that whisky in your blood?"

Little Ismail let out a giggle, batting my hand away. "And doesn't your God say you shouldn't whore around and do unspeakable things with other men?"

I gasped, dramatically. "All the things I do are very speakable of, thank you very much."

We laughed.

"All right, enough. I let you sleep. Georgie has been suspiciously quiet for far too long now anyway." I rose to my feet, but Little Ismail caught my hand. Raising my eyebrows, I looked down at him.

"Thank you for letting me stay." he said, quietly but with a tone in his voice that spoke of him needing to be heard, "You know, sometimes I think God is love."

My expression slipped into blankness. I thought of the people I had loved, thought of the people who had claimed to love me, thought of the fact that I had been so busy negotiating half of a bed that I had not even realised that for Ismail this meant he could've been kicked out of George Langston's apartment altogether, thought of the emptiness inside my chest. Eventually, I gently retrieved my hand and smiled. "And I sometimes think God is hope. At least that would make him impossible." A single grain of weight. "Goodnight, Little Ismail. Know that I will always fight for your right to stay here."

There was a door that isolated the big space of the living room area from the backrooms, and because I had well noticed how George Langston had slipped the two little packs of what-ever-the-fuck-the-white-shit-had-been into his pockets before laying Little Ismail down on the sofa, I was preparing myself for another fight. Fight meant noise, and noise meant waking Little Ismail up, and I could not have that. So I closed the door. Tight.

"Georgie," I called him and Minush's chirping led me to the bedroom. There they both lay on the bed, he with all his limbs extended away from himself, Minush sitting on his chest. I assumed she had been dozing there, but upon hearing my voice, she had woken up. Coming to the corner of the bed, she craned her neck towards me in the hope of some scritches. "Hey, you." Willingly, I ruffled the fur of her neck while waiting for George Langston to come to his senses. "Georgie," I called again.

He grunted and sat up. His toupee was a mess.

I sighed. "Tell me the real reason why you didn't want me to stay here."

George Langston looked pained, either because he knew where this was going or because he really didn't and in both cases, it made me need the answer even more. "Because of me being a gross paedophile who sleeps–,"

"The real reason, Georgie."

Pain further contorted his drugged-up features as he continued trying to come up with cheap lies. "Um..."

"Did you start taking again?" I had no time for lies. I was tired. Hollow and light, yes, but mostly just tired. "I saw the white powder on the sofa. I'm not blind, Georgie. Be honest. Did you start using again?"

George Langston had completely given up looking at me. His head was ducked, and his hands folded in his lap like a scolded schoolboy.

I held out my hand, palm up. "Show me."

Hesitation. Then he reached into his trouser pockets and pulled out one of the packs I had seen earlier. "Sorry," he mumbled.

Ignoring him, I took it and looked at it through the clear plastic, mushing it up between my fingers to guess what it was. Especially now that I had grown so fond of Little Ismail, I could not bear the idea of poison lying around like this in this apartment.

I had not had much experience with drugs as I had always made sure to stay away from any addictive stuff, usually for all the wrong reasons, one of them namely being me being too greedy to spend my money on that shit. When I had walked the streets, I had seen enough people take all sorts of things, and even the least deadly of them, cigarettes, alcohol, had all led to consequences. I had learned. Keeping my money, sanity and free will in my sequined purse when I had nothing else to put in there. So once I knew what the powder was, knew that my worst fear had come true, I slapped George Langston across the face. "You're a fucking asshole and I'm disgusted by you."

I had not hit him hard, but the way he was now holding his cheek, tears pooling in his eyes as he looked up at me. Like an over-dimensional puppy.

"Why did you do that?" I hissed, keeping my voice down solely for Little Ismail, "You were clean for a year. Why did you do that? Don't you remember how much this shit wrecked? How hard it was to get you sober? Have you no respect for Loretta? Is this really worth it? Is it? What if Ismail were to ask you for some, would you let him? Is that how it is? Have you given up on seeing it as it is? That it can get you killed? That has already killed you once? You fucking moron, you idiot, I–..."

George Langston had caught my wrists, and my voice died as he made me look at him, his eyes glassy and pain-stricken. "I'm sorry," he repeated in a whisper.

I took a sharp breath. I hadn't been shouting, so perhaps that was why I sounded more serious than earlier that day. But the truth was, no matter the accusations I made, no matter the impact they had –

and I wanted there to be an impact – I wasn't angry. Anger is one of the first that you lose. I was just very serious. No accentuated feeling, my chest filled with nothing but mild annoyance. The breath I then exhaled took away this, too, though. "Why?"

George Langston shook his head. "Someone offered and I said yes."

I lowered my hands, and he let me. Minush had gone into hiding on the other side of the bed, and I couldn't blame her.

Quietly, George Langston took the pack from my hands, slipping it back into his pockets, then replaced the space in my palms with his fingers. "I would never let Ismail try, Antoni." Our gazes met. "Nor have I forgotten Loretta. I didn't–... I didn't think properly. I just did it, and then it was too late. I'm not–... There was no other reason to it. I'm not proud of it. I'm tryna-, I'm tryna–... It's just that–..." He took a shaky breath. "It's a fucking pointless life without her, you know." Then his lips quivered, and a second later, he curled up around his own middle like a fern, falling silent.

I watched him cry for a moment, unmoving, then turned to go take a shower.

. . . .

Theory.

Secondly, I will build my theory on you.

Are you a Mamma's boy who longs for some warmth and compassion?

Are you an arrogant bankster who has worked their whole life to be at the top of their company, leaving everyone and everything they ever loved behind, just to now find yourself so lonely and empty that even five loadings straight into their throat can't make them feel any less hungry for more?

HOW TO GROW FEELINGS LIKE FLOWERS

Are you someone who just wants some fun for a night but is too lazy to actually go through the trouble of finding yourself a 'real' guy, as you call it?

Or are you someone who just pretends they're too lazy because, in reality, you're just terrified of the rejection 'real' guys could give you?

Are you with me because you think I can't reject you?

Are you in college and your friends dared you, but your oh-so-high education does not allow you to treat me with disrespect, and disrespect means any sex that does not involve a penis and a vagina in missionary, so we'll spend the evening drinking coffee until my stomach feels bloated and I excuse myself to go read your physics papers on the toilet?

Are you a macho with muscles so thick you can hardly fit through the door and an ego so big that you cannot possibly allow your girlfriend to know about your soft side, so you come to me so I can take you hard and from behind? Or cradle you, little spoon?

Are you curious? A virgin? Simply a little lonely and tired of your right hand? Left hand?

I need to know. And I will know. And once my theory is set, I will lean back, and spend the rest of the dinner to confirm my theory, finding out whether I was right or not. Usually, I am.

· · · ·

We called her Queen Virgin because her name was Elizabeth and her hair as fiery as her soul.

She had worked herself to the peak of her career with nothing but shoulder pads and pantsuits, and whenever someone had asked her when she would finally settle to have children, her spite to climb ladders only grew. What did she need a man for but to sit on his face as she wore nothing but her high heels?

You see, there was an unwritten rule around us people of love, which all those who had once gotten into the hands of a brute and preferred to never relive that, took very seriously. It said that if you did not want to lose control over your client, you should never lose control over the situation. You should always be the one managing the scene, always be the one knowing what was going to happen next, be the one who was mentally on top, even while being the one taking it, the one who never, not even once, loses control over your senses.

That morning, I had brought Minush back to Mrs Potter. I did not want her to accidentally chew on one of George Langston's powder packs. I needed her. Even if all she had done during last night was sitting on George Langston and happily kneading his neck, ignoring me completely as though I wasn't the one who had taken her in after finding her and her siblings in a dumpster. I had almost felt happiness when she had come out of the burning building alive, but all she gave me was a disgusted expression whenever I tried to pet her. It was maybe ridiculous to feel so hurt over a cat's rigorous cleaning routine. But I was.

At home, we used to have a family dog, a German shepherd who had already been old when I was born. And although I had grown up with him, I had never felt as connected to him as I did with Minush. Our dog had been like a gentle but slightly demented relative, who everyone willingly accepted and probably also loved, but who we all appreciated finding asleep on a couch or quiet in his garden hut. Minush, however, she was like my own child. She had come to me when all else had disappeared. Found a spot in my vacant heart to keep it warm. If I got up in the morning, if I was not yet cold as a corpse, then because of her.

When Mrs Potter opened the door, her eyes grew wide with wonder. It was long after nine in the morning, so Mr Potter had already gone out for work, which meant that, unfortunately, I could not see his reaction either. I would have to trust Mrs Potter when she said that 'Harold will just have to accept the facts', and hope that Minush would feel happy in the empty living room at night. And in the end, it was only for a couple of days, right? By Monday at the latest, I would have my own apartment back, whether the old or a new one was left to find out.

We did it on the washing machine. It was Mrs Potter's favourite way to climax. Sitting at the machine's corner with her legs spread and her large, offensively beige panties still on, she was probably doing it even when her husband was at home. With the thundering noise of the machine's climax, her own voice not heard in the living room. My job usually just consisted of holding her breasts or listening to her impassioned speeches while the machine did all the rest. When she had first introduced me to her secret lover, I had been quite impressed. To think that women went to such great lengths to get somewhere, while all men did was stick their hands into their pants and hope for the best. In a way, there was also something charming about it, and so I had eventually grown fond of Mr Bosch.

Today, as I listened to her, my mind was distracted. At least Mrs Potter was a good person. At least Mrs Potter would keep Minush safe. At least I would not have to dwell in my anxiety that something bad could happen any second.

So when Mrs Potter had brought me to the door and started rummaging through her wallet, asking me how much she owed me, my eyes obviously grew wide.

"Oh. No, no, Mrs Potter. Please. You don't owe me anything at all."

Mrs Potter seemed surprised by that. "Why not?"

"Because you let me sleep in your house? Because you kept care of my cat, and because you're keeping care of her again? Because you're being incredibly kind to me already? Should I go on?"

"Yes, I'd like to hear what else you've got on your account." Mrs Potter retorted, dryly but with that sweet, amused smile on her lips. "Boy, you've got your price and I've got my money. When a handyman comes to my house and fixes my sink, then I pay the full price, do I not? So why would I constantly skip payment with you just because you give me the joy of caring for Minush? I pay you because you're good at what you do, and I let you stay at my place because I am fond of you. Not because I'm obligated, not because I wanted a free session with you."

She had talked over me ruthlessly, no matter how often I had tried to interject. Even as I now tried to repeat that I, on the other hand, hadn't come here for extra money but because I trusted her, she refused to listen.

"Boy, sometimes you just need to let people help you."

Thus, with two hundred pounds extra in my already far too heavy wallet, I bid her goodbye and promised myself to never use that money. Perhaps, one day, Mrs Potter would find herself needing it, and then I could return it all and prove how grateful I was.

As I passed the building on my way to the bus station, my eyes went up to floor number eleven and the ones above it. There was nothing burnt about their appearance, the windows were intact and the walls were as pale grey as always, no soot tainting them black. Who knew, perhaps we'd all be back home by Friday night. Perhaps I would indeed get a chance to see and thank Lev.

It was then that the sound of someone weeping pulled me out of my thoughts.

A woman sat on the side of the road, dressed in wide, loose clothes that covered almost her entire body. In her pain, she was rocking herself back and forth. At least it looked like it, but as I stepped closer, I saw that she was holding a baby pressed to her chest.

"Ma'am?" I carefully asked as I approached her.

She startled, looking up at me with wide eyes. For a brief moment, I thought she would go back to crying, perhaps in some form of act for monetary compassion – many people did that, however, only a few tried it in our neighbourhood. Most of them knew that there was more to get in the richer boroughs in the south and that begging for money here barely even paid for the bus ticket out again. But this woman was not crying for compassion. On the contrary. She quickly wiped her tears and scrambled to her feet. "I'm sorry," she said. "I'm okay. Please, don't worry."

I looked at her and her baby, her reddened eyes and blotchy face, and I frowned. "Did something happen?" I asked because, yes, I was a lightweight with more pounds in my wallet than on my body, but I was more than ready to go and confront whichever husband had done this to his wife and their newborn child. "Should I call you a cab?"

But the woman shook her head. "And where would I go?"

I followed her gaze to my building, and suddenly I understood. "Oh! You live on this block, too?"

"Lived," she corrected me, and as her eyes watered again, I was reminded of Mr Potter, who had said the same thing.

"But, ma'am, please don't cry," I said, stepping a little closer and trying to look into her face, which she was hiding in her baby's chest now. "By Friday, we'll all be back inside, living happily as though nothing happened."

"No," she wept, "No, I won't." Once again, I thought of the theory with the abusive husband, but what the woman then said went in a totally different direction. "They say it was my son who set the fire. Even if we are allowed to move back in, I won't be able to follow. I'll have to pay."

"Your son? He looks kind of young to be setting fires, though." I mumbled, looking at the baby.

She raised her gaze to me, glaring. "This isn't my son. This is the daughter of my husband and his whore. I am just keeping it because I understand the meaning of the word 'consequences' and because I've got a good heart and not just a good fanny."

I raised my hands defensively. "All right, all right." What a dramatic turn this had taken.

She sighed. "My son is at school right now. He's sixteen. Just a sixteen-year-old innocent boy. Even if we get to move back in on Friday, someone will have to pay. And none of us has the money. I'll have to pay. I'll have to leave all of them alone and pay for it in prison."

I stood a little perplexed, a little awkward. Those was a lot of information I had not seen coming. Especially not the paradox of 'sixteen-year-old boy' and 'innocent', but, hey, who, if not I, knew how mothers glorified their sons. "Um." I looked around, almost hoping there was someone else I could hand the responsibility to. Of course, there was no one, though. And of course, even if there had been someone, what would they have done? Criminality was everywhere here and whether accidental or purposeful crimes, at the end of the day, everyone had to fight for their own bread. No one here had enough money to buy a kid out of jail.

Well.

I looked back at her. "On which floor do you live?"

"Twelfth."

"Right above mine. If you lost your place, I probably lost mine too."

She kept wiping the heel of her hand over her eyes. No wonder they were that red and puffy, gosh. "At least in jail, they have a warm meal every day, don't they? At least in jail I won't have to see this ass of a husband anymore." But as soon as she said that, she burst into tears once more, and she cried into her baby's chest. "He's just sixteen, I cannot leave him alone."

For a moment, I considered hugging her, but her shoulders were shaking so much that it would have been quite an uncomfortable hug. So I stood there, hesitating. "You know, Ma'am, if it's just for the money, I can give it to you. I–,"

"Your whore money?!" she exclaimed, her voice suddenly harsh.

"Wh–..?"

"Do you really think I want any of your filthy sin money? My Anthony is better than that, if he survives and goes to uni one day, it's because of hard work and honest labour and none of your sin."

I blinked. "Okay. Did not expect that?"

She raged on: "I am done with you and your repulsive kind. Don't you think I don't know how to recognise you? How you go in and out of other people's houses, stealing everyone's husbands with your dirty hands? Be off already. Be off and don't ever think I'd let you lot help me ever again."

"Your son's named Anthony?"

There was a hiss in a language I did not speak, but the intentions were clear nevertheless.

"All right, all right." I huffed, mostly taken aback by the sudden change of mood, but slightly amused, too. "I'm leaving. It was just an offer. And it still stands. If ever you get bored in jail and stuff."

As I turned and left, I heard her wailing behind me. What was it with people that they thought one kind of work was better than the other? As Mrs Potter had so aptly put it: Whether you fixed sinks in other people's houses or their libido, what was the difference? In both cases, you just used your hands, no?

However, even if used to such offensive, ignorant opinions, I could not stop thinking about her. Some people really couldn't be helped, but who knew, perhaps her son was a little more evolved? Had he really set the building on fire? How much would it cost to pay for the renovations and the fire brigade, and the police investigation? For how long would his mother have to go to jail for him if no one paid the bail? Would he show remorse? Had it perhaps been an accident after all? A stray cigarette, secretly smoked inside his bedroom? Anthony, floor twelve. I would find out more, I was sure of that.

Who, if not someone as privileged as I, had to help?

So when it was time to submit myself to our Queen Virgin, I did not pretend that my needs were worth more than hers. There were so many people out there who suffered a rigid future, who would never be as fortunate as I was, so who was I to pretend like I deserved even more than that? And you know, when our Queen Virgin calls you and her fingers curl into the collar of your shirt as she drags you into her penthouse, you do not refuse. You do not try to impose your own rules and habits. You obey. And you're grateful for it. She wasn't just a client, after all. She was regal. She was the monarch of all butterflies, the Venus of all Botticellis, the Ninth of all symphonies. When she called you, you obliged, and it was thus that for her I was giving up all unwritten rules and allowed her to push me down with the cleats of her high heels.

And then you pray to God just like Little Ismail predicted it, because you are just too aware of how damn lucky you are to be able to give up control when you need it.

• • • •

"You're back already?"

"She didn't want me to stay over," I said as I crossed the room to open the window.

I had showered and scrubbed the smell of sex off my skin and was now wearing my tracksuit pyjamas. But it was warm, far too warm for the heat and the stuffy air inside the bedroom. Thus, after tipping the window open, I pulled the curtains to the side to let more fresh air in. The light of our two moons was now falling into the room and revealed that a sleeping Little Ismail was curled up next to George Langston.

I had expected so when the couch in the living room was empty upon my return.

"Antoni–..." George Langston started, ready to defend himself, but I shook my head. Tonight, I was too tired to argue. And Minush wasn't around.

"I'll just pretend he's naked because it's so warm, okay?"

George Langston nodded.

Third of a bed, then. Wordlessly, I climbed between them, pulling the thin sheet of a blanket from George Langston and over Little Ismail instead. As I wrapped my arm around him, he shivered against me, probably because my skin was cold from the shower. It didn't wake him up, though.

"Did you have a good day?" George Langston's voice was low, soft.

I thought about the long bus ride home, about the dominance of our Queen Virgin, about the crying woman and her baby, about saying goodbye to Minush, who had not even seemed to notice my departure. "And you?" I asked instead.

"It was a good day, yes. Going to museums with someone cleverer than you turns out to be hella entertaining."

I smirked. I could imagine it well. Little Ismail, so overly well-educated, excitedly rambling on about a random Rembrandt they found in the National Museum of Art. But the smirk fell when George Langston's hand came to rest on my shoulder.

"But how are–,"

"Don't touch me, Georgie."

He retrieved his hand. There was a moment of silence, then I heard him shift. When he spoke again, his voice seemed more distant, and I assumed he had turned around and away from me and Little Ismail. "I don't-, I'm not high right now, you know." Despite distant, I could hear the frown in his voice. "I haven't taken anything since yesterday. I'm not-, It's not ... bad. I just do it for fun, not because I have to. Sometimes! Rarely. Only a little bit. Besides, I'm done with needles. You won't ever-... You know."

I didn't believe him. In a way, I did not want to. How often had I heard him say those exact words, believing them, hoping that one day he'd open his door for me, looking healthy and sober? And how often had he woken from a crash, crying, because he had once again failed to join Loretta? The memories were eager to swamp my mind, but I did not let them. I pushed them away, all of them, until there was only emptiness. "Good." I shrugged. "Because you know that Loretta will slap your ass if she learns that you died before your time."

George Langston let out a soft chortle. "Do you think there's such a thing as ass-slapping in heaven?"

"I sure hope so. You deserve it."

"Well." He sounded amused. "I guess that if there's ass-slapping, it does sound like heaven."

I didn't mean to, but a tiny laugh escaped me. "You're a moronic lunatic," I mumbled. For a moment, I wanted to turn around to see his face, see him alive, even if pale under the cold moons' light, but with Little Ismail in my arms, I could not move much, and after all, it was me who had told him not to touch me. So instead, I freed one of my icy feet and slipped it between George Langston's warm calves.

"For fuck's sake." he hissed out, and I smirked.

"Tomorrow I'll make you dumplings."

"Well, if that's the price."

I smiled. "Good night."

"Good night, curly fry."

The next morning, I did as promised. While George Langston slept until noon, Little Ismail and I prepared the pierogi, the little radio playing music in the background. We talked a lot about a wide variety of topics, but neither of us really asked about where the other was from, how we had come to know George Langston. It turned out that the little conversation about faith we had had the other night really hadn't been out of character for him; Little Ismail was a bright young man who not only knew how to talk incredibly well, but who was also more than capable of understanding my sometimes clumsy, heavy English. When the topic of our conversation would turn a little more complicated, he never showed any sign of impatience as I scrambled for words, and in return, it gave me the patience to involve him in the cooking process more than just commanding him around. I told him of the origins of those dumplings, about how we usually ate them with sauerkraut but that I hadn't been able to find any in the local store, and how two years ago I had first cooked them for George Langston. He showed himself curious and interested, and the closer lunchtime approached, the more I hoped he would try to get away from there as soon as possible. I did not want to see his life ruined.

Ironically, just as George Langston rose from his sleep and shuffled into the kitchen, greekly dressed, the radio played a certain song by Huey Lewis & the News that caused me to turn it off completely. "Good morning." I smiled. "Lunch is almost ready. I couldn't find sauerkraut in the store, so we made some salad with bits of bacon in it instead. I hope that's all right?"

George Langston waved it off. "You know I'd eat shit if you were the one serving it to me."

I chuckled and watched Little Ismail hastily washing his hands so he could then hop over to George Langston and press a good morning kiss to his lips. Casting a glance in my direction, George Langston hushed Little Ismail away to set the table.

Much like all three of the backrooms of George Langston's apartment, the kitchen was narrow and long. And because one side was furnished with the kitchen counter, stove and fridge, leaving only a one-way path to bring you from the exit to the table at the very end of the room, it was even more narrow. However, because it had all been painted in a yellowish kind of peach tone, and the sun never ceased to shine through the two large balcony windows, it was a beautifully bright room. Warm. I had made and collected many happy memories here, and I was sure that almost everyone who had once had the excellent coffee often served here, or the even more excellent company, had fallen in love with the welcoming appearance of this room. With the white cupboards and counters, there was something clean-cut and modern about it, without making it feel clinical or staged. But what made it feel so welcoming and alive was the way George Langston had decorated the door and all the cupboard surfaces with the licence plates of old, unused cars from the city he was originally from. I had always wondered how he had come to own so many cars, but suspecting that it was for no cheerful reason, I had never dared ask.

As we pushed the table away from the wall a bit so it could accommodate three instead of its usual two chairs, Little Ismail started babbling about the recipe and how he was excited for us to try it all. He looked so ridiculously proud that I could but smile fondly. I still didn't know what had made him a refugee in George Langston's arms, and although I was wary of it, I knew that no other place could've given Little Ismail so much momentary happiness. Who but I knew that? Just because a situation was dangerous didn't mean it wasn't also happy.

"Dear God, Antoni! Are you trying to make me explode?"

"Oh, shut up. It's not that much." I rolled my eyes as I set the giant pot full of pierogis on the table before them.

"It's hella too much!" George Langston courageously tackled another heap of dumplings anyway.

It was a cheerful meal. I watched them talk about their plans for the upcoming days, noticing how no answer George Langston gave was in any way insincere or filled with annoyance. He truly did enjoy the prospect of spending time with Little Ismail, whether at the London Dungeons or on a boat on the Thames, and I felt a little less guilty for not having reported the kidnapping of a child. Little Ismail, in return, seemed just as delighted about his time here. He was from London, he told me between his second and third serving, but he had spent so many years in boarding schools and colleges far away that he had never actually gotten around to doing any of the touristy things. So being here was quite like a holiday far away from home, despite needing as few as two underground stations to be back in his childhood room. Why he stayed here, though, he kept to himself, and I did not dare ask. In a way, I didn't need to anyway. A gay young man from a family made of pure gold? Come on. What could possibly be the reason?

"How long have you been here, Antoni? Have you been to the Tower of London yet? That's where I want to go tomorrow."

"Five years, almost, but no, I haven't been yet. Tell me how it is, yes? If you say it's interesting, I'll make sure to give it a try."

In the end, George Langston kept right. We really had made too many dumplings. Despite our valiant ambition to finish the pot, there were still a dozen dumplings left, and not to speak of the mostly untouched salad. But the minute we came to that conclusion, I already knew what I was going to do with them, and started packing all of them into a smaller pot.

"Stay away from the fumes when he smokes," I told Little Ismail on the way out. We had talked so much over dinner that it was already past 3 in the afternoon.

"What's wrong with the fumes?" Little Ismail asked, looking at George Langston curiously.

"Nothing," I answered. "As long as you don't breathe them in." Then, after leaving a small peck on both of their cheeks, I gave George Langston a last warning look, then left, my pot o'pierogi under my arm.

It was funny how, back when my mother used to make them for us, I had never particularly cared about this dish, but how now I treasured her recipe like a piece of home itself.

Did everyone feel that way about memories from their home country? As though it was of no particular worth until you didn't have it anymore? Was this the explanation for forty-odd California license plates? What if I ever returned to Poland? Would I suddenly feel sentimental over a plate of fish and chips?

• • • •

"Hi."

"Hey, honey." I smiled and pressed a gentle kiss to Lenny's lips. "How are y–... Did you cry?"

"What?" His eyes were glassy, and his nose a little red. He was either sick or had been crying moments ago, and knowing Lenny, both were equally likely. "No, no, I-..." He waved me into his apartment. There was a distinct smell of citrus soap in the air, which meant his cleaning lady had already been there this morning. Usually, she came on Fridays, right after I left, sometimes our paths even crossed. She was a nice Spanish lady, probably far too intelligent for such a banal job. But everyone had to do what they could do in this economy, didn't we? "I just worried something had happened to you."

I turned back to look at Lenny, a frown on my face. "Am I too late? What time is it?"

He nodded towards the big wall clock. "Quarter past already."

This meant that despite having left far too late from George Langston's place, I had still managed to be here relatively on time. Fifteen minutes. My mother would call that being forty-five minutes early. But this was Lenny. And if I had learned something from working for him for so long, it was that you did not mock or point out how ridiculous his fears were. "I'm sorry," was what I therefore said, smiling in the hope of reassuring him. "I forgot that the buses take longer from Georgie's place."

I had not meant to drop the bomb right away, knowing that a topic such as me seeing George Langston again wasn't one Lenny could just let slide. And indeed. Drop, explosion, impact.

"You're back at Mr Langston's place?" he asked, his eyes growing wide with wonder and confusion. "Why? Did you make up? Or do you have trouble paying rent or something? Do you need money?" His eyes grew even wider. "It's not because of Mr Langston, right? Nothing happened to him, I hope?"

"No, no, everything's fine. We made up, him and me. There was a small incident in my building, so they evacuated it until they were sure it was safe to go back in. Given that it's Georgie who signed the lease, I thought it would be best to stay with him until they contact and inform him."

Lenny nodded as his eyes chased my words through the room, but his expression showed that my answer satisfied and relaxed him. "So it's just some good ol' bureaucracy?"

I chuckled and nodded. "Yes. Just some good ol' bureaucracy that makes me stay with Georgie."

"And you're okay there? You–, you know with–, but that's–, It doesn't make things complicated, does it?"

"Always worrying about the well-being of others, aren't you?" I teased. Thoughts about George Langston's bad habits came to my mind, and for a moment, I considered telling Lenny the truth, but what did this rich, privileged boy from the upper class of England know about the struggles of us immigrants who had doomed ourselves to death in their search for free love? So I shook my head and dismissed the thoughts. "Ah, you know, things are always complicated with me and Georgie. But, no. We're fine. It's just that currently, he has a guest over, so I had to clean up and cook and all that." I nodded towards the pot o'pierogi. "That's why I'm late. I'm sorry."

Lenny mirrored my smile. "I know that you're important to Mr Langston, and it was making me sad that you've been fighting and not talking for so long." Lenny's hand shyly caught mine, barely touching it. "And don't worry about being late. It's just fifteen minutes, I'm just overreacting. Especially if you're taking care of Ismail, I shouldn't complain. I–, Oh no."

My eyes grew wide. "Ismail?!"

"Oh darn."

"How-, What-, How do you know about that?"

Lenny lowered his hand very, very slowly, and behind his eyes, I could read all the excuses he was trying to come up with right now. "I ... don't?" was the one he ended up using.

If I hadn't been so surprised, I would've laughed. "No, but–... Did you talk to Georgie recently or what?"

Lenny looked down between us. "What's that?" He pointed at the pot under my arm, but I ignored him.

"Lenny. Why do you know Ismail?"

Lenny's eyes closed. "He's an old school friend of mine." He glanced back up at me, to the door, to the wall, to his feet. His fingers had started fumbling with the buttons of his shirt, busying themselves as he straightened against his fight-or-flight reflexes.

I stared at him. And stared. And stared. And suddenly it clicked. "You're the one who introduced him to Georgie?!"

Realising there was no way out of the reveal now, Lenny caved. "He has trouble at home, so he came here, but you know how nervous it makes me when people are here, I-... He used to be in the school choir with me, and he was always nice to me, never said anything mean to me, not even behind my back, so I didn't–, I couldn't–... So I thought about Mr Langston. I-, I mean, he has the financial means, and he's helped me before and-... I mean-, I mean, he used to take you in, right? That's what you told me, right? He helped you out when you had nothing, so I thought–, so I thought maybe he'd be good to Ismail, too."

I took it all in silently, thinking about them even moments after he had stopped speaking. He wasn't wrong. A kid without money, especially one who is used to always having enough of it, couldn't survive alone for long. And while I disliked the idea of 'fresh meat' being brought into the den of George Langston, I disliked the idea of Little Ismail being sent back home to a hateful family even more. At least there was warmth and laughter at George Langston's place. My thumb brushed over Lenny's cheek. "You did quite the right thing," I said, emphasising the words. "Thank you for taking care of Ismail." For a brief moment, I could see Lenny's eyes, then they lowered again. "I just wish there was a safer way to take care of all those kids who get kicked out of their homes. A place where they can go without having to prostitute themselves."

"Prostitute themselves?" Lenny scrunched up his nose. He didn't like that word.

"Well, sleeping with someone to not sleep on the streets is what I call prostitution, yes. And the last thing I want for Little Ismail is Georgie making a whore out of him as well."

That was a word Lenny liked even less. He scrunched up his nose harder. "Don't you like your profession?"

Profession. I huffed out a chuckle. "I do, but–..." I thought of Mr Hendrikson and the hand that had escaped him. I thought of the woman in front of the building yesterday, and how she had hissed at me. I thought of my mother and all the lies I told her. Of Minush and how I was not able to rent an apartment for both of us without someone else's help. Of Lev and how offended they were when I had touched them. Of The Second and how he flinched with disgust whenever I took his son's name into my mouth. "I do enjoy what I do. But I hate how the world is trying to make me hate it."

This was something, even sweet, innocent Lenny could understand. He kept fumbling with the buttons of his shirt until I took his hand into mine, and for a moment we stood like this in silence. "You know," he eventually said, "you know that if you wanted to, I could ask Papa to give you a job at the company, right?"

I felt my expression melt into fondness and adoration. "Oh, sweet, sweet honey," I murmured, caressing my fingers over his. "Who allows you to be so precious? Come on, I want to dance with you. You asked me about the pot, right? Go put on some music while I hide this in the fridge, so it can be a surprise for tonight, yes?" Without waiting for confirmation, I turned to go to the kitchen.

In the same way, George Langston's kitchen was perfectly welcoming, Lenny's was perfectly hostile. There were no windows at all, and the only light source was a glaring white lamp without a shade at the top of the high ceiling. White. Clean. It was cold. It was unfriendly. It was the kind of room that was never being used because it did not look like it wanted to be used. The only good thing about this monstrosity was that it had a gigantic fridge in it, which always carried the most wonderful ingredients. Especially untouched exotic fruits, which, due to being so expensive, weren't something I ate anywhere else but here. But tonight we'd have the leftover pierogi, and so I put the pot into the fridge, glad that at least my stomach had stopped aching from having had too much of them already and withstood this rich-in-vitamin temptation.

"I mean it," Lenny said behind me. Of course, he had followed me into the kitchen.

"What do you mean?"

"That I could ask Papa to give you a job at the company."

I chuckled. "I know, honey. But he'd never hire me."

"Why not?" Lenny asked back, almost immediately, as though he had expected me to say that. "He hired you once already? He trusts you to do a good job. He doesn't like you, but he trusts you.

He knows you've never broken the contract by skipping a date and or telling anyone about us. He knows you're diligent and kind, and loyal and terribly intelligent."

I laughed and closed the fridge, turning around to Lenny. "I'm not intelligent. I never even finished school."

"You are! That's exactly why you are! I mean-, I mean you regularly-, you quote Marx and Smith and all those people in your newspaper when you're upset, you read Victor Hugo and Cervantes, your English is self-taught and nearly perfect, and I bet you still do that thing where you calculate the speed of whichever vehicle you're in just by eye-measuring the distance and time, just for fun. And if I remember right, you picked up Hindi just because you wanted to converse with the people in the deli near where you live. Stupid people don't do that. And I–, I mean I went to Harrow! I know what stupid people with an expensive education look like, and I still think there's hardly anyone out there, whether in the schools I attended or my father's company, who could ever be more quick-witted than you are."

"You're sweet, honey."

"I mean it. You're bloody brilliant."

Never in my life, never, had I heard someone say such a thing to me. Except perhaps my family, but how honest was your own mother with all her biases? My teachers had always been on the verge of desperation with me, infuriated by how I never found the focus to do a single task without getting up and walking through the classroom intermittenly, click my pen, tap my foot, and, gosh, how often had my preachers kicked me out of our faith lessons because I could never shut my mouth? I was sure that all of them would have burst out laughing hearing Lenny talk like this, too. Strange, though, how heavy it made my chest feel... For a few breaths, anyway. I refused to acknowledge it. "You're aware that you don't have to say that to get me to sleep with you, right?" I teased instead.

Lenny jutted his lower lip into a pout. "I'm not flirting. I'm saying it because it's the truth. You're the only person who makes me curious about the world."

I didn't dare let it affect me. "So what you're saying is I should actually do your father's job at the company?"

"Yes. Antoni! Don't laugh at me! You really are fit for a position at the company. And admit it, you'd love to have a job that requires you to use your brain."

"Yes, but I also do love sex."

Lenny fell silent.

I sighed. "Listen, honey." I clung to the pet name. "I don't think sitting at a desk all day and doing boring paperwork is exactly my kind of job. I need to be around people. I need to move, to talk, to engage." I gently squeezed Lenny's hands in reassurance. "Plus, you know, I earn more getting off than I would ever earn at your company, considering the positions your father would actually offer me. You see, even if I were to stop seeing everyone but you, I'd still make twelve hundred pounds a month, which is, if I'm not mistaken, as much as you have after paying your rent and taxes, no?"

Lenny nodded timidly.

"I don't want Little Ismail to do what I do because, as long as people think of it the way they do now, it's not a safe job. And, fuck, you said he went to school with you? That alone means he's had more education than anyone in my whole entire family. He could rise to the heights of society and change the world from up there. Not client by client, but with the help of institutions and laws. He deserves better than old men's dicks being shoved up his arse four times a week. You should ask your father if he wants to hire him. But I could never accept your offer. I'm not made for the world of 3-piece suits and legal money." Lenny was still not replying to anything, so I pulled myself up to my tiptoes and pressed a kiss to his cheek.

"Besides. If I were to do honest work, we wouldn't see each other anymore, would we?"

"We could, though. No? For real this time. I mean, Papa just doesn't like you because he has to pay for you, but if we were together, you and me, for real, Papa wouldn't have any reason to mind you anymore. We–... We could go to the company's parties together. I could introduce you to my friends, dance with you in front of everyone, I–, You-, papa would finally let me talk about you at family dinners. You could be there. Always. And I–, I'd never have to be afraid again."

My chest felt heavy. So, so heavy. It nearly suffocated me. "Oh, honey," I said, and although I said those words often, my voice shaking with the struggle to enunciate them now. "You beautiful, beautiful person." My hold around his hand tightened as I breathed, breathed against that weight. "Whatever we are to each other will not suddenly become honourable just because your father stops paying me." In his silence and the way he looked at me, I could read his doubts, his hesitation, his fear that I'd never see him again if it wasn't for the money, and because I didn't know the answer to that either, I sealed his lips close with a kiss. "We're happy, no?"

Lenny stared at the fridge. "Yes," he nodded. "Yes, I think we're happy."

"C'mon. Let's dance."

• • • •

We knew almost the entire choreography by heart, having watched the movie a thousand times whenever we could, and while we were both merely mediocre dancers, we had far too much fun mouthing our way through the entire musical as though we were the ones singing, just like Kathy later did it in the storyline of the movie herself. At first, Lenny had put on *You Are My Lucky Star,* but I had needed something more cheerful, so with a totally accidental kick of my foot, I had forced the record player to jump back to *Good Morning* instead. And it was a good decision. Lenny and I had choreographed such a great – read: brutally embarrassing for anyone who was to watch us – routine through his apartment over time, which included a part where we improvised the languages in which 'Good Morning' was being sung, that at the end of it when in the movie Kathy, Cosmo and Don fall down on the sofa and we copied it by falling down on the bed, our laughter was always genuine.

At least twice as breathless as they were, we held each other and giggled until our voices faded away into exhaustion.

"God, she's adorable."

"I know many are in favour of Gene, but I much prefer Donald O'Connor. He's the real star of *Singing in the Rain*. And very adorable, too."

"Of course you'd prefer the goofball," I smirked, genuinely not surprised by Lenny's choice.

"He's not just a goofball! You think the movie's about an evil company getting rid of their leading star, or about the other boring star getting even more successful by stealing other people's ideas, but that's wrong! The real story is the story of the sidekick who, despite being just as good and despite working as hard, has been ignored and mistreated for years. And now, finally, thanks to the invention of the talkies, he is being given the chance to show the world his musical talent and shine!"

Lenny had dramatically gestured through the air as he explained all that, and it had me curling up with laughter. "Justice for Cosmo!"

He dropped his hands, grinning at me for a moment before his features turned sober. "Can I ask you a question?"

"Only if it's dirty."

Lenny smiled at me but it felt half-hearted. Looking for something to do, he rolled onto his back, reached for a teddy and held it over his head, looking at it for a while, lost in thoughts. Or maybe avoiding the ones I had made him avoid.

"You're going to make me jealous if you look at Teddy like that."

Lenny chuckled shyly. "Don't worry. He's not my type."

"Why? I think he looks cute. Is it because he's too chubby or too small? Or because his tail isn't long enough for your taste?"

"It always comes down to the tail, doesn't it?" Lenny grinned, turning the teddy to look at the fluffy bunny tail.

"I only come down to the tail when the tail doesn't go up first."

"Antoni!"

This time, we laughed together again, heartily, despite all those jokes being so terribly low-hanging.

When silence returned, I watched Lenny look at his old teddy with childlike interest. He did not talk to him out loud, but I could see in his eyes that he was holding a conversation with him nevertheless. I remembered my first plushie, a teddy, too, very similar to the one Lenny had. My grandmother gave it to me on my first day on earth. My mother and I were still in bed, there were pictures of us lying there, looking exhausted. Growing up, I had loved my teddy a lot. Contrary to Lenny's teddy, it had soon lost its beauty because I would drag it around with me everywhere, and literally no one could remember anymore just how often its button-eyes had to be replaced because I would chew them off. Eventually, I had deemed myself too old to love a plushie, so I had abandoned him. Now, pretty much ten years later, I regretted it. A child makes no distinction between a doll and a real person; both of them are true friends to it, and as I watched Lenny nudge his teddy's nose, I had no doubt that the company of this lifeless friend was not worth any less than mine. Well. At least he never had to be alone. "Lenny?"

"Yes?"

"What did you want to ask me?"

Our gazes met and held each other, then Lenny's jumped back to his teddy, leaving me alone. I watched him some more until, eventually, he said: "Nothing."

I frowned. Carefully, I moved between Lenny's arms and the teddy, gently pushing myself into his vision, my weight causing Lenny to release his breath. It was shaky. "Are you sure?" I asked.

Abashed, Lenny nodded. "Are you still thinking about Kathy?"

I could hardly hold back a laugh. "No," I answered. "No, on my mind and before my eyes, there is no one else but you."

I didn't know where the teddy went, but soon I felt Lenny's hands driving deep into the back of my jeans, pulling us close together. Our lips met, so did our tongues.

Letting yourself be unguardedly happy, even if happiness is long nothing more than a beautiful memory, is dangerous. Such a state of mind can make you very foolish.

· · · ·

The balcony of George Langston's apartment showed east, which meant that as I came home early in the morning after Lenny had called me a cab, - "You're a cab, Antoni." - I was able to drink my freshly brewed coffee under the first rays of the sun.

Before I came here, people always said that England was the land of rain. That I'd always have to walk around with an umbrella if I didn't want to grow webbing between my fingers. And they thought I'd only stay for two months. But now, five years later? Well, perhaps the Summer was a little greyer than the simmering dry heat of our Summer at home, but apart from that, I never felt like there was too much rain. Especially the Autumn was beautifully golden sometimes. Today wasn't going to be one of those golden days for long, thick clouds threatening the horizon, but for now, there was some sun.

HOW TO GROW FEELINGS LIKE FLOWERS

"Happy birthday, Pia," I murmured into my mug of coffee. *"I hope you have a beautiful day, a beautiful party. I hope that my gift pleases you, that it makes you happy, and that you know that I love you. And I promise, for your eighteenth, I'll be back home, I'll be there."*

I wished Minush could be here. Her warmth brought more comfort than this small mug, and at least she would've rolled up against me while I sang Pia a quiet little happy birthday song, just like she had done last year. Now I had to sing alone, and my voice sounded strangely muted, even before it had a chance to disappear amongst the street noises below.

"You sing quite well," a voice behind me said.

Surprised, I turned. "I don't. But thank you."

Little Ismail smiled, stepping closer. "What language was that?"

Perhaps I was a tiny bit embarrassed that I had been caught singing Happy Birthday into the street canyon to my feet, but as with most emotions, this one passed soon, too. "Polish."

"Ah!" Little Ismail looked delighted, paused, looked up at the sky, then declared, grinning: "Dj-en dob-reh."

I blinked, then understood, and let out a laugh. It was free of mockery or offence. On the contrary, I found it adorable. "Good morning to you, too, Ismail."

He kept grinning proudly. "The wife of our concierge is Polish. She taught me much more when I was younger, but I'm rubbish at languages. My mother hates it. She's been trying to teach me Arabic for years, but I can't get it into my head. Except for the prayers, but I think it's the music that helps with that. As I told you, I'm more of a maths and chemistry kind of person. So, sorry if I just totally butchered that."

I chuckled. "You didn't. I bet I'd do much worse if I were to try Arabic. Come here, though, don't stand in the door like that."

"Oh," he mentioned behind him into the kitchen, "actually I wanted to ask if I could steal some of the coffee you made."

I told him that, of course, he could have some of it, that I had made far too much anyway, and after he served himself, with plenty of milk and sugar, he came to join me on the balcony again, leaning his back against the balustrade. We talked about languages and how funny it was that you would go into a country, and after a week, you could suddenly speak three times as much as after several years of learning that language at school. Then we talked about this country through the eyes of immigrants – my impressions versus the stories Ismail's grandmother used to tell him – and that he planned to go to America after graduating from university. This led to me asking if that meant he didn't plan on staying here with George Langston, and him smiling sadly.

"I think there are certain cages you have to endure for a while before you can run away without dying under freedom's weight," he said, and I felt those words resonate within me more than I wanted to.

Perhaps he knew. Because then he asked me if I had to go to work today. I told him yes and reminded him of the date with Richard Leaflet, George Langston had arranged for me before, remembering that Little Ismail had been asleep during that conversation. "A bankster, apparently. Tonight at six. We'll have a little aperitif in a café, then we'll go have dinner and see if we click."

"And you're here so early because of the phone call from the landlords of your building?"

I nodded.

"How come Mr Langston is paying your rent? You don't sleep with him, do you?"

"No, I don't." I laughed – reminded of something, and thus started to rummage through my coat pockets. "And he's not paying my rent. He's just the one who signed the contract for me, for cases like these. I'm here pretty illegally, and I work black. Usually, when you sign leases, they want to know what your income source is, and, well." I let a vague hand gesture finish my sentence. Little Ismail obviously had no issues understanding. He was perhaps rich and privileged, but not spoiled and innocent.

"I hope they call soon, then," he smiled and looked so very genuine about it.

When I found the piece of paper I had searched for in my pockets, I handed it over to him. "There. A note from an old school friend of yours."

Little Ismail looked a little surprised, then quickly freed one hand from the coffee and took the note. "Oh. It's from Leonard," he smiled, delighted, then plunged into reading it.

I had watched Lenny write it, so I knew it wasn't particularly long, but not much more. Nothing about the content.

Little Ismail laughed. "Excuse me." Placing a hand on my shoulder, he leaned over to plant a quick kiss on my cheek. "There, delivered."

I huffed, rolled my eyes, then tried hiding behind my coffee mug. If I felt warm now, it was because of the coffee's heat, I was sure.

"I didn't know you knew Leonard." Little Ismail went on as though nothing had happened. "But I mean, it makes sense. Mr Langston introduced you, I assume?"

I nodded. George Langston had introduced us, yes. And still, I felt warm. Felt a little out of place, out of my own skin. Like when you take off your sunglasses and suddenly realise that the people you were just secretly staring at could now look back into your eyes. Or like when you were just the tiniest bit tipsy on wine, feeling your hands being a little numb and heavy. Or like when you accidentally wake up far too early in the morning and suddenly find yourself in the silence of a grey sunrise, and the sound of the birds pierces through your wakeful state without you quite being able to relate to them. Perhaps it was just the lack of sleep, though. Lenny and I had talked until late at night, after all. Lenny, the sweet fool. Gosh. Did he not know better?

• • • •

"*Good news, Mama!*" I exclaimed as soon as she picked up the phone, making sure to sound as joyful and excited as I could. "*I can move back into my apartment! The landlord just called; everything is fine, no one got hurt, and there are only three apartments one floor above me that need real renovation. Isn't that great news?*" It was. It meant I didn't have to deal with finding a new place to stay. It meant not being all too dependent on George Langston again. It meant finally not having to clean up after those two men anymore. Left for one of their daily adventures hours ago, and the apartment was a glorious mess; I planned to clean before going to see Richard Leaflet. It meant having my entire wardrobe back and being able to shower whenever I wanted to instead of having to wear Baker's perfume and clothes all the time. It meant finally sleeping in my own bed again. Not a third, not a half. No, the whole thing for myself. Well. And Minush. My Minush. I hoped she had been doing well at Mrs Potter's. For a moment after I had hung up the phone with my landlord, I had considered calling her, but then I decided that Pia was more important.

So I settled down on the sofa, had called home. Albeit still feeling a bit off and misplaced, as though I kept squinting one eye close, then the other, then the other again, making my reality a constant shifting, I also felt much more grounded. We were back on track. I could go back to how things were. Nothing had to change just yet.

"I'm so relieved to hear that!" my mother said, and I noticed how she immediately picked up on the tone of my own voice.

"I am, too. Everything is going well, I–,"

"Antoni has his apartment back!" my mother yelled away from the phone.

"Is that Antoni?!" I could hear Katharina's voice. And then a moment later, from much closer: "Hello, Tolek! We love and miss you!"

I laughed heartily.

"You heard your sister, Antoni," My mother was back on the phone, "are you back in your apartment already?"

"No. I'll move back tomorrow morning."

"Call us then, yes? We have to go now. Everyone's already waiting at the community centre."

"But!" I blinked. "I want to say happy birthday to Pia!"

"It's too late, my son. She's already at the centre. But I'll tell her you called. She'll be happy to hear that."

"But, Mama!" I was clutching the phone a little tighter now, as though it would keep my mother from hanging up. "Did at least my gift arrive?"

"Oh, yes, yes, it did. She was very excited. You will have to tell us how you got your hands on something like that."

"I will, I–,"

"You know that God is watching you, my son. Do not disappoint us."

I fell silent. What?

"Call us tomorrow. Pia will be happy to hear from you, but now I really have to go."

"But–,"

"We love you, Antoni. Have a good day!" And then, suddenly, she had hung up.

Moments ago, my feet had been planted in dirt; now I was back underwater, sounds were muffled, light met me brokenly, and I felt... No. My eyes grew wide. I scrambled back to the surface. I couldn't do it.

I had to shake that feeling off. Now.

• • • •

Experiment.

It starts at the door.

Do you want me to hold it open? Do you want to hold it open for me?

Will you pull my chair back? Should I do it?

Who will call the waiter first? How do you look at me when I order? Do you order for me instead? Am I allowed to speak? Are you scared of speaking for yourself?

I am touching your arm. How hard can you blush? Not at all. What if I reach out to your face? A glance towards the other people in the restaurant, perhaps? No? A brave one you are. But what if I go in with the pet names? Ah. I knew it. You are a sweetie, I know that already.

How will you hand me the envelope? Proudly? Secretly? Will you wait for me to ask you for it? Do you think it is impolite to make me feel like I'm only here because you pay, or have you come to terms with it? With me?

It slides across the table, and I ask if I can count here or if I should go to the bathroom. You give it a shrug, which I know means bathroom.

Will you let me try some of your food? Should I offer first, perhaps? What about the dessert? Do we share? Will you go wild and trust me to choose one for you?

You're making a lot of jokes. Is that your anxiety or your flirting? Do I make jokes back? No, you seem irked by that. What if I simply laugh and tell you how funny you are? Indeed. Who knew you could smile so broadly?

HOW TO GROW FEELINGS LIKE FLOWERS

Now that the bottle of wine has emptied a little, I can see your eyes glisten. Yes, don't worry, I catch every single one of your sneaky glances. Even the ones I am not returning.

The bill. You pay fearlessly. A grand gesture. So you are not scared that other people will know of your filthy little gay secret? Or do you really think we can pass as brothers? No, you have stopped caring. I let you guide me out of the restaurant and hold the door open for me. You might be striding proudly now, but when will you dare to kiss me?

Will there be hesitation as we pass taxis? Will you get cold feet and not ask me up to your room? Will there be a room?

What if I ask if you want another drink? Ah, look. You do have an opinion. You do not want to extend the night outside. You want to move it to the inside, am I right? Your glances have started moving again. Perhaps I should make the first move and ask for more? You laugh. Embarrassed. Pretending you had totally forgotten about that because you had such a great time with me. Do I laugh and let a blush bloom on my cheeks? Or do I call you out on it, playfully, but letting you know that I can see right through you?

Today, I try the former, and I am right. Your lips crash into mine, and I smile. You think it is because you have mastered making me happy. I know it is because it is the other way around.

• • • •

Richard Leaflet ran away the moment he saw me.

I knew it was him because of the way he was looking at people across the café and by how wide his eyes grew when he realised that no amount of head-ducking and behind-hands-hiding would stop me from walking straight up to him. He was ordinarily handsome, wearing a suit and a scarf, his chestnut hair sleekly glued to his head to give him the appearance of a slug, and his smile, which he gave me as he apologised and ran away, wasn't all too horrible either. But well.

In the end, he had the courage of a pony, and I found myself standing in the middle of a café, alone, surprised, and unemployed.

It wasn't so much the fact that someone ran away at the prospect of sex on two legs literally walking closer, which puzzled me. On the contrary. I was quite used to that. Not so much anymore, but back when I had walked the streets with Loretta, there were a lot of Johns, who, when you went up to them to talk to them, pretended it was a perfect coincidence that they had been standing here for half an hour watching us, and who then suddenly became very busy and hurried away. Especially the younger men, who would drive down the street, grouped together in a car with their noses glued to the windows, and who, as soon as one of their desired objects stepped closer, would screech and press the gas pedal as hard as possible. Sometimes, we would even take bets on them, sending the girls who were manlier than those Johns themselves, and watch the ordeal with popcorn in our hands. But anyway, since I had left the streets, and most of my clients were hand-picked and had to make a private appointment with me, which in itself already cost time, patience and courage, overzealous and ungraceful exits didn't happen that often anymore.

"Excuse me, Sir?" the delicate waitress asked.

Hmmm?" I blinked. I had not noticed her approaching.

"Can we bring you something, Sir?"

I looked around. Most everyone in the café was looking at me, and those who didn't were very careful not to. "Oh." I felt awkward. Not because of having been stood up – literally. But because I suddenly felt so out of place. A place so grounded in reality. A reality I was only ever paid to join. Who were those people? Why was I in the same room with them? Why was I in the same country, on the same planet? I was so different from them, and they knew it. Wild red curls. Darker skin. Outdated fashion from turtleneck to plateau shoes. Too much perfume. They knew that whether employed or unemployed, I did not belong. How could I have? After all, what was I? "I–..." The last meal I'd had was with Lenny yesterday evening. Thanks to Richard Leaflet, though, I had no money on me to buy a meal. Enough for a drink, but not a meal, and drinking – whether coffee or wine – on an empty stomach was just such a bad habit. "No, thank you." I therefore said, giving her a hasty smile, then I hurried out of the café, as though the world outside would welcome me more.

The church tower was just starting to chime six in the evening. It was good, I tried to convince myself. Everything was good like that. Now I would have time to go see Minush at Mrs Potter's house and maybe see if they had already reopened my building. Who knew, maybe I could already sleep in my own bed tonight? Would that not be wonderful? Was it not good that Richard Leaflet had run away? It was.

It was, it was, it was. Just another one of those unfortunate happenstances of an unfortunate week. By tomorrow, everything would be back to normal.

"Hey, careful where you're walking!" a man barked at me.

"I'm sorry." I chased after the hat that had fallen out of the man's hand as we had collided.

He looked me over. "Fucking faggots. And here I thought you were supposed to stay in your red cesspit district."

"What?" I blinked as I managed to get back on my feet.

The man tore his hat out of my hands and spoke, in a hiss, as though he simultaneously wanted no one and everyone to hear his words: "This is a street where children walk. You shouldn't be allowed here."

Baffled, I watched him turn and storm away. Same for Richard Leaflet running away, I was not surprised by the animosity itself – after all, I was rather used to such pointless aggressions, and usually I would've found something to retort, something to say – but why was it all happening while ... everything was supposed to be as always.

• • • •

The building was still closed. They had by now removed the yellow tape warning of fire and police brigades working here, but the door was still locked. And then I noticed it: They had fixed Door. Of course, I knew that they had meant to do that for quite a long time now, and while I had been a victim of Door's moods myself, I didn't know how to feel about her silence. No matter how much I let her rattle in my attempts to open her, she remained silent.

Pursing my lips, I turned to leave. Enough. It was just a door. I wanted to say hi to Minush.

Minush would make it all better. Mrs Potter would tell me that I was just a bit hungry and needed meself a good cuppa, that Minush was okay, and that by tomorrow night I'd be back in my own home with her warm and purring in my arms. Her being Minush, obviously, not Mrs Potter.

"Antoni," Mr Potter asked when he opened the door, blinking in surprise upon finding me behind it, "Antoni Pokorny?"

"Is Mrs Potter home, Sir?" I asked, holding myself to the door frame, feeling a little wobbly on my anxious feet.

"I fear she's not, boy. She went to the store only a moment ago. But I'm sure she'll be back in an hour if you want to come in and wait for her?"

He looked so cheerful, so light-hearted, despite his surprise. I did not understand. It confused me. His presence seemed wrong. Of course, it was long after seven in the evening, of course, he was back from work, but why wasn't Mrs Potter there, why was she at the shop, why had she left when I needed her reassurance?

"Antoni?"

"What? Oh. No. No, I'm–, I'm fine, can I just see Minush for a moment? Is she–, How is she doing?"

I was too busy looking past Mr Potter into the apartment, searching for Minush, to notice that his smile was slowly but surely slipping off his face. "Your cat is doing fine. Henrietta makes us care for it like our own children."

"Her."

"Pardon?"

I looked at him. "Her. Minush is a–, She's a girl."

Mr Potter frowned more in confusion than irritation, though.

"Of course. Well, you can come in and see her if you want. But weren't you supposed to pick her up tomorrow anyway? I thought–,"

A black bolt passed me out into the streets.

"Minush!" I exclaimed, panic washing over me. For just a moment, I thought she was running towards me, but she hadn't even recognised me. "Minush!" I yelled again, but she had already made it to the other side of the road, and before I could even take a step to follow her, she had disappeared between the bushes there.

Behind me, I heard Mr Potter speak, but I ignored it, dashing after Minush.

Behind the fences of one of those abandoned playgrounds where you never let your children go out of fear they might swing themselves right into tetanus, I caught sight of her again. Walking towards our building, her tail high in the air. "Minush!" I called – thoughtlessly. She cast a glance behind her, then darted away, around the corner, "Minush, no!" Of course, I knew she was walking towards our building, but the door was still closed. What if the scents of our building had changed too much for her to recognise the right floor? What if she then wouldn't find her way back to Mrs Potter? What if she ran in front of a car? My breath hitched, and I began to run – only to stop a mere moment later.

Lev.

They sat there, on the side of the street with Minush on their lap and a Walkman in their hands, and seemed as stunned to see me as I was to see them. With their dark, wide eyes on me, they took off their headphones. "You're back already?" they asked.

I pointed at Minush. "That's my cat."

They looked down at her. "I'm aware."

"Are you? Be–, because this is the second time she's in your arms when she should be in mine."

Lev hesitated, frowned, then their expression evened out. "I didn't kidnap her," they said, monotonously now, then grabbed Minush and – in patches and plaster-covered hands – held her up and out for me. "Go on. Take her then."

The running had made me feel dizzy. Maybe that was why I couldn't breathe away the panic, feel relieved that she was safe now. I reached for her.

But Minush, already very displeased by being held in such an undignified way, clawed at me.

I flinched, stumbling back. "What the fuck?"

Lev, stone-faced, had quickly moved her away from me and was now holding her tight in their arms, where she seemed quite happy to be. When I stepped towards them and reached out for her the second time, Minush puffed up her fur and hissed at me loudly. "But Minush..." I had never seen her like that. Never had she hissed at me this aggressively, never had she chosen the lap of someone else over mine, never had I felt so unsure if this was really Minush. But it was her. The white spot on her chest belonged to her, and only to her. But then why was she acting like this? "What did you do to her?" I breathed.

Lev's eyes closed, as though trying to remain calm. "Excuse me?"

"You heard me."

"You know, you're really not who I imagined you to be."

"Answer me! What did you do to my cat? Why is she like that?"

"I didn't do anything at all." My voice had risen in volume, theirs had lowered. "I don't want your cat. I haven't seen her since the fire. Perhaps you're the one who treated her badly?"

But they didn't care about my answer. Rising to their feet, they simply let Minush fall to the ground, then put their headphones back on and stuffed their plaster-covered hands into the pockets of their leather jacket with a shrug. When they turned to leave, Minush followed immediately.

My throat felt tight. "*You're an ungrateful creature,*" I eventually managed to push out. "*I've kept you alive for two years!*" But I was ignored, left behind without a single glance, left wondering what the hell had just happened, left staring at the pair that, albeit black in their appearance, dragged all the colours of my life away with them. I shivered.

"Fine." I whispered, "Fine, then leave. Go back to your dumpster. It's not like I ever asked to have you."

Like I'd ever wanted to care about you.

• • • •

On the bus, I hardly managed to resist the sound of the motors and the motion of the vehicle to lull me into sleep. The only thing that kept me awake was my stomach demanding food. My head resting against the window, I watched the small, crumbled and dirty houses of the poorer boroughs turn into modern buildings with excessive use of windows and the colour grey. The cars below on the street looked small from where I was sitting, their front and back lights blaring through the early night, and only the fellow red buses on the opposite streetside allowed me to catch a glimpse of the people within. Some of them were dressed up for a night out, but most of them were on their way home. Their tired faces from long days at school and work looked out the window with glazed eyes, not noticing that someone was watching them with nothing on his mind, with nothing in his heart.

Near Piccadilly, I got out, finding myself a supermarket and buying the prettiest – yet cheapest – bottle of wine there with the

113

few coins I found amongst the dust in my pockets. Walking through the aisles, I ignored the meal deals and 3 for 2 offers of crisps. I forced the hunger to be still, telling it that we'd soon have dinner, soon, before that bottle of wine was even opened and shared, and kept my mind on the goal: to not be unemployed tonight and get things back to normal.

It was well needed because walking through the restaurant-filled West End with the smell of delicious food around every corner didn't make it much better. At least night was falling now, and the stares of the people around me were less obvious. Soon. I'd soon be at Lenny's, and there'd be food and warmth, and someone who needed me, who wanted me.

• • • •

I should've remembered by the time I heard the upbeat jazz music thundering through the door and down the hallway. But I was more willing to believe that I had gotten out of the elevator on the wrong floor than to believe that such music truly came from Lenny's apartment.

I rang.

Never had I shown up without calling first, and rarely had I ever come by on days that weren't Thursdays. So, I did not question it when it took a moment for the door to open. Perhaps I should've. Perhaps this had been my last chance to keep me from drowning for good.

"Mr Pokorny?" The man who opened the door looked like Lenny, but it wasn't him. His hair was shaved short, his beard grey, and what were big, friendly blue orbs in Lenny's face, were icy, glaring slits in his. I felt my heart sink deep into the emptiness of my guts. "May I require to know what you are doing here?"

The party.

Lenny's birthday party. "Fuck." I breathed.

"Excuse me?" Leonard Rudolf Maria Kensington II asked, his eyebrows rising, a hint of indignation appearing on his cold face.

"Who is it, Mr Kensington?" a voice, a far too familiar voice with a far too familiar American accent, asked. A moment later, George Langston appeared in the shadows behind The Second, groomed and well-dressed, with an expression of surprise on his face. "Antoni."

My eyes widened. "I'm sorry. I forgot about the party."

The Second was a tall man, but he still cocked up his chin to look down on people. It could make you feel small even while standing on ten-inch platform shoes. "Then what about your ... gift?" he asked. His arms were crossed behind his back, so it took me a second to understand what he was referring to.

"Oh." The wine. The bloody bubbly wine I had bought for Lenny and me. "It's not–..." I didn't know how to explain it.

"I think I made it clear enough," The Second went on, and while he did not shout but spoke calmly, there was a tremor in his voice that permeated the air, drowned even the music behind him, "that I do not and will not tolerate Leonard to be seen with you." To be seen with you in public was what he meant. Be seen outside of this little apartment that Lenny called his refuge, which usually was the only place on this planet where he felt safe – but which was, tonight, invaded by said outside world. The public was allowed in tonight, and so I was not.

"No, I know," I nodded, ducking my head.

"I see no reason for you to be here, and Leonard knows the rules, which only leads me to the conclusion that you ... convinced him to invite you?"

"I didn't, I swear–, He didn't invite me."

"So you showed up unsolicited?"

"Mr Kensington." George Langston interjected. "How about we call Leonard, let him explain the situation and accept his present, then continue with the evening?"

"No. Do you really want to tolerate their little plan to go behind my back? What's next? Inviting him in?" The way he spat out the 'him' said more than anything else. "No, Mr Langston, I will not risk anyone seeing Leonard with this–, with this–, with this." This was the first time his hands appeared from behind his back, and only so he could motion towards me and everything I stood for.

"But Mr Kensington," George Langston tried, but The Second persisted.

"My word is final, and it will remain final!" This time, The Second's voice had risen, enough to reach inside the apartment.

Reach Lenny.

With his big blue eyes widened and full of curiosity and confusion, he appeared in the doorway, halting when he recognised me. His gaze jumped to my shoes, the wine bottle, to my shaking hands, then to my face. "Antoni?" For just the split of a second, it looked as though he was smiling, as though he believed The Second himself had invited me here. But the hope was crushed as soon as he caught his father's expression. Then, he, too, ducked his head.

"Did you invite him, Leonard?" The Second asked.

And before I could stop him, Lenny nodded. "Yes."

What happened next was a blur. There was a flinging hand that I remembered. There was Lenny, letting out a scream, his cheek turning red, me trying to help but being pushed away.

"Are you okay?" I remembered calling, but George Langston brought his large arm around Lenny and pulled him away. No matter how much I called, I was kept outside; even George Langston pretended he did not hear my begging, and soon, the door shut in my face.

• • • •

People always say that solitude, silence, stagnation makes you feel heavy. But that's not true. It makes you feel hollow. That night? I felt empty and light, as though every single one of my bones was filled with cold air. With helium. Moving my hand was not defying gravity, it was defying the wish to just float away, to become part of the clouds, of the sky, of all the atmosphere's layers which draw the air of your lungs until you implode. You see, when people think it's solitude that they're feeling, then they're wrong. What they're feeling is the sadness, the pain, the desperation that comes with it, and that is what makes them heavy. But real solitude is none of that. Real solitude is the lightness of complete lack.

. . . .

Trousers, shirts, socks, perfume, toothbrush, scarf, notebook, pen, keys.

When I came back to my senses, I found myself on my knees on the floor of George Langston's empty apartment. My hands were shaking. Why was I staring at all my stuff?

I had come here to have a reason to never come back, to leave George Langston and his ever-same betrayal behind. And here I had thought that asking George Langston for help would turn him into a good man. But quite obviously, I didn't really know him. I had thought he was different from Louisanne, that he didn't care more about his clients than the people he sold to them. But how I had come to that conclusion, I couldn't remember now. After all. Loretta was dead because of him.

With blurred, shifting vision and a headache, I looked around. What else did I need to leave this hellhole of a deceitful trap?

Trousers, shirts, socks, perfume, toothbrush, scarf, notebook, pen, keys. Wine bottle! What else?

I paused. Where was my wallet?

My little leather wallet with oriental ornaments on it, with the envelopes? Where was it? Had I taken it with me to Richard Leaflet's date? No, that's why I hadn't ordered a meal. Where was my head tonight?

I, once more, looked at the corner on the ground where all my other stuff had been. But nothing. With trembling fingers, I reached deep into the hidden pocket of my bag and found – nothing.

No wallet, no envelopes.

I reached deeper. Took the bottle out again. The notebook. The toothbrush. Even the keys. I turned my bag upside down. Pound coins fell out. No wallet, no envelopes.

My blood froze within me.

The bag slid out of my hands and landed on the pile of mess on the floor. I turned, crossing the room to look through the nightstand, went to the kitchen, looked at the table, helplessly felt my fingers run over the walls as I tried to steady my walk, over the license plates of all those dead people, went to the living room, checked the sofa. Breathing hurt. I inhaled. The piano.

"No," I whispered, and with hands so sweaty and shaky that the wood kept slipping from them, I opened the key cover. "No." I exhaled. "No, no, no." Packs after packs after packs of heroin fell to the ground, all having been neatly stocked there – amongst my empty envelopes. Mr Hendrikson. Lenny. Mr C. Baker. Mrs Potter. Queen Virgin. Every single envelope, there, slipping off the keys from their hideout to the floor, where they lay, exposed to what the money inside them had been used for. My throat let out a cry. My nails dug into the packs of heroin, clawed at them, ripped them open until their content was spread over the ground, crushed into the rug with the heels of my hands until it was unusable, gone.

I had sent a large sum to Pia, yes, but of what I had saved, one could've bought a house back in my hometown, one could've lived in my apartment in London for at least a year. One could've afforded a hotel room for tonight...

I searched the pockets of my tracksuit pyjama bottoms and found the three remaining ten-pound notes I had ended up not using for Minush and my feast. Thirty pounds. It would've been more had I not bought canned food for myself. Had I bought that kid those chewing gums. Holding them in my hands, I saw Louisanne's before my inner eyes, laughing, throwing her head back, her sound filling the air and my blood with cold, cold fear.

My lungs were burning.

Blindly, I lined up the envelopes on the living room table. With a tight grip on my pen to keep my hand from shaking, I wrote: BUY – YOURSELF – A – FUCKING – HEART. Each envelope marked with one word, and below the thirty pounds.

Sweat was dripping down my forehead.

Where would I go without it? All the leftover coins I had paid for only two short bus rides. Richard didn't want me. Lenny couldn't want me. George Langston had never wanted me. What was I supposed to do?

And suddenly, I knew who to call.

· · · ·

Conclusion.

Lastly, I draw my conclusion.

I know now whether I should wait for them to call me or if I should call them again first. I know now how to dress the next time I go to see them. I know now if I come up with a special location for the date, or sex afterwards, or if we will skip the date, or if we will skip the sex. I know now if there are movies I need to watch or books I should read, or if I should do neither to make sure they will always have enough to educate me about. And more importantly, I know now whether I will bother to see them again or not at all.

I know everything now. Not about them, of course, that would be boring. I am not delusional enough to think that just because you have figured out someone's sexual preferences in the first two minutes of your meeting, it means you have figured them out as a person and will, from then on, never be surprised by them again. On the contrary. I firmly believe that there is always more to learn about a person, no matter how long you've known them. There will always be secrets that will bubble up, always moments that will make you adore them a little more, always be smiles that will look a little different than the first smile you ever saw on them. Often, if you give them a chance to evolve with you, they will get to know themselves along with you, too. That is the beauty of what I do. People have a way of opening up after climaxing that is perfectly unique in its kind.

So in conclusion, if you are kind to them, and let them introduce themselves to you, and assess them and your position in their life right, and make sure to always make them happy, even if that means giving up everything you are for the time being, if you do all that, and do it with pleasure, then they will share their best versions of themselves with you. You will make truly wonderful friends who will also give you truly wonderful paychecks.

Chapter Four – Water your seeds and ask the sun for some warmth (don't be scared to ask for help)

. . . .

This was the second time Mr Hendrikson hit me.

Always five minutes early, he used to come to, as George Langston would put it, *swoop me up* with his company car, where we'd sit in the back, chatting, while his driver would bring us to whichever chosen restaurant and hotel Mr Hendrikson saw himself eating and sleeping in tonight. During the chatting, we would brush topics like politics, how his day had been, or, when we felt particularly culturally integrated, the weather.

There had been a time when my English was still so broken, well, I'd say unpolished, but really, it was still very *polish*ed, that we would talk about pop culture instead, clumsily making our way through our opinions about various horror movies we had enjoyed seeing in the theatres recently or retelling particular scenes from certain science fiction franchises that would make the other laugh. I remember a few instances to a time long before I had even heard the name George Langston, where we would forget to get out of the car altogether, sitting side by side, talking, talking, talking until the sun rose and it was time to return to a life less simple.

Who needed restaurants and hotels when the inside of this Mercedes became a refuge? A safe haven from the kind of darkness that was real outside, but nothing but a piece of conversation inside?

A year later, when my English had just started to be as appropriate as my clothes, meaning, when I had stopped confounding vowels and stopped wearing lipstick-red mini shorts and midriff-exposing tops so thin that the icy winter air would blow right through my guts, Mr Hendrikson would still *swoop me up* regularly. But now he did so knowing that I was well capable of holding entire conversations about American elections, British economics and political riots – even if I found none of it remotely entertaining. Sometimes, he would then ask me about home, sounding careful, but I think he soon learned that his attempts to get me to talk about failed communism, about potential martial laws and a hunger-driven country, would, in the end, only have me change the subject and talk about royal weddings instead.

There were things I did not allow myself to think about, not even then, not even when I had still been capable of feeling. And in a way, I knew him well, my Mr Hendrikson and I knew that he found happiness in those moments of ease in his car, where for once, he didn't have to talk about the future of his company, of his employers, of his marriage. Where he could just allow himself to speak his opinion about Harrison Ford and Tom Cruise and the unspeakable beauty of Peter Riegert in a Scottish landscape. So we'd come back to talk about action movies, about film scores, about the weather. It was easy. It was simple. It was beautiful.

Yes, I knew my Mr Hendrikson well, so when I entered the car today, on this numbing Saturday of fading steadiness and pouring rain, I immediately knew something was off.

I was waiting by the bus stop, as agreed upon, when I was jolted out of my thoughts by a loud car horn. The street was not an empty one, so for a couple of seconds, I looked around in vain, not even entirely sure if the honk had been for me. When I found no one, I sat back down on the bench under the station roof, only to immediately be honked at again. It was only then that one large bus from the other side of the street moved, and I caught sight of Mr Hendrikson's driver, Liam, leaving the car. I immediately rose back to my feet and met him halfway, apologising that I hadn't seen him and that he had to put himself out in the rain for me. He greeted me, hushed me amicably and offered me his umbrella.

Feeling dizzy from rising and having walked so fast, I was glad when I finally reached the car.

"I'm sorry, there was a bus, I couldn't see you," I explained as I put my bag onto the seat next to Mr Hendrikson.

"You could've walked around it. We had no problem seeing you, after all," he replied, not returning my smile.

"I should've, yes. Just because of the rain–,"

"Which is now all pouring into my car. Will you sit down and close that bloody door, please?"

I blinked. It wasn't so that I wasn't used to Mr Hendrikson's cursing, but I wasn't used to such a rough tone for no reason. Silently, I nodded and sat down in the car.

Because my fingers felt so numb, I had trouble handling the seatbelt. It slipped from my hands twice, and just as I managed to pull it over me and almost got it to stick in its holder, Mr Hendrikson's patience was lost. He sharply clicked his tongue, slapped the seatbelt out of my hands and let it crack back to where it came from, then pushed me harshly into the backrest so he could reach over me and close the door. "For Christ's sake," he hissed.

Startled, I watched him sit back again and give the window between us and the driver an impatient knock.

"It's hardly drizzling," I said, looking at him from the side.

"It was pouring in," he replied, and his loud voice filled the small space all too much.

I looked at him. "Right. Sorry." Then breathed in deep. Gosh, I was so sensitive today. This hadn't even been a real slap. He was right. This car cost more than my entire life, so obviously, he didn't want the leather to get wet. Everything was fine. And I had nowhere else to go, anyway. "Where are we going for dinner tonight?"

"Italian?" His voice was gentle again, patient, and he looked just like the man who had given me hope at a time when my life had been built on nothing but instincts of survival.

I smiled. "Italian sounds fabulous."

* * * *

The restaurant was the kind of restaurant where you immediately feel at ease. It was dimly lit but with plenty of small lamps and in a way that the orange wallpaper shimmered friendly, giving the room a comfortable, clean and yet warm atmosphere. A few paintings, copies from the great artists of the Renaissance, were decorating the walls, and their colours were as soft as the waiter's voice as they came to take our order.

Mr Hendrikson had made me sit with my back to the door, and although he did not explain why, I soon realised that it was so he could keep an eye on it during dinner, again and again, checking that whatever he feared so much wouldn't enter and surprise him.

As always, he made sure that I ordered a whole menu of at least three courses and as always, our little banter of me only agreeing if in return, he'd order nothing but a salad for himself, unfolded. The only difference from usual was that when the waiter did come, and I ordered nothing but a soup, Mr Hendrikson was too distracted with his pocket agenda to notice it. I considered it luck and ordered a salad for him.

That all our conversations ended with his eyes becoming glazed by thoughts unfathomable to me, his responses being nothing but hums and half-hearted nods of the head? I pretended I didn't notice, deciding that it was fate that we both felt a little off today. At least in the many moments of silence, before he'd snap back to reality with an 'Oh, sorry, I must've missed what you said, can you please repeat?', I had time to reimagine this day, dreaming up decisions I never took. That the decision of leaving Mr Hendrikson as soon as possible should've been my priority didn't cross my mind. He was stressed. I was tired. And then he ordered us two espressi, not noticing that I had not yet finished my soup.

"Do you mind if I pay now?"

"No, of course not. I feel a little tired, so I–,"

"Your call came so spontaneously that I had no time to book a hotel room yet." Mr Hendrikson simply interrupted me. Not out of rudeness, though. I doubt he even noticed it. And in a way, I was glad that I didn't have to explain myself. I felt so tired. "So we might have to be lucky to get a good room tonight."

I smiled and nodded, sipping my espresso in silence.

When Mr Hendrikson gallantly pulled my chair back, as he always did, and he helped me to get into my coat, as he always did, I felt safe. Because this was Mr Hendrikson. And that he forgot to also hold the door open after I took the time to bid the waiters and chef good night? Quite obviously, he was just lost in thought again.

"Liam? Let us try the Dorchester, please."

The driver gave it a nod, and Mr Hendrikson turned back to me, smiling. "How are you, Antoni?" he asked. "I asked you before, but I must've forgotten what you said. Why was it important we see each other tonight?"

I had, indeed, answered this question multiple times before. Each time differently. "I'm fine. I missed you. That is the sole reason."

Mr Hendrikson chuckled. "And the real reason?"

His hand was heavy on my knee. I reminded myself that I liked his hands. "A few of my clients cancelled, and you know me. I don't like sitting at home doing nothing. I try–,"

"No! No, no, no, Liam, not down Hyde Park." Mr Hendrikson had leaned forward and snapped the window to the driver open again. "Not down Hyde Park. What did I tell you about big streets? Take a right turn, now, for Christ's sake."

The window was left open then, and I stayed silent.

Mr Hendrikson did not seem to notice that our conversation was never continued.

We did not park in front of the hotel like we usually did, but in a side street, in which Mr Hendrikson asked me to wait while he went to ask for a room. The car door fell close with a thump, putting an uncomfortable pressure on my ears. What an ugly silence. What an ugly street. What an ugly weather.

I shivered. "This is quite the day and place to be murdered, don't you think?"

Liam looked at me through the rear-view mirror. "Who would be the murderer in your scenario?"

I chuckled. "Now, now, let's not make it too easy for future detectives." Liam's eyes in the mirror smiled. I smiled back. Who knew. Perhaps if I kept smiling, it would all pass eventually. And at least I was inside a car, where it was warm, where it was safe, yes? So I scooted closer to the window, which separated the back seats from the front seats, looking at Liam with my chin propped up on my wrists. "How are you doing, Liam?"

"Well, thank you, Sir."

"I'm glad to hear that. And your wife?"

"Oh, she's brilliant. We're expecting our second child."

I responded with a gasp. "She's pregnant again? How wonderful for you! When is the due date?"

Liam's smile remained polite but his voice was undoubtedly filled with mirth. "In December, if everything goes well. We'll most likely have to move places, though, our flat is getting a little small."

I chuckled, pretending that the oddness of that day was forgotten now, that this was a sign, that it was all going to be okay now. "My sister's pregnant, too. It's her first child, though, the first grandchild for my parents."

"That must be very exciting."

"It is! I mean, I didn't have a chance to talk to all of them yet, but I think they're all very excited." I tried to imagine what it would be like to be an uncle. To spoil the little bean with gifts and time. Would it look like Laura with her bright eyes and chiming laugh, or would it look like Milosz with his dark hair and sturdy build? Or, who knew, maybe the little bean would look like our father, and I'd finally not be the only one looking like him anymore. "You'll have to tell me when it's time, Liam. I'll help you with the moving and bring a gift for Baby Rogers."

Despite not leaving the street ahead with his eyes, I could see his smile broadening. "You're very kind, Sir."

"Shush. You better pick me up on that offer. I don't look like it, but I do know how to carry boxes."

Liam gave it a nod. "Voluntarily. But, if I may, please do not tell Mr Hendrikson."

"Of what? The moving? You've been working for him for so long, Liam, I'm sure he'd be elated! Maybe even contribute to it with some extra Christmas money."

"He might. Mr Hendrikson can be very kind regarding such matters. But, no. I meant my wife's pregnancy."

I frowned. I knew of quite a few women who had lost their jobs because of a pregnancy, or even just the risk of it, but not of me. Mr Hendrikson had children himself, and he was such a generous boss, I could not imagine him reacting badly. But before I could ask, a knock against the car window interrupted the conversation.

I hurried to unlock the door, looking up at Mr Hendrikson through the window, who stood there, looking impatient and irritated.

"Where are you?" he asked as he pulled the door open harshly.

I blinked. "Here? You told me to wait."

"No, I told you to come follow me after I'd booked a room."

Through the rear-view mirror I could see Liam's frown. No, Mr Hendrikson had not said that, we had both heard it. But, licking my lips in order to give me time, I decided not to point it out, eventually just showing myself understanding instead. "Sorry," I climbed out of the car, "I must've misunderstood something." Putting on a smile again, I closed the car door behind me, only to have Mr Hendrikson groan out in annoyance.

"For Christ's sake, Antoni. I still need to talk to Liam. Think a bit for yourself, yes?" He pushed me aside and onto the street, from which I hurriedly stepped away and onto the other side, finding a safe sidewalk to wait on while he talked to Liam. But perhaps I should've stayed closer to them because as the car drove off, Mr Hendrikson shook his head disapprovingly. "What are you doing? The hotel's that way." And he turned, without waiting for me.

I only caught up with him in the lobby.

"Mr Hendrikson?"

"Don't be so slow, Antoni. I cannot always wait for you." He sounded annoyed. Resigned. The way you sound like when you know you're in the right and think yourself above arguing about it. And suddenly, I found myself doubting my own memories. Who knew, perhaps he had told me to follow him? Perhaps he kept interrupting me because my voice was too quiet? Is my language too slow? I had long realised that the ache in my throat and the dizziness in my head were probably the symptoms of a cold. Clearly, I was not at my best, and maybe Mr Hendrikson was in the right, taking care of me the way he did.

When we stepped into the elevator, and Mr Hendrikson told me how glad he was that this hotel still had a room free, because he felt like we hadn't really talked in a long time, I could but agree with that.

"I love the Dorchester. It's such a beautiful place." I made sure that the smile on my lips looked bright and genuine. He deserved that, my good Mr Hendrikson.

"I know you do. That's why I chose it." Mr Hendrikson returned the smile, and his hand came to rest on my shoulder. It was heavy. "Do you come here often?"

"Just with you, Mr Hendrikson."

"What about, ah, what's his name? Our friend, Mr–..?"

"Langston?"

"Yes! Mr George Langston. How is he doing? He's not–... Is he?"

I looked at the elevator boy. "He's doing very well. The illness seems to react differently with everyone, it still doesn't show any ... signs." My tongue burned as I forced it to swallow the 'yet' at the end of that sentence.

"Good, good." Mr Hendrikson nodded, looking reassured. "What about you?"

My eyes widened. "Me?"

"No! Just because–... You look a little pale today."

I tried a laugh but could not quite shake the discomfort. "I just didn't sleep much last night." I placed my hand on top of his, the one on my shoulder. Somehow, that made the touch lighter. "And my day was a little nasty. I need a shower. So I'll do that while you get comfortable, yes?"

"Sounds good." His smile was warm.

"I'm very glad you had time for m–,"

"That's your floor, Sir," the elevator boy said, and we got out.

A shower surely would do me some well. I could already imagine the icy water cooling off this rising heat within me. So after Mr Hendrikson led us to our room – they always looked the same, didn't they? – I gratefully went straight to the bathroom to set down my bag. It was much lighter than usual with no toys in it and all the clothes taken out. On the one hand, my shoulder appreciated it, on the other hand, I felt a little bit less prepared.

"Mr Hendrikson?"

"Yes, Antoni?" He had taken a seat on the large chair in the mirrored corner and opened a newspaper.

I chuckled. Two seconds here, and already busy with the economy again. "You brought the clothes I asked for?"

"Yes, of course. They're in the plastic bag over there. Why, do you need them now?"

I cast the bag a glance, then shook my head. "No, but if you hadn't brought them, I would've considered asking the hotel to do my laundry. For tomorrow."

"Ah, and here I thought it was a new form of payment for you. Considering how you are dressed today, I'd not be surprised."

I looked down at myself, down at the black turtleneck and elephant trousers Mr C. Baker had given me, incapable of hiding my amusement. "You don't like it? I find it looks quite Disco at the Funeral."

Mr Hendrikson laughed. It was good; laughing would keep him distracted from the fact that I was, indeed, entirely dressed in another client's clothes. "I'd prefer them on the ground."

I put my hands on my hips. "Oh, would you, you old dodger?"

He only laughed a little louder. "Yes, yes, I would."

I clicked my tongue and shook my head. "Well, what choice do I have, then?" I gave it a dramatic sigh. "You know too well that I can't resist your wishes." Bringing my hands to the hem of the sweater, I stepped around the bed to show myself to him fully, then took the sweater off. It landed on the ground. For a second, breathing easier again, I did exactly that, just that, breathing. Taking all the time in the world to inhale, to exhale, trying to soothe the burning in my throat, trying to free myself of the dizziness that wanted to wash over me, trying to gain control of this day that had simply been too difficult for me to grasp properly.

I returned Mr Hendrikson's eager, amused gaze with a patient one, watching it linger on me as the AC tickled my glistening skin.

"More," he demanded, and thus 'more' I gave him.

First, the shoes and socks, then the trousers, and finally all underwear. My gaze stayed fastened on him the entire time while his gaze roamed over me, growing hungry. After letting him look for a long while, I motioned to the pile on the ground. "Is that how you like them?"

Mr Hendrikson's amused smile turned into a grin, eager and sombre, a wolf's grin upon spotting a carcass to devour. He nodded.

"Good," I said, my voice still light and playful, all too used to being looked at like that. "I'll see you after the shower then." I turned.

"No."

Surprised, I glanced over my shoulder and saw Mr Hendrikson rise to his feet. "Yes, Mr Hendrikson. I smell." I smirked because I really did. "I need a shower."

"No, you don't," he said, taking a step towards me, and perhaps it was at that moment that I should've noticed how all playfulness had left his gaze. We were no longer in on the same joke. "Stay."

I didn't. I just rolled my eyes and huffed out a chuckle, turning to the bathroom. "I'll see you in two minutes."

His hands caught me, yanked me around and back towards him. "Who are you to say no to me?" he asked. His wild, hungry gaze was fastened on me.

I fell silent, made sure not to overreact, made sure to look back at him. This was just Mr Hendrikson. He'd let go of me any second. I just needed to smile. "What the hell, Mr Hendrikson?" I forced my voice to sound soft, smoothing out the tremble with humour. Smile. Just smile. "I'm not saying 'no. ' I just want you to wait for a second–,"

"Stop lying."

Carefully, I tried to free my arm, just wanting to make it to the bathroom now. "Just let me take my shower so I don't–,"

He hit me.

It drew all air from me. I stared at the ground, listening to the thousand thoughts thrashing through my mind as they all tried to justify, all tried to soothe, to calm, or at least to rationalise with cheap jokes, until big hands came to my cheeks, lips pressing against mine, and brought everything to a brusque halt.

Apologies were planted into my skin, kisses that trailed down my jaw, down to my neck. "You're okay, Antoni," he murmured against my skin. "Please forgive me." His plea sounded urgent. "I'm sorry you want to leave me, but you can't. I'm sorry. I'm sorry, but you can't just do that, you can't just lie to me, it's not my fault, I'm sorry, I'm yours. Please forgive me."

I felt my knees wanting to give in, too weak to hold the weight of my veering mind, my disgust, my burning cheek. "Stop." I breathed, but the kisses didn't stop. One by one, they wetted my skin with apologies I couldn't feel. "Stop," I repeated, a little louder, but my voice failed to carry my fear, and even as my arms tried to twist out of Mr Hendrikson's grip, my body refused to obey. The more I struggled, the harder Mr Hendrikson pushed himself against me, the more urgent his apologies and the way he spread his saliva over and into my skin, making me his, just the way he repeated it, again and again. "Don't you love me at least a little?" His voice was pure hunger now. "Don't you pity your old Mr Hendrikson? Here, I told you I'm sorry, feel me, feel how sorry I am, make me–,"

Finally, my throat let out a scream. My body woke up and I freed a knee to kick him, but just as I had been taught so many times before, resistance only led to greater attacks and before I knew how to escape, his hand struck my face once more, crashing into the bone around my eye, and I stumbled backwards into the bathroom. I felt the tiles cold under my feet, the light burning in my eyes. Strong, angry fingers wrapped around the back of my neck, at first trying to push me down, then, as I blindly tried to turn out of the grip to stay upright – *don't fall, don't close your eyes* – pushed me forward. I knocked against something white, cold, hard. The bathtub.

"Well?! Go on then!" he barked, "Go take your bloody shower."

My voice echoed through the bathroom, yet sounded so meek, so weak. I tried to open my eyes – they had closed, hadn't they? – for the split of a second catching droplets of red in all this white around me, ruddy shabby red in luxurious porcelained white, but the light pierced through my eyes and my head pounded nothing but blackness into my vision. I had lost control.

And then there were these hands again, one on my neck, the other on my upper arm. They pulled me up. "Now, go on. Get into the shower."

I was pushed forward, and I fell into the tub. A sharp pain shot through my elbow before I could understand where the ceiling was and where the ground was. If I screamed, I did not notice it. I just knew that there was water then, and it coursed into my face and into my mouth, making me cough and wheeze and fight the weight on top of me with all my might – in vain.

"Stop moving, Antoni, you're hurting yourself. I'm just–, I'm just cleaning you." He sounded so nice, and without knowing why, I tried to move my head and look at him, to see that niceness in his face, to give him a smile. Perhaps a smile would help. But a large hand pressed my head to the side until my cheek met the ground, and my neck trembled from trying not to crack. I swallowed water. "You do need cleaning from this smell of all those lies."

There was a cry and I assumed that one of my blindly aimed kicks had found him, but I could not open my eyes; there was water everywhere now, in my mouth, in my eyes, in my ears, and suddenly my body was turned around, handled as though it was a mere, lifeless puppet, a carcass indeed, my face was pressed to the bottom of the bathtub, and my left leg turned white with pain. I did not know where my arms were, then. I just knew that Mr Hendrikson was on me, against me, in me, over me, done with me.

The water stopped.

Silence.

I lay still and watched the water take the blood with it down the drain.

And then it took the groans and the huffs, eventually even my coughing. Even when the weight got off my back, I didn't move. My own breath sounded distant, rattling in a throat that didn't feel like my own. My body was drowned by long-gone water. I lifted my head. Pulling my arms off my back, they ached as I propped myself up. I couldn't remember when one of my eyes had gone blind.

Mr Hendrikson sat by the bathtub, on his knees. His suit was drenched, the belt undone, his face red. With wide, fearful eyes he was looking at me. "Antoni…"

I slapped his hand away as it came out to reach me. "Don't touch me," I whispered. A whisper? If I had been able to, I would've screamed. But my throat burned, my voice cracked, and I could only see through a white veil of pain.

Shakily I rose to my feet, ignoring the biting ache that came from my knee, and took my bag. I dressed, left. Mr Hendrikson did not follow. He did not beg for me to stay anymore. He did not move, said nothing, and the silence drowned all pain.

This silence. This emptiness. Making each step light. Too light. As if nothing tied you to Earth anymore. It was all too familiar.

. . . .

The bottle was empty when Richard Leaflet found me.

I had started filling it with sand and blades of grass, bored and incapable of finding rest on the shore. I had left as fast as I could, but while my feet carried my body through the city, through the joyful umbrellas, past the trafficked streets, past the restaurants, down to the Thames, my mind had stayed caught in the hotel room, replaying and replaying and replaying the same memory, over and over and over again until my hand had found the wine in my bag. Whenever I closed my eyes, vivid, flashing images seized me, and so I kept them open, staring at the river flowing past. *Take it*, I thought. *Take it all away*.

I should've left earlier, I should've left when I had sensed that something was wrong, just like Loretta had taught me all those years ago, just like Louisanne had forced me to learn. Had they not taught me well? Had I not learnt right? When would I? Control. *Always stay in control*. It was such a simple instruction, and yet.

My knees hit the ground of the shore, and the blood seeped into the pebbles, and I emptied my stomach into the river, watching the water carry it away. This city-poisoned water, awhirl from the storm, passing by with no fear of leaving. Would it carry me away, too?

Tonight, I drank until the bottle was empty instead.

In the flickering shadows of the street lights, I picked up sand corn after sand corn and let it rain into the bottle amidst the small blades of grass which grew between those lifeless pebbles. I was still on my back, watching the stars turn, and I was quietly humming a song to myself that my mother would sometimes sing to us before she tucked us all to bed. Those nights, when we'd all snuggle up in our parents' bed because extended family was coming to visit and needed our beds, or because it was just very cold outside and our heaters had fallen out again. It had always been cramped and full of childish fights for blankets and foot space, but gosh, how we all loved looking back to those nights. Those were the thoughts the wine brought me. Thoughts of a time when leaving people behind had not yet been necessary, when bathing was a fun pastime. Not a necessity.

Thoughts, interrupted when a group of young, finely dressed men walked past me.

Shamelessly curious, I tilted my head far back and watched them, cursing the eye that had grown blind in the last few hours. They were all quite handsome men. The kind of high-class handsomeness which fades quickly once you see them in jeans or pyjamas, but which you still find a little too charming to ignore. And then my eye caught one of them in particular, and I sat up.

"Hey! You! Aren't you Richard Leaflet?" I shouted.

The poor man startled. "Excuse me? Who are you?" he asked, and in his face, I read that he was now going through every possible reason why a drunk fist-fight-inclined homeless person could know someone like him.

"Anthony Pokorny?" I asked back, not hiding the half-mock, half-serious offence in my voice. "The hooker you ordered for today and then left standing in shame without even paying what I should get for at least getting my arse up and all across town?"

Leaflet's friends started laughing, half of them because they wanted to believe it, half of them because they believed I was just an old friend fooling around. And apparently, that was the quick-witted way out Richard Leaflet chose, too. Perhaps he wasn't all that stupid after all.

"Oh, it's you, Pokorny!" he laughed, and for just a split second, I was surprised by how convincing he sounded in his relief. "I didn't recognise you. Mate, you look bad. Did your night not go well?"

I smirked and ignored the hand he offered me. Mine was smeared with wine and sand, blood and vomit. His was clean. "No, not really. My girl ran off with another guy," I played along. "I refused to let her go without a good fight, but you know I've always been the weakest in PE. How are you? I'd offer you some wine, but, well." I nodded towards the bottle in my other hand, and with his back to his friends, I could see how Leaflet's expression changed.

"I'm sorry to hear that," he said and sounded genuinely sorry. I was putting him in quite a compromising situation, as much as I was also the only way out of it. He looked from his friends to me, then back to them. "Guys, this is Anthony Pokorny, an old-school friend." And back to me. He hesitated.

Smirking, I waited.

So? What was he going to choose? Was he going to dare a night with me, finally? Would the state I was in, the blood, the exhaustion, the stink, deter him from doing so? Or would exactly this be the reason he'd stay? Help me? Pay me? Make things go back to normal?

The moment seemed to stretch for hours. And then, finally, he chose his friends. "I'm gonna call him a cab."

"I don't want a cab!" I laughed.

His friends were visibly uncomfortable. They believed I was but an old school friend of his, sure, but that didn't mean I was part of their world. "Just let us call you a cab, mate," one of them said. Another looked around for a telephone box. "Where do you live?"

My laugh felt hollow.

I let them leave. Go back to where they belonged, far away from the city grime and the darkness in which my people worked.

For a long while, I kept my gaze down the street where they had disappeared, then lay down in the sand again, listening to the water rushing by. City-poisoned water, rushing without fear of flight, without fear of taking everything with it to far-away places. How often had I imagined it taking me with it, too? What if I were to immerse myself in it now? Would it carry me, would it wash me to distant shores where no one knew my name, where I was safe?

My fingers found the bottle of wine instead. It was heavy due to the sand inside of it, and as I glanced over, I saw it standing next to a half-buried, old water bottle. The wine and the water. The poison and the remedy. The remedy for a remedy that had once been a remedy, too.

Well, perhaps this was the end of this circle. Hadn't everything started with Louisanne, the Thames and me? "Good night, you two,"

I whispered, caressing my fingers over their glass and trying to maintain my smile as long as I could, already feeling it slip off my face as sleep took over, and pushed them a little closer to each other.

"G'd night, Ant't't'ni," the water bottle rattled.

"Thankssssss for not letting usssss spend our lasssssst few hoursssss alive together," the wine bottle agreed, the sand inside of it whispering through the night.

Head pounding, throat burning, chest aching, limbs unmoving, eyes shut tight. Voice whimpering, hands searching, stomach revolting, fearful grasps at the nothingness and the constant feeling of falling. There were people speaking, far away in the darkness, and sometimes they came to touch me, and my world became cold. I had no strength to move, but I felt my inner everything flinch away from their cold clothes and drinks on fire. I was dead. I knew I was dead and that this was hell, not because I had been brought to this land of never-shining-sun, and not because the only music being played here was a never-ending chorus of a Bee Gees song, but because at one point, many, many years into this blind helplessness and fear, an angel appeared. Their genderless self towered over me, and with their hands so fine that porcelain dolls would've been jealous of them, they inserted ice into my body, transforming it into an eternal shell of blue checkers and making me scream in soundless vain.

"I'm sorry," I begged. "I'm sorry, I know I shouldn't have..."

With a voice greater than the universe itself, the angel laughed. "And you won't ever again."

I clutched their beautiful hand, but it was torn away from my hands as I fell, fell, fell, and I knew it was all my fault. All those people I had refused to be friends with, all those I should've protected, all those I should've shown kindness and mercy to, real warmth, all of them, they were dead now, and their last hours had been spent in loneliness, for they were the untouchable, the unlovable, the damned. And I was to follow them now, for how was

I, he who had distanced himself from them in an act of wisdom and the wish to live, any better than those who had condemned them to their death? I was going to die with them and suffer until all eternity, and the angel shushed me quiet, pressing its deathly kiss to end my earthly pain.

Hands relaxing, voice failing, eyes fluttering, limbs long forgotten as silence arose. With a chest barely heaving anymore, for breath had hardly come in hardly through the burning throat and was now almost giving up on trying at all, and a head that had long forgotten how it was to lift itself without the heaviness of all its memories, I knew that this was the end.

I became weightless.

Pure, perfect weightlessness.

One last time.

. . . .

When I was little, my siblings and I would often go to the river, which graced our small village. It wasn't a particularly large river, just deep and wide enough to learn how to swim. Although I was the oldest, I was the last to master this very discipline. There had always been something intimidating, something inescapable about moving water. While most children had no trouble overestimating their strength and skills, I had always been a very careful child, preferring to consider all possible outcomes before throwing myself into an adventure. The idea of voluntarily submitting myself to the force of this river seemed insane to me.

It had been on Laura's eleventh birthday that I overcame my fear.

There was one great oak, casting some shade, onto which we had tied a rope and from which we would swing ourselves into the water. When you let go at just the right moment, you could swing particularly far, flying through the air so high that for a split second, you could almost pretend you were a bird. Unfortunately, when you let go a little too soon, you would fall onto the tree's roots and the shore. It hardly ever happened, but one of those times, it was Pia whose small hands failed to hold onto the rope long enough. It was starting to get dark, and everyone had already gone home; only lovely little Pia had wanted to stay a little longer. Being the oldest and 'so very sensible', my parents had trusted me to keep the watch. For about thirty minutes, I enjoyed my newfound responsibility, but then Pia slipped, her head met the hard roots of the tree, her body started floating lifelessly down the river, and I regretted everything.

I screamed, running along the stream and hoping my voice would wake her up, but it was of no use. And eventually I had to face the truth. I had to get into the water and swim.

I did.

I saved her, and two days later, she was back on her feet, smiling and beautiful as always, going back to the River without missing a beat, fearless, careless, happy to enjoy her never-lost life.

I never grew comfortable with swimming in moving waters, but it was true that after this incident, something inside of me changed. I felt less powerless. Less small. I would still not stay in the water longer than needed, would still prefer staying close to the shore than swimming to the very centre of the river, but I relaxed. When my mother, one day, asked if I was less scared of the water now, it was Pia who answered with: "Of course, he isn't scared. He can save everyone now."

I don't think I can save everyone. But it was true. Perhaps the part of me which had been so preoccupied with death until that point had gotten lost in the river that day. Washed away by the stream.

Water. Water was everything. It made you soggy and heavy. It made you everything. Feel everything. Only many years later, I realised it could also wash it all away again.

HOW TO GROW FEELINGS LIKE FLOWERS

What a beautiful river. So many Summers, picnics, card games and first kisses had been shared there. Would I ever go back there? Would my body ever feel that heavy again? It did now, didn't it? And moving my hand, the friendly lapping of water was to be heard, the sound piercing despite its gentleness, piercing through my consciousness, meeting me in my fever sleep. Fever sleep.

I awoke with a start.

A pale pink ceiling was above me; that was the first thing I saw. A strong scent of sage, thyme, and, honestly, I had no idea, but perhaps something like lemongrass, was the first thing I smelled. And the sound of water as I moved my arms? It was the first thing I heard. I felt heavy, but the water helped me float; there was a bitter taste in my mouth, and I was terribly, terribly disoriented, but other than that? My headache had disappeared, my stomach wasn't cramping any more, and neither my knee nor my eye were still sending me those blinding, throbbing waves of pain. In fact, I felt so perfectly, beautifully fine, that I would have just closed my eyes again and given in to the temptation of relaxation and heavy well-being if I hadn't been so deeply puzzled by the fact that I was lying in a fucking bathtub.

It was a pink bathtub, too, did I mention that? Pale pink, dusky rose, grandma red, whatever you want to call it. *Pink*. And yet, that still wasn't what caught most of my attention. No, there was something even stranger to be found as I turned my head and looked around. Something that truly, full-heartedly and thoroughly put me into a state of grand puzzlement and confusion: every inch of this bathroom, as far as I could identify it as such, was filled with plants.

Flowers. Herbs. Green stuff. *Everywhere.*

Snake Plants, Begonias, Air Plants, Lilies, Aloe Vera, Orchids, Fern, Rubber Trees, Azaleas, Spider Plants, and all *sorts* of differently coloured greenage that I had never seen, never even dreamed of, and definitely didn't know how to name was placed all around me, on the dresser, on the sink, on top of the wall cupboard, and all along the walls. On the ground and thus also on the border of the tub stood tiny pots of flowers, small-leaved, big-leaved, in a wide variety of colours and strange forms, some of them hanging down into the tub water – which, by the way, had white petals in it - some down into the sink's drainage, some up through the ventilation slits, some creeping away from their initial potted home over the ground as though seeking to meet their friends on the opposite side of the room, leaving only a small path that led to what appeared to be the door and exit. The mirrors, there seemed to be quite a few of them, and the windows were hardly visible due to their hanging, hugging, embracing leaves. In glass bulbs the size of large fists, which seemed to float in the air without anything holding them to the ceiling, were planted little cacti, some with, some with delicate flowers at their branches, and even the entire ceiling was covered with winding ivy and vines.

The only patches of wall that were actually visible showed how the pink colour had peeled off due to the humidity inside this room, mould probably thriving in every corner all around me. No wonder the air was so heavy that breathing felt like inhaling pure water; what I had initially thought to be steam from the hot tub was quite obviously mist that hung in the room, filled thick with scents from the flowers and herbs around me. A sauna, which filled your lungs with the realisation that you were alive.

Life. So much colour and life.

And I could but lie there with my mouth wide open, dazzled, incapable of not being absolutely, perfectly, entirely overwhelmed by all this. Smitten. It was beautiful. Simply beautiful.

Whose bathroom was this? Too amazed and relaxed, I did not ask myself this question until the answer came through the door.

There was a clicking sound, the door knob was pressed down, then snapped back up. The clicking sound repeated itself, the doorknob moved downwards, this time enough for the door to actually open.

In came Lev.

Humming a little melody, in their hands a tray with tea cups and a teapot on it, they closed the door behind them with their foot. The melody stopped abruptly when their gaze rose to me and found that I was looking back at them. There was a pause, silent, motionless.

"Hi," I said.

They cleared their throat and nodded. "You're alive. Cheers." Their voice was low, rough, dry.

"Hooray," I said just as bluntly, watching how they shook off their motionless state and moved on.

The tray was placed on the ground, next to the bathtub, then they settled down and started pouring tea into the cups. Their hands were once again covered in tiny patches and plasters. All in silence still, they then handed me a cup.

"Uh..?"

Lev tilted their head to the side, eyebrows raised, looking at the cup as though searching inside of it for a reason why I didn't accept it. "It's tea. Jasmine."

I blinked, frowned, looked around, then tried to sit up a little straighter to take the cup. "Thanks?"

"You're welcome." Lev nodded, giving it a shrug before picking up their own cup.

I stared at them as they, calmly and as though all of this was a perfectly common scenario, blew air into their tea, then carefully tried to sip from it, looking at the plants by the window. I thought that, perhaps, if I gave them enough time, they'd come around to explain. But quite visibly they didn't feel like there was anything to explain. And thus, we sat there in silence for a long, long while. "So?" I eventually asked.

They glanced at me, at my hair, at the cup in my hands, then at their own, their blank face somehow managing to look puzzled. Then they seemed to understand. "Oh, I didn't ask if you wanted sugar, but if you want some?"

Seemed. "No, that's ... fine?"

"People have the cruel habit of putting milk and sugar into their tea as though that doesn't kill the taste of the plant. Seriously, if they want to drink something unnecessarily sweet, they should just drink soda or something and stop wasting tea for it."

"Lev."

"But if you want sugar, I can go bring you some?"

"No. Lev. You know, I'm rather concerned with the fact that I'm in your bathtub." I cast myself a glance. "Naked."

"Oh." Lev fell silent. Their eyes narrowed a bit, but they were steadily on either mine or their teacup. "Now that you say it, it does seem like a thing a serial killer would do."

My mouth opened, closed again. I hummed. "I'm glad you're the one pointing it out."

They did not return my smile. Their expression had grown very serious. "You do remember that you nearly died, yes?"

I chuckled it away. "I tend to be dramatic like that."

"You were unconscious," they insisted. "Last night. Do you not-... You fainted on my doorstep?" They paused, waited for a reaction. "You don't remember."

I shrugged.

They hesitated, mirrored my gesture. "I was just making sure you're okay. You were running a fever."

"So you stripped me off my clothes and put me in your bathtub?" You had to admit, it was a funny thought.

Lev apparently thought differently. Their shoulders straightened. "What else should I have done? I'm not going to let a stranger into my bed, am I?"

"No, but I would've been very fine with a couch, for example."

"And you wouldn't have been confused to wake up naked on a stranger's couch?"

"What, but-..? Why must I be naked in that scenario to begin with?!"

Lev stared strainedly at their cup.

"I mean, I don't mind. Unless you actually do go serial killer on me, I do not mind a little bathtime nudity, but. You know. We're not particularly on good terms."

Lev turned their head away.

I had to admit. I was the one who hadn't been friendly with Lev. They had just been their strange self, causing me to fill their silence with my own interpretations. For all I knew, just because I couldn't make them like me, it didn't mean they'd ever disliked me.

I watched a white flower petal float around my knee. "How did you do it, then?"

"Do what?"

I nodded towards the water. "I hardly feel any pain anymore."

"That's the belladonna."

"Belladonna? Isn't that a poison?"

They hardly gave it another shrug. "Would you prefer writhing in insufferable pain?"

I laughed, thinking it was a joke – no one would just say such a thing in such a deadpan voice without actually joking, right?—but Lev cast me a brief glance and it was so dark with seriousness that my voice cracked when I asked: "You seriously drugged me?"

No response.

So I decided to play along. "So. You're telling me ... you saved my life."

They snapped to respond: "If anything, I'm saying that I kept you from dying. Don't act like I did something heroic."

This made me smile. "No allusions to accidental heroism, all right."

They yanked their sweater's sleeves over their hands, busied themselves with their tea.

In the silence, I let it sink in. *Accidental heroism.* They were different from what I had made them out to be in my head. I'd been wrong with my assumptions, again and again. Perhaps it was time to stop assuming. To actually let them act before trying to find out ways to react.

"I'm sorry I yelled at you," I therefore said. "And that I accused you of getting me here for ugly reasons. If I made you feel like I was in any way ungrateful or like I'm thinking badly of you, I'm sorry. I'm not, and I don't. Really."

A moment. And then the dark of their eyes did not look that dark anymore. When they spoke then, there was a softness in their voice. "You had wounds all over you. Some were beginning to close up, but they were infected; they needed cleaning. Your knee was dislocated, too. Not to mention the bruises all over your body. They were maybe a week old, but deep red, it was haunting. You could hardly breathe, so I assume you had pneumonia. I don't know where you've been or what happened to you, but you needed to be taken care of. I'm genuinely sorry if I crossed yet another boundary. I just wanted to help."

I smiled. I believed them. They did not give me much to work with, but what they gave me, I wanted to believe. As earnestly as them, I asked: "And you couldn't have helped and brought me upstairs to my own apartment?"

"I feared to leave you alone. You were running a fever."

"So?"

"A heavy fever."

"You could've just let me sleep it off alone."

"Antoni," they said, suddenly more forceful, "you had no heartbeat."

Finally, I fell silent.

I understood.

It ached.

Oh, Lev.

Ached?

Slowly, very slowly, I lifted one hand out of the water, felt how heavy it was now, heavy where before everything had been light and without consequences, and brought it to my chest.

There.

Beneath my collarbone.

A beat.

My hand splashed back into the water. Eyes wide, I stared at them.

My breath quickened. My mind awoke, struggled, tried to make sense of it. I knew that now was the time for a million questions to arise, to interrogate Lev and my existence, to beg for any of this to make sense, and I knew questions upon questions were growing silently somewhere in the back of my mind, and yet—I exhaled, slowly. The heaviness in my heartbeat, of my very own heartbeat, remained. For the first time in a long while, I realised I had no desire to figure out the person before me. I just wanted to let it happen.

Slowly, carefully, I turned my attention to the life around me instead.

"Are they all yours?" I nodded to the pots of plants around me.

"No," Lev replied after following my gaze, theirs then falling and lingering there as their expression grew softer still, "they belong to themselves."

Have you ever looked at someone and watched them think? Watched them piece mental puzzle pieces together and dwell on complicated memories? Yes? But have you ever watched someone dream? The way their soul opens itself to the worlds of future tenses and what-if-constructions, the way their breath inhales the air of things not yet real and exhales all the possibilities of changing that, the way their eyes become so glazed that it feels as though you could see those dreams yourself if only given the chance to redirect their gaze towards yourself. You cannot watch a person dream and not dream about them in return. Even in the realms of reality, certain things remain impossible.

A rattling sound beyond the bathroom door startled both of us out of our thoughts.

Lev blinked and cleared their throat. "I mean-, Of course they belong to me. Or do you think I found them in my bathroom one day and decided, oh well, might as well respect their personal space and never move them away again?"

Such a long moment had passed since my question that I had no idea what they were talking about. And perhaps I would've asked had my attention not been caught by Lev's sweater. Or rather... The *thing moving inside of it*. As if a dozen hamster-sized animals had suddenly started to run all over Lev's torso, their sweater was bulging in all sorts of lively ways. My eyes grew wide.

"Antoni."

"What?"

All movement inside of the sweater stopped. "Your cat."

"My cat?"

"Minush? She's with me? The noise, that's her. She's outside. Do you want me to..?"

There was no doubt they had noticed the thing moving inside of their clothes as well, but with their almost defiant casualness, Lev was simply looking at my tea cup and it made me doubt if I had seen right. And why not. A fever hallucination, perhaps.

"Oh." I blinked, tearing my gaze away to the door. "Right. Minush." And then the realisation settled in. "Minush!" I scrambled to my feet, grabbed for a towel. It was humid, but I didn't care. Wrapping it around me, I noted: "Oh, my tea!"

Lev was sitting immobile, as though focusing on something on a random spot on the wall. "Would you mind finishing it in the kitchen?" Their voice was almost strained because of how soft it was. "I'll join you in a moment. I'm just going to–..." Their gaze travelled—slowly, carefully—to the water in the bathtub. "Tidy everything up real quick."

"Sure."

"And be careful. Your limbs must feel a little numb due to the belladonna." Their voice, their expression, their gaze. Everything had turned into perfect blankness. Were they annoyed? Angry? Just really in need of a pee?

I had no idea. But I heard more noises from outside now, and knowing that they all came from Minush? My beautiful Minush, well and happy and alive? I did not need to be asked twice. Struggling against the weight of my own limbs, I exited the bathroom.

The door snapped closed behind me immediately. Strangely, I was not sure if Lev had actually moved from their spot on the ground.

The way to the kitchen was like a jungle, even with a dizzy, hazy mind like mine, even with only a few light sources standing around here and there. Every inch of the ground was covered with pots of flowers, plants and cacti. They hung from the ceiling, covered the walls, made you duck your head, and filled your sight with unspeakable, healthy green, but most importantly, they stood along the walls on the ground, allowing, just like in the bathroom, nothing but a small path to walk along. Following it tentatively, I was brought into the wide-open kitchen.

That I recognised it as a kitchen despite the literal tree which covered most surfaces with branches and leaves was thanks to the fact that Lev's apartment was directly below mine, and thus shaped the exact same way. The entrance hall was the kitchen, and the kitchen was the living room. Or something like that. Because while I had filled mine with a bed and a couch and two barstools for the kitchen counter, theirs was, yes, a jungle. The second difference was that they had probably fused two apartments together, meaning that not only was their bathroom giant compared to mine, but also that there was most likely a door somewhere that would possibly lead to a proper bedroom. Or whatever proper could be called in this case. So, no abusive family. Just a slightly strange person. London, eh?

I was smiling.

It was strange, yes. But it was charming. I had never cared much for plants, but I did enjoy unabashed eccentricity. After all, in this case, it seemed like a sort of magic, didn't it? To be able to create and raise life like this? To grow flowers like...

"Minush!"

The small black cat had jumped onto my foot. I let out a scream of pure joy. Minush was there! As I picked her up she licked my fingers and purred just like she had always done it, ever since the very first time we had met. I laughed, the sound was filled with genuine happiness, and squeezed her into a hug.

She did not fight, she did not try to escape, she just buried her head into the crook of my arm and purred as loud as a freshly oiled motorcycle ready to hit the road.

I felt happy.

"You dumb little cat, scaring me like that. What was it all for? Why were you so awful to me?"

Minush chirped in response, repeatedly, excitedly, as though eager to explain everything to me.

"Hold on, hold on, not so fast, you've been away for so long, I've kind of gotten out of practice."

Minush turned her head away, then looked back up at me and mounted to her behind-legs, putting her tiny paws on my shoulder to reach up to my face. She sniffed me, curiously, and I let her, grinning from ear to ear.

"Oh, was it my smell? Did you not like Mr C Baker's perfume? Is that what-"

She put her tiny paw on my mouth.

"All wight then," I mumbled. "I guesh that'sh fair."

Happy.

Heavy.

So, so heavy with happiness.

I found us a little spot next to a patch of – were those pumpkins? – flowers, where we stayed until Minush fell asleep on my lap, until her purring ebbed away into perfect peace.

. . . .

"Shite," Lev whispered.

I blinked and looked up. I had no idea how long I had been mindlessly staring at the blob of black fur on my lap, allowing myself to feel perfectly at ease.

Lev had put on a second sweater. Their thick, dark hair was tousled, making it look amusingly spiky, and their eyes were fixed on Minush.

For a moment I thought they were angry that she had not rejected me again, but I soon enough noticed that this was those treacherous assumptions again, contorting reality.

But then why the "Shite?"

Lev shrugged. "That's ... cute." They motioned towards us. Their hands weren't wrapped into their sleeves anymore, I noticed, instead, they were patched up with even more tiny little plasters, most of them soaked with a droplet of blood in their middle. "Cute to, erm, look at. I'm glad she recognises your smell in here."

I took my eyes off their hands. "What do you mean?"

"I've been trying to grow Nepeta recently. She probably smelled that on me. And that's most likely why she kept trying to come into my apartment."

My mouth was open with bafflement. "Catnip?"

After a time lag, they nodded. "Hm-hm."

A laugh escaped me. I covered my face with a hand. "For fuck's sake." Out of all the apartments in the world, out of all the people on this planet, out of all the days in a year, my immediate plants-obsessed neighbour had decided to grow fucking cat drugs in scent-reach of my cat, just when I had coincidentally been so stupid to start wearing a perfume I didn't even like myself. "Really? *Really* now?" I was shaking with laughter now. It was all just so fucking dumb.

"Easy there," Lev said. "Remember, your lungs are still recovering." They handed me a large, blue jumper to wear.

Swallowing down my amusement, I put it on, not questioning where my own clothes had gone as I wasn't so certain I ever wanted to see them again. Then I picked up my tea, sipping from it between the chuckles that refused to be contained. "D'you want to sit?"

"Nah, I'm good." Lev was still standing in the kitchen with their shoulder leaning against the wall and their arms crossed.

"C'mon. You look uncomfy. Here. I make you a bit of space." And as though this was my own apartment, I started to move the pots of plants around to make some ground-space-near-wall free for Lev.

"Careful. Some of them like to hug and to never let go," they mumbled, dryly, and after watching me, unimpressed, they sat down after all. Now that we had talked about smell, I was incapable of not noticing how nice they smelled. *Floral?*, one might think now, but no. It was more than that. I had never been good at describing and recognising scents, but it was a warm scent. Full and rich, round and very, very warm. How strange. The note of eucalyptus I had noticed the first time was still there, though, but this might just have been the bath-air that was still caught in my nose.

Through the window fell cold moonslight, shining right onto their face. It was only now that they sat so close, that I noticed that, much like their hands, their face too was full of tiny droplets of blood. At least ten on the side that I could see. "You're bleeding?" I asked.

For the blink of a second, Lev's eyes seemed to widen, but before I could be sure of it, their expression had returned to blankness. "I shaved," they replied with a shrug.

Narrowing my eyes, I leaned a little closer to their face - like a magnet, they moved away from mine. "You don't look like someone who needs shaving"

"Perhaps I'm just *that* good at shaving."

A laugh escaped me. "Quite obviously not."

Rolling their eyes, they pushed a single finger against my shoulder and pushed me away.

I grinned. "How old are you, anyway?"

"Twenty-nine."

That surprised me. "You surely don't look your age."

"Younger or older?"

"Younger."

Their brows creased. "How much younger?"

"Ten years younger?"

They huffed, and the crease disappeared, indifference returning. They hadn't looked at me since sitting down, not once. "Nonsense."

I smirked. "How do you know? All your mirrors are covered by fucking plants."

Their response was a blank face.

"I'm twenty-three. Almost."

"Good on you."

"And? Do you think I look my age?"

But it didn't work, Lev wouldn't look at me. They said nothing.

I pursed my lips into a pout, trying to think of what else to say. This was like sitting next to an immensely delicious cake and only being allowed the tiniest of bites. It was frustrating. But then again, I had promised to no longer assume. So what choice did I have, stuck here with Minush on my lap, then to learn the truth? "When did you move here?"

"When I was your age."

This had me smile again. So at least I knew they were listening. "That's six years. Never thought about finding yourself a nicer neighbourhood? I mean, those sirens can keep you up at night, don't they?"

Lev shrugged. "I did move. Twice. From the third floor to the sixth, then, two years ago, here, to the tenth."

"Oh, twice? Always into bigger apartments? Because you were given a raise at work or something?"

"No." There was a pause, eventually they went on. "First into a bigger apartment, then ... back into a smaller one."

And maybe it was this very pause they had made, or the slightest tint of heaviness that was in their voice, that stopped me from asking for further details. There were not many reasons why someone would first move into a larger, then a smaller space again, were there? "I moved here two years ago, too," I said instead, keeping my voice light.

"I know."

My eyebrows raised, I looked at them, catching how they realised what they had said, how they shot me a glance, then tried to recuperate: "Not a serial killer, remember?"

I laughed.

"Door told me."

My still-laugh-parted mouth formed an 'oh'. "So I'm not crazy!" I grabbed their arm. "Door really did talk to you, too!"

Clicking their tongue and freeing their arm from my grip, Lev nodded. "Not sure about the former, but yes about the latter."

I beamed, and if it hadn't been for snoozing Minush on my lap, I would probably have turned around to face them properly. "So your name really is Lev?"

They gave me an impatient look, "And you are Antoni and she is Minush, great, now that we've introduced ourselves, how about you finish your tea?"

I shut my mouth. I had not meant to annoy them. Tease them into conversation to learn more about them, yes, but not become an overbearing piece of regret. Apologising, I picked up my tea and sipped it. It was still far too warm for the humid heat in here, but I did not want to seem ungrateful. I'd just drink it up and then go home. They had done quite enough.

"Do you-... Do you like it?"

I blinked.

They had their arms crossed and their shoulders pulled up while their chin was tucked against their chest, giving them a defensive look. "The tea," they explained. "Do you like it?"

"Oh. Oh, yes! Yes, I do."

"I did not add sugar, but if you want some, you can go get some from the kitchen? I find it an insult that-... What? Why are you grinning like that?"

My smile had indeed returned almost immediately. "You already asked me that, Lev."

"Oh." Surprise. There was real, actual surprise on their face! For almost three and a half seconds, before they seemed to catch themself and clicked their tongue again. "Well, the offer still stands."

My smile remained. "It's very good tea, though. Thank you. Just a little warm. I feel like I could need iced tea instead. But don't worry now! I'm fine, really. I'll just take a moment to finish it up and then go home, promise."

Silence.

"Unless you ... want to offer me to stay in your watch for the night?" I teased. "In your bed, perhaps?"

Lev let out a sigh and rolled their eyes to the green ceiling. "You'll do quite well in your own bed. I'm sure it misses you, after all this time."

I laughed. "Probably. Even though I really did appreciate your help, you know. Did you study that? Professionally? Working with plants? Or were you born with a naturally green thumb?"

"Definitely wasn't born with a green thumb."

"So, what are you working as? Gardener?"

"No."

It was a joke, but Lev's serious response and their defiance not to look at me just made me want to continue teasing. "Botanist?"

"No."

"Horticulturist?"

They sighed.

"Arborist?"

"You can stop now."

"Turf manager!"

"What on earth is a turf manager?"

"Well, you know, the people who keep care of the grass in football stadiums and all that? Oh, no, I know!" I grinned. "You make the bouquets at weddings!"

"Dentist!" Lev interrupted me. "I'm a dentist, okay?"

"What?"

They sighed. "I'm a studied and trained dentist. I practised in a private surgery for five years. Never particularly enjoyed it, never was particularly good at it, but it was a job, and I did it. The plants-... They came later." They propped up their legs to bring their knees to their chest, resting their crossed arms on them. Hiding themselves even more. "I never cared about plants. They were just there and, I don't know, eventually started to grow on me. They're very fragile, but sometimes very nice." A pause. "They don't talk as much as certain human beings."

I nodded, baffled. I had not expected that. And yet, again, I could but find myself a little charmed by that twist. "You had medical training then?"

"Basic one, yes."

"So that's why you knew how to help me."

"Yes."

I grinned, tilting my head back to rest it against the wall. If this had been any other person, I would've asked why they hadn't simply said that right away when I had woken up in the bathtub. 'Hi, I'm medically trained, you fainted, so I helped. ' It would've cleared things up a little faster. But this was Lev, and ... I struggled to finish that thought. No assumptions allowed. This was Lev. Period. "Aren't you going to ask me what my profession is?"

"No."

I laughed. "Will you tell me what happened to your face?"

"I thought I already had?"

I made an 'eh' kind of noise.

"It's not my fault if you don't believe me."

That was only fair, too.

"Will you tell me what happened to yours?"

Wall. White. Water. Blood. I shook my head.

"Okay."

I made sure to breathe slowly. Habit; it alleviated nothing. Eventually, I glanced over again. "And what's in the tea?"

"Tea?"

I raised the empty cup.

Lev followed the motion with their eyes. "Tea ... is in the ... tea. I don't-, What exactly are you asking about?"

"I mean, you said you gave me painkillers, so I assumed you did that by–,"

"By putting them in the bath. I wouldn't make someone swallow something without their consent. Besides, you were hardly conscious enough to make you drink anything." Their voice was pointedly quiet. "You're really eager to paint me as the villain in your story, hm? Is that something you do with everyone or just with me?"

I didn't answer. I didn't know it then, but this question would stick with me for a long, long while. "But then why were you so eager to have me drink up my tea?"

Lev's lips briefly twitched before they spoke. "Because it's really good tea." They took a breath as though they were going to say more, much, much more, but then there was nothing but a sigh.

"I promise this was the last time I'll assume anything about you. Especially that you're trying to murder me."

"Okay." Detached boredom was on their face.

I nudged their shoulder with mine.

No reaction.

"Hey, Lev."

Still no reaction, only an annoyed click of their tongue when I nudged them again.

"Leeev."

They sighed and looked at me, and the moonslight was caught in the black of their eyes. Their soft, glistening eyes. We were so very close, breathing the same air, sharing the same very second this far-travelled light decided to reach the earth.

What had I meant to say? Ah, yes. I smiled. "It's really good tea."

The corner of Lev's lips twitched again. What I had read as a sign of displeasure moments ago suddenly appeared like a smile to me. "You need sleep." They stood up.

I agreed. Carefully picking up Minush, I followed Lev to the door, leaving the towel behind now that I had the sweater to engulf most of my body. Despite the darkness in the corridor, Lev trod the path through the pots and plants without hesitation. Instead, there was ease and lightness in each of their steps, almost as though they were dancing an old, choreographed dance that told them exactly where to place their feet. Mesmerised and clumsy at once, I followed.

Cold air poured into the apartment when they opened the door. I stepped outside.

"Hey, Antoni."

"Hmm?"

"I lied."

I grinned. "I knew it. You actually *are* a turf manager!"

A sigh. "No. About the tea. It did serve a purpose." Their eyes on me, as though expecting another stupid comment, they paused. But I just let them. "Did you ever hear of the phrase 'a hug in a mug'?"

"I have now?"

They continued: "Tea is good for that. It–, it makes you feel less lonely, like someone hugging you. People always think that healing a body is all about the body itself, but they forget how powerful our minds are. Sometimes–, sometimes there's nothing better than the comfort of a friend, or the illusion of one, to help you get better." Their hand drove through their hair - some of the paper patches fell off - and another shrug graced their shoulders. "All that to say that I–, I'm glad you've got Minush back."

As so often, they were not looking at me, and because neither of us had turned on the light in the stairwell yet, I could hardly see their face, only scarcely the beautiful shape of their features and that small-framed sexless body that always held itself as though it was timidly confident and confidently timid. And yet it seemed as though something about them changed. I couldn't pinpoint what it was, but something was different. "You're really different from how I thought you were, too."

They knew what I was referring to. I heard it in the way they answered: "You still don't know anything about me."

"True." I paused, then smirked. "I mean, I do know you used to be a dentist! That's something, right?"

"Oh, Christ, go home already."

"Going, going." I laughed. "But I'll be back. And I'll find a way to thank you properly. Even if it's a gift that can't be wrapped in with a bow."

They looked at me strangely.

I grinned. "Good night."

"Antoni." They had caught me by the sleeve. The mere gesture made me remember I had a heartbeat now.

"Hm?"

I then understood what the change on their features was, and everything else was forgotten: A smile. A real, genuine, soft, warm smile was gracing Lev's delicate features. Not a smirk, not a contorted frown, not a look of mocking arrogance. No. Lev was smiling, and it was the most beautiful thing in the whole world.

My lips parted in wonder.

"I'm here if you need me," they said, speaking softly, "You're not alone." Their fingers curled around mine. And their smile was beautiful. "Please don't forget that."

"I won't. I-..." I could not finish my sentence. My eyes grew wide. No, the smile was not the only change in their features. My newly sprouted heart missed a beat.

Lev stared back at me. "What is it?"

"Your ... nose." I exhaled, raising my hand to point at it. "There's-, there's a flower growing on your nose."

Chapter Five – Sing your flowers some love songs (don't forget to appreciate their beauty)

. . . .

"You're alive!"

"Georgie?"

George Langston stood in my door, a brown paper bag under his arm and his orange toupee wet and sticking to his forehead. It had been raining all morning.

"Thank God."

And suddenly, I was in his arms, engulfed by the scent of his cheap cologne and the moist warmth of someone who had just walked up eleven floors. Perhaps I would've given in to it, just for a moment, just grateful that there was warmth at all, just glad that someone was keeping me up on my legs as my body filled with a weight I was no longer used to.

But I had to push him away. "What the fuck are you doing here?"

"Did you not receive my messages? I've been calling you all week!"

I frowned. A week?

"Anyway," he pushed past me into my kitchen. "This is for you. It was hanging on your door, I put it right here, yes? Next to the telephone? And I–, let's see, I brought you bread, apples, butter, milk, uh, what's this? Ah, right, a bit of cheese, a few packs of rice and, here, the news." He emptied the brown paper bag onto my kitchen counter. Only the newspaper was directly handed to me.

I took it, incredulous. *Anyway*, he'd said. As though what had happened could just be pushed aside with an *anyway*.

"What is this?" I asked.

"Just open page two, you'll see."

"I mean you being here."

George Langston, starting to cut me bread and smashing thick layers of cheese on top of it, waved me off. "Page two."

I did, and my heart sank deep into the crook of my guts. "*Fuck*." My eyes scanned the headline, the pictures, the names that appeared in the blur of the text.

"That happened yesterday. Today all sorta shit is going down."

I took a deep breath. Exhaled the tight feeling in my throat, hoping it wouldn't come back. But despite my chest easing, my body remained heavy.

"Underground organisation or not, people are not just going to let that pass."

I held myself against a wall. "Can you open the cat food can, please? Minush hasn't eaten yet either."

"The state will have to respond to that and, mark my words, if it doesn't do that right, your country is going to blow up."

"And put it on a plate, too, please."

"What did you say your mother works as? Isn't she a laundry lady or something? Surrounded by workers all day, isn't she?"

"It's too bad it's raining, isn't it?"

"Close with people in the unions?"

"I wanted to take a walk today."

"Hopefully, she's keeping quiet about where she gets all that money from, or she might end up being in trouble from all sides."

"Maybe I can take some fresh air on the roof."

"I hope you–,"

"I hope you're also worrying about your own country, Georgie." I interrupted him, my voice now sharp, cracking a bit under the sudden volume I forced upon it. I couldn't. I had tried to breathe indifference into myself, but I couldn't. Couldn't anymore. My throat felt tight, and my heart hammered against it incessantly. "I hope you're worrying about your own actions. What is this?! You betrayed me, you–, You've betrayed me again and again in the past, and you promised to better yourself, and then you did again. Why the fuck did you not say anything at Lenny's party? Why did you let his father hit him? How can you–, How can you just bring people together but then not ensure their well-being? I know The Second is your boss, but surely he'd listen to you? Surely you've got some power in the situation? Why can't you ever use your power?" My palm smacked against the wall, then pushed against it to keep me upright. "If he doesn't let–, If Lenny never gets to see me again, that's your fault! It'll all be your fault, and you know that. So I ask you again, why are you here?! How can you just pretend like nothing ever happened?! How can you just continue bringing in powerless boys to sleep with when you know you're ill?! How can you just keep using if you know it was the drugs that killed Loretta?! How–, How can you stand here, in my apartment, and 'anyway' everything away like it didn't fucking kill me, like it has killed me before?!" I was out of breath, my throat hurt, and I barely managed to stand on my feet. But my eyes were fixated on him, and for the first time in years, I wanted him to see the emptiness in them. The reason why I could not look at myself in the mirror. The reason why I fit into other people as though I was perfectly crafted to be their counterpart. I wanted George Langston to see it. To see what he had done, even if today...

And George Langston looked back at me and saw it. Or rather, saw something. "Antoni Pokorny," he whispered. "Are you alive again?"

I felt a shiver run down my spine. "Out."

"Antoni, where have you been for the last couple of days?"

The fear. The happiness. Now the anger. I shook my head, tiny, brusque, lost motions at first, then, when George Langston didn't move, more heftily. "Out!"

He did move, hesitantly, taken aback, but at the door, he paused once more. "Understand, Antoni, I got a call, I tried to contact you, nothing, and days later–,"

"I don't care about your excuses anymore. You didn't care. You've never cared. It's always just been a heartless game to you, at the expense of others. What's it to you whether I die or live–,"

"Antoni!"

"I could've died."

"Since when do you care?"

I was shaking now. My eyes were stinging, my vision blurring. "Out. And don't ever speak to me again." I threw the door shut behind him.

My heart was racing, pumping pain all through my body, making it feel heavy and slow as well as frantic and lost at the same time. I tore the newspapers apart. No, no, this couldn't be real; this couldn't be true. I had nearly died so many times before; never had it brought me back to life. Blindly, I grabbed for what George Langston had put next to my telephone, where a red light blinking indicated that he was saying the truth. The thing was a small pouch, and without thought, in the hope of distracting myself, I ripped it open. Out fell a multitude of white petals and the scent of jasmine.

Something inside of me broke then. Like a seed.

I fell to the ground, gasping for air, clutching my chest, clutching the pouch, clutching the pouch to my chest. It hurt. I was hurting. Deep throbbing pain was what this was, this heaviness. My lungs; I sucked in air and there was some. Convulsions took over me. it was a cry but no scream, a gasp but no shock. My head; it was dizzy but clear. My knee it ached, but was not broken. No. What hurt was that heavy, jittering thing inside my chest.

And I did not understand until my hand wiped over my cheeks. I froze. "Tears?"

Flowers.

That Lev hadn't been a dream, I was rather sure of. But had there really been a flower blooming on their nose? Had my fingers really touched a blush of pink carnations? Had the vines growing up their legs really tried to reach for my ankles? Or had my fever and Lev's belladonna caused hallucinations? The belladonna… Had they grown it themself too?

I didn't know when I stopped crying. I just knew that eventually I had reached into the pouch and drawn out something that looked like tiny balls of rolled-up leaves. It was the green tea they had offered me, wasn't it? Memories of a blooming bathroom and trust flooded me along with the scent. Letting out a shaky breath, I exhaled the air, but the scent remained. I supposed this was how it was going to be from now on.

Was it all real? I had a feeling that I didn't care to find the answer. What mattered was that it had changed me. That it would change me even more from here on in. How, why, when? These answers would come when they were ready to be given. Maybe with time, I'd be ready to hear them better, too. For now, I needed to find out what to do with it. Brew it, I supposed. Drink it.

· · · ·

I carefully climbed down the stairs, holding the empty pouch to my chest with one hand and myself to the railing with the other. Making sure not to put too much weight on my knee, I watched my feet attentively, and so I lifted my eyes only when I reached Lev's floor.

There they already stood. Their dark eyes on me, as though they were a statue, having waited there with a patience of stone. Dark eyes, so black that you could not read them, not the depth, not what they contained. Obsidian mirrors.

Their chin was slightly cocked up, but not in an attitude of arrogance. It was more a manner of confidence, of calmness, and so was the way they had propped up one foot against the door, heel on the ground, toes against the door, holding it open while they leaned against the opposite wall with their arms hanging so loosely down their shoulders, that their thumbs had been stuffed into the back pockets of their jeans. They were barefoot, yes, but everything else, every other part of their body, was perfectly covered: their ankles, their legs, their knees, their waist, their chest, their arms, their shoulders, their neck. All of it was covered in loose, washed-out grey-black clothes that hung down their body so vaguely that it was impossible to guess any forms of or beneath it. Their body was already of an optical-illusion kind of size, making them look tall and lanky when they were even smaller than me, just like making them look broad, without any sort of meat to it. The loose fabric veiled all this while at the same time emphasising it. Only the feet, the tip of the fingers, and the face allowed the porcelain white complexion of their skin to shine out, building this strange, almost ghost-like contrast between the darkness of their clothes and their surrounding. In short: They were drop-dead gorgeous, but I could not even begin making sense of them.

"Hi again."

A single eyebrow was raised, the same colour as their hair, and so different from the sharpness of their cheekbones and the smallness of their nose, this very blackness of their hair took all shadow from it and made it impossible to recognise form and shape. They blinked, once, slowly, their head moving ever so slightly as they took a breath, and perhaps this was the only thing that made them look human in that moment.

"You're late."

I smiled, without being able to help it. "I didn't realise you were waiting for me."

"I didn't realise you needed me to tell you."

It was a bit ironic. The only person who refused to reveal their thoughts and feelings to me was the first person from whom I needed it. If I never found out who they were, what they were, then how was I supposed to know what they had done to me? Their face was patient marble. "Well, I would've been here a little earlier, but I'm one of those Vitamin-D-lacking fools who prefer the company of the moons to the sun." George Langston never left his apartment before noon. "I can't seem to wake up early in the morning, ever. Maybe I'm a vampire."

And then it happened. The only thing I had so strainedly kept my eyes away from, this singular, minimal, infinitely beautiful dot of colour in all this formless, achromatic appearance, curled into a smile, and my heart released a beat in their name. Red. No. *Pink*. A soft hue of pink and the very epitome of worthshippable lips. Smiling. Lev was smiling, and I never wanted to look away from them again. Unfortunately, it was gone in a blink. "I've made tea."

Lev had tidied up. Yes, everything was still a small jungle, wilderness within a city too grey for its own good, and everything was probably still full of bugs, but somehow it looked less ... messy. There was more space to walk around. Less pots stood around without purpose, appearing placed in a more elegant, more aesthetic way, the vines that had hung down from the ceiling had been trimmed – trimmed, not removed – and the larger trees looked as though they had been freed of draining branches and dead leaves, making everything feel less ... threatening. I could recognise the door to the bathroom now, the window, and the shape of the kitchen. So they really had been waiting for me. I had forgotten how hearts contract when you smile.

"Do you want a refill?" they asked as they handed me one of two mugs that had been waiting on their, let's call it, stove.

"Oh." I looked at the empty pouch, then happily handed it over. "Yes, please!"

A moment later, I held a new jasmine pouch in my hand. It, too, had been waiting for me. Upon seeing my raised eyebrows, Lev clicked their tongue. "I do not take psychic abilities to know a man longs for caffeine at three in the afternoon." They tapped against a small pot of sugar to indicate I could take some if I wanted to. "Or might want another cup of the jasmine. It is good jasmine."

I was not too surprised by their deduction. After all, this was how I had survived for the last five years. All until, I suppose, I hadn't. "That's almost disappointing," I said. "I was ready to hear my own life story told back at me through your mouth."

"Alas." They nodded towards a rocking chair made of bamboo. It had marks of vine residues all over it, painting it almost green. Quite obviously, one of the many things the cleaning had brought back to life.

As I shuffled over to it, I tried to imagine Lev existing mundanely. It was oddly difficult. I knew they had thoughts and hobbies of their own, but I was not privy to them. The only smiles, the only emotions I had caught of theirs so far, had been in response to me talking about myself. *You know, you're really not who I imagined you to be.* I could still hear it in their voice. I settled down on the rocking chair – the coffee almost spilled as I was so suddenly swung backwards – and I proposed: "What if I tell you three things about me, two lies and one truth, and you try to guess which is which?" Who knew? Maybe that was the key to Lev. Maybe if I shared about myself, they would have to share as well. And then it was only a matter of time before I'd have my answers.

"Thrilling," was, however, their rather unexcited response as they sat down across the small room by the wall, where we had sat yesterday. All of their movements were pointedly slow, in a way careful, as though they were moving through water and considering and considering and reconsidering every single action before committing it. They had moved a little oddly previously, too, but today it was far more pronounced, far more noticeable.

I decided not to dwell on it. After all, perhaps they were sick or disabled or something like that, and it felt rude to stare and point it out. Even if there was nothing I wanted to do more than stare and point and find out more. "All right. Let's think..."

"You really don't have to play a g-..."

"Oh, I know! One. I'm really good at waltzing."

Lev let out a huff. Was it a sigh? Was it a chuckle? I focused on myself.

"Like, dancing the waltz. Well, you know what I mean. Two. Despite my origins, I hate vodka. And three." Three representing fingers were up now. "I still have no idea whether you're a girl or a boy."

Their eyes shot up at me, then immediately lowered themselves back to the cup of coffee. It was the first line of action that wasn't slow with calculation. Their lips were parted, letting out a breath that made them return to expressionless blankness. It reminded me so much of myself. Except that I had learnt how to emote. "And now?"

"Now you have to guess which ones are the lies and which one is the truth."

With their cold gaze directed at the window in front of them, they were completely still, and I was about to prompt again when their eyelids fluttered, as though they were waking up from a sleep. "None."

"What?" I blinked.

"None of those are lies." And then there it was again. That smile, so soft, so pink, so suddenly turned into a smirk before it vanished. "Am I right?"

"Maybe." But I knew I was blushing. So, what? Had I lost the ability to lie, too?

"You're not playing fair, Mr Pokorny." They did not look like it, but there was pride in their voice. Almost something like cockiness.

I adored it. "You know my last name? Did Door tell you that, too?"

They shook their head, blowing into their coffee. "Nametag on the mailbox."

"Right. Stalker. Your turn."

"Two lies and a truth?"

I nodded.

Pensively, they blew into their coffee, then: "I've lived in London my whole life. Every Saturday, I go to the National Museum of Art. And I-... I've never danced a waltz."

A quiet 'oh' left me. "All of them are lies?" I tried.

Lev clicked their tongue. "*I* play fair."

My mouth stayed open as I tried to find the answer. It was well possible that they had lived in London their whole life. It seemed more likely than the other two. Right? "The London one is the truth."

Lev shrugged. "If you say so."

"Hey!" I laughed. "You have to tell me what it is now!"

They ignored me. Slowly they took in a sip of their coffee, and leaned their head back against the wall, closing their eyes. This dot of pink in a sea of black and white in a world of green in a universe of grey.

"Let's play again. You go first this time."

"Later, maybe."

I pursed my lips and narrowed my eyes. I wanted to know more; it was infuriating. I wanted action, reaction, palpable smiles and truths. Not for myself! Not to know how to act and react, no. Fuck that. Them! I wanted to get to know them! Not because the obsidian mirror scared me, but because I yearned for the colours behind it.

Alive. I was alive again because of them.

But now that I didn't make them talk, they didn't talk at all. It was positively unfair. And I could feel my guts itching with impatience. "Lev?"

"Hmm?"

"Is now 'later'?"

They rolled their eyes to the ceiling.

"Lev?"

"No."

"Please."

They sighed and looked at me.

"How did you know I was going to come by today?"

Silence again. But this time, it was charged with my question and all the answers Lev struggled to give. "Because there are things you still want to know."

That was quite the way to phrase it, yes. "Too bad you're never answering my questions."

"I'm trying to," they replied, quietly, and after another pause: "I just need you to stop trying to ... reveal me."

Reveal them.

For a long moment, we just looked at each other.

I understood. I understood but I did not like it. Part of me wanted to lie and agree and still slyly continue with my game anyway: *Let me reveal myself and we shall see what it achieves.* The other part of me, the less nasty, the more selfless side of me, wanted to tell them that it was okay. That they were safe with me: *Trust my game and it will all be fine.*

But that is what this was. A game. My old familiar game of Theory, Experiment, Conclusion. Wasn't it? And here was Lev, looking back at me, looking straight through that game, and revealing it for what it was. Revealing me for what I was: Hollow.

Hollow and thoroughly dishonest. There was a lump in my throat. "But how will I get to know you then?" When I spoke, my voice was shaking. I suppose that is what happens when you let go of control.

"Why do you want to know me?"

"Because you've made my heart beat again, and I don't understand why and how."

"Why does it matter?"

Because I'm scared. I failed to open my mouth. My jaw, my throat, my lips, my whole body was tight. Sealed and waterproof. It was as if any attempt to say now what I had not allowed myself to even think for three years was once and for all going to burst me wide open. The gash within my chest, in which had lived nothing for three years but two round yellow eyes, in which the seed of a heartbeat had been planted just a few nights ago, it would at once fill with a river of past happiness and the memories of inescapable terror. Irreversibly. *Because I'm alive, although I don't deserve it. Because I'm scared.*

At last, Lev lowered their gaze. "Would you like to tell me about yourself, Antoni?"

I exhaled. "A performance?"

"If you must."

I felt myself relax. "I can do that." After all, what was the truth but the well-executed interplay of gestures and facial expressions? My back straightened. My legs crossed. My shoulders rolled back. My lip corners pulled. My eyes began to shine. And I declared the first and easiest truth of them all: "I'm gay!"

Lev did a flinch that looked like a laugh and made a sound that sounded like one, too. "I would have never guessed that," they replied, so dryly that it wasn't dripping with sarcasm but cracking with. Like the Nevada desert.

I laughed, too. Bright and easy. Waterproof. "Yes, okay, fair. But it's only so obvious to you because there's one-third of a chance that you grew up in London. You're surrounded by your clichés of how gay people talk and act and live, but where I'm from, there are no gay people. Or *weren't*." I frowned. "*Are*. Hm. In my town, well, village, really, there was, ha, once a week, there was a party. In a barn. It was the event of the week; on Monday, we'd all talk about it in school as though it had been the biggest event in the world, but really, even when every youth from the surrounding villages came, we still never exceeded more than a hundred people." Fucking barn. How I had hated it. How I had loved it. When would I see it again? "I always knew I was gay. Not even just in the deeply emotional and slightly psychologically twisted way. But also in the very plain 'Karolina, I'm flattered, but I like boys' kind of way. No doubts, really. Never. I have three sisters, and when they cooed about boys and talked about marrying them, I always joined in because everything they said just made sense, you know? But I also knew that no one else knew it, just like no one else wanted to know it. So I didn't even bother to get into anyone's knickers. Not necessarily because I was scared of the consequences, but because-... Because I knew there'd be no consequences."

Lev glanced at me.

"I mean, where would it get me? Boy kisses girl, girl allows him to hold her hand at school, everyone plans their wedding, and three years later, they're married with six kids. But boy kisses boy?" I shrugged. Even when the consequences weren't stained with violence, they were never as beautiful as they should be. "It was just so ... futile."

Lev's expression was quiet, attentive. They did not play along with my jokes.

I cleared my throat. "And then I come here and," I laughed, "fuck! Almost twenty years of thinking I'll never get near a dick, and then I come here and suddenly I'm paid to touch dick!"

The sound from earlier returned. Airy, close-lipped, very, very quiet.

"It's true. It was amazing. And I didn't think it would be that easy. The first time it happened, I was at a bar, and flirting with this really not-ugly man when he said: 'I'd give everything to take you home'. He was obviously just flirting, being smooth and all that, but I was broke and high, and so I replied: 'It's twenty pounds, but if you make me enjoy it, I'll give it to you for free', and he just took it. He just took the fucking deal. It was amazing."

"I bet," Lev mumbled, not particularly amazed.

"I mean, you know what they say: Prostitution is the oldest profession in the world. And I'm all for tradition."

Lev downed their coffee.

"Too much?" I wanted it to be too much, I realised now.

But Lev only shrugged with their eyebrows. "Go ahead."

I did. Images of a long bygone time were beginning to flood my mind. "It was pretty draining to never know if I'd find a client that night, though. Plus, all the extra money that got wasted on having to buy drinks and stuff. It was annoying. So I asked around until I found street where your typical, local whore walks, and made it my, um, office. Business picked up from then on. I mean, I didn't make much, but you know, just enough not to starve. At least for a while. Unfortunately, it turned out that the street belonged to someone, and I only learned about that after working on it for like two months. Sometimes I wonder if she kept me in the dark for so long on purpose, you know. Because when she caught me, she threatened me, and when she had me begging for my life, she offered me a deal. She said I could stay until I had paid off my debt with her, all the money I supposedly made her lose, and then she'd reconsider whether she was okay with me staying or not. She was a scary lady, Louisanne. Grand. Iconic. But scary." I still remembered the way she would tower over her girls, drenching them in her shadow, blackmailing them into ceaseless work. I still remembered the way her nails would dig into my skin when I would once again lose her so-called 'great patience'. I still remembered the stench of fake Chanel n°5 announcing her arrival from yards away and would make us jolt out of our sleep at night when our unconscious mind caught a whiff of it. So many years later, and I still remembered. Still steered away from perfume. I took a breath. It only smelled of herbs in here. "As I said. At that point, I didn't have a place to stay, nothing real at least, so this was pretty much the closest to a real job offer I could get. I hardly spoke English, you know. And she offered me a bed in a real house. With a real roof." So that at least at night you didn't have to worry about the junkies and those who the dirt of the street had robbed them of their mind over the years.

"Did you manage?"

"Did I manage what?"

"Did you manage to pay off your debt?"

I nodded. "Pretty soon, too. Turned out that none of what was happening out there kept people from wanting to have sex. It just made them have it in silence, in the shade. And who was there? Waiting for them in this very shade? Me. Us. The only ones dumb enough to give them what they wanted while the stench of disease flooded the city."

Lev's gaze was on me, lost in the memories I presented to them.

So I continued. "It was paradise, really. A dirty, stinky, dark kind of alley-paradise. For the first time in my life, I made my own money, you know, and for the first time in my life, men were – not so literally – queuing up for me. And I met nice people there. They were all as … consequence-less as I was, and it made me feel like I belonged, more than I ever belonged in that bloody barn." I chuckled, shaking my head. "There were women who sucked dick and men who sucked dick and women with dicks who sucked dick, and I-… I belonged. Those people? They didn't care. They didn't care about where you were from, where you'd go, what your past was, or who you aspired to be. There was just them and the now, and while most of them were really, really nasty people, some of them were just the most … beautiful angels the world had ever had the right to see. I mean, I can't and couldn't call them friends, because calling someone a friend meant to cry over their tomb, and fuck, there were so many tombs we had to erect every day that we eventually lost the ability to cry, but—, Maybe some of them were friends after all." I saw her face then. Her beautiful, dark face with the thousand-pound smile. "Loretta," I said quietly, seeing her dark curls and even darker eyes in the reflections of my coffee, seeing her twirl around herself in a new dress, seeing her in all her beauty, with all her liveliness. "She had the purest heart. The warmest soul. She would always share her meals with those who hadn't made any money that day, always defended those who couldn't defend themselves, and always had an extra blanket lying around for when the nights were a little colder, a little lonelier than usual." We had all loved her so much that we had chosen a random date on the calendar to celebrate her birthday, because she had refused to tell us her real one. She joined the celebration for us. "After I paid off my debt for Louisanne and before I started saving for myself, for my family at home, I paid off Loretta's debts, too. She wanted to get married, you know?"

Lev's face had softened. Though perhaps I also just imagined it, just wanted to see it, in honour to Late Loretta Langston.

"She left the streets and disappeared. I thought I'd never see her again, but a few weeks later, she was there again, more radiant and magnificently beautiful than ever before, and she invited me to tea at her new place." I chuckled. "It was a wonderful new place. With a kitchen and a bedroom and a bathroom all to herself, and the tea she served, she'd bought herself and cooked herself and served herself. She'd found a place to lead her new life. We had so much fun together, oh, after the tea party, too. We would meet again and again, and it was never boring. There was so much life in her, it was addictive." I remembered something and smiled at Lev, who was still observing me. "She loved flowers, you know. She would always wear some in her hair. It kind of made her look a bit old-fashioned, but also kind of ... free. As though she was always saying: Hello, world, you may think I'm odd, but I am happy anyway!" And how much she *glowed* with happiness when the surgeries were over, and she was finally able to find beauty in the sight of her own body. Quite like George Langston had looked at her all along... And in a way, it made sense. That day, when Loretta had finally been able to see herself as the woman she had always been, she had seen herself the way we had always seen her, in all her beauty, and she had fallen in love with herself like we had fallen in love with her a long time ago. This love hadn't been an act of selfishness or arrogance, but an act of embracing what once had been hated so violently. "It didn't take long before she introduced me to her husband. I mean, you know, they couldn't really marry, but she called him her husband anyway, and we called them Mr and Mrs Langston. In a way, they were married more than most married couples ever will be." Love. Nothing but love. "His name was George. He came from America, ah, San Francisco, and had this," I chuckled, "this weird twisted way of being nice, and always accidentally insulted everyone by being a bit too polite. The first time he saw me, he said that I looked like a curly fry dipped in ketchup, and when I was admittedly a little taken aback, he apologised and said that at least I was a cute curly fry." *Oh, Georgie.* "But he was a good man. A really, really good man, and the only one worthy of Loretta's love." I had understood that soon enough, and never stopped believing in it.

My breath felt a little shaky. I took a deeper one.

"One day," I continued, "a few weeks later, Georgie told me that he worked in this fancy-shmancy company and had overheard that his boss had a newly outed gay son. Boss was worried that his son might start going out and get himself into trouble over a stupid hook-up simply because he was too curious and naïve and knew nothing about anything. So Georgie told him that he'd find him a boy for his son, someone that would satisfy his curiosity but also not hurt him, someone who was clean and nice and possibly looked like a cute curly fry dipped in ketchup." I pointed at myself and grinned.

A one-sided smile curved Lev's lips momentarily.

"I was pretty fucked at that time, because Louisanne, the lady who owned the street on which I was still working on, right, she had started demanding more and more money from us, and I mean, we already didn't earn ourselves much." My family had never owned a lot, and yet, although we were four kids, and it had been anything but easy times, we had always had enough to eat. Something that I couldn't say of the time when I had still worked for Louisanne. "Eventually, the ten pounds left at the end of the month wasn't worth the way the clients treated us, so when Georgie suggested I should go to meet with his boss's son, I was obviously thrilled."

"Obviously," Lev mumbled, their face still very calm, their gaze still on me. "And did you? Go?"

I smiled. "Yes." I couldn't remember the first time I had seen Lenny's face, but oh, how well I remembered the first time he had started babbling about music, how handsome he had suddenly become, filled with life. I remembered the first time we had kissed and how flushed he had looked. I remembered the way he had grown comfortable around me and how much I had grown to like him in return. "Yes, I did. First, to the doctors, of course, a full check-up, from head to toe. I never had that in my life before, so that was really fun. Turns out I have a lack of iron in my blood. No idea what that means, but from then on, I made sure to lick random pieces of metal more often."

Lev's smirk grew. Unfortunately, so much so that they became aware of themselves once more and hurriedly went back to hiding inside their – probably by now empty – coffee cup. A performance, wasn't it? All of this, all of us, we both. The way we had taught ourselves to survive.

"I still do." I continued, "I like him. His—, his name is Lenny, and he's got those big, blue, innocent eyes that never stay still because he's always—, I think because he's always a little scared." A week, George Langston had said. I'd been gone for a week. I had missed our date on Thursday. Would he forgive me? Would he be worried? I'd have to call him eventually. "He's not particularly great in bed, though."

Lev made another one of those quiet, high sounds.

I liked them. "Anyway. Georgie would talk about me to his friends, or people he thought trustworthy, and they would then call me to make up a date. Pay me. Bring me home again. Be respectful. It worked wonderfully. I mean, there were always a few spoilt fish in the mix, but at the end of the day, there were more positive points to be found than negative ones, and the fact that they were colleagues with Georgie and didn't want to anger him helped a lot. So, then, one thing led to the next, years passed, and now I'm here."

"You never attempted to get a real job?"

I blinked. "This is a real job."

Widening, Lev's eyes shot over to me. "I'm sorry. That's not how I meant it."

"Just because I-... I mean, whether I work with my hands to build a house or work with my hands to jerk someone off, it's still work. I'm still tied to work hours, I have to dress a certain way, I have to stay healthy, and I have to be professional. The only difference is that I bring pleasure to people, not headaches from construction noise."

But Lev had already long spotted their own mistake by the time I had called it out. They nodded. "I know," they murmured. "That's really not how I meant it."

I couldn't tell if they were just ashamed of their judgment or if they hadn't meant to judge at all. I supposed that this was part of my lesson, not to assume and to control, but to trust. "I'm content, you know. I'm well-paid, and I have enough regulars not to be pressured to go out every day. I can be sick and still have enough money. I can have a cat and a place to stay, and it's-...." I shrugged. "I did try to work at a Deli first, you know, when I first came here, and it was all nice and fun until it turned out that I really sucked dealing with the money. I constantly gave out the wrong amount and got fired a month in."

Lev closed their eyes.

"I doubt I could've had more luck. And—, I don't know. People are amazing, it's fun to work with them, literally work *with them*. They're just-..." I thought of Mr Hendrikson. A shiver ran down my spine. For a moment, I closed my eyes, too, and took a breath. When I exhaled it, though, the feelings did not leave my chest. Right. Things were changing.

"They're just very real." Lev finished my sentence.

Surprised, I looked up. "Yeah. Yeah, they are."

Their fingers were playing with the rim of their cup. "What about your friends? Mr and Mrs ... Langston?"

"Oh." Loretta and Georgie. Mr and Mrs Langston. It was strange how often I had used those names when they had still been together, inseparable, intertwined, and the way they were spoken was like a melody, something irreplaceable, an unchangeable sound. Mr and Mrs Langston, the two who had meant to be together forever. "Overdose."

Lev was still. "Both of them?"

I shrugged. "Can you imagine? You survive a pandemic, immigration, racism, prejudices, you survive a surgery that cuts off your balls, you survive all the hate and disgust society has in store for you, a fucking war because you're just that fucking strong, and then you accidentally poison yourself. From one day to the next, you're gone." For months, there had been a suffering greater than life, a series of goodbyes that had filled me to the brim with pain. And then? Then my life changed in a single night. Lightness. Emptiness. Silence. This was how I used to feel when I thought about Loretta from that moment on, for years. Hurting in a way which only brought silence.

Now I felt it. Felt it all over again.

Fuck. I pressed the heel of my hand into my chest. "Can you imagine? Being *alive* so much only to *die* because of a stupid mistake?"

"Yes, I can," Lev whispered. "I can imagine that." Their hair had fallen into their face, but it didn't manage to hide the pain that had begun to move their porcelain neutrality. Pain, visualised. At last. At last, the obsidian mirrors gave in, and the depth and volume of their emotions flashed up. At last, I understood. They, too, weren't empty, were they?

"Lev?" I asked.

They took in a breath, a deep breath, as though there was never going to be enough air to breathe it all away. I did not expect their gaze to meet mine again, but it did, and their eyes were veiled with unspoken thoughts, with words so heavy that no tongue could carry them, with gentleness. Without intention, neither from my side nor theirs, they revealed themselves to me.

Carefully, I reached out, my fingers catching the small petals of a clover leaf which had started to grow out of Lev's neck. "You're blooming again."

Silence.

A breath.

Then everything happened very fast.

"Shit."

The mug crashed to the ground, the leftover coffee spilled everywhere. Lev ran to the bathroom and threw the door close behind them.

I followed instantly. "Lev?"

"Don't come in!"

But I had already opened the door, and it was enough for me to see Lev leaning over the sink, scissors in their hands, and clover growing all over them. Well, or at least from what I could see, on their neck, face, feet and hands, as everything else was, I finally understood, *preventively* covered with clothes. The scissors were huge kitchen scissors, and their hands were growing so green that it seemed impossible to hold them properly. They were also shaking. Heavily. Even from where I stood, I could hear their panicked panting, even from here, I could see their already pale skin losing all colours underneath all the green. And with almost every stem of clover they cut, a little hiss of pain surpassed Lev's lips, a little flinch went through their body, a little ache twisted my stomach. "Lev." I tried again, but I was once again not allowed.

"Please, leave me alone! I'm sorry, I–, I'll be right–," They winced. "Fuck."

It was obvious that me being here did not help them at all, but while of course I did not want to cause even more panic, I also doubted that me just going outside would calm them. Not now that they knew I was right there, waiting for them to return, aware of what had happened. Aware of their truth.

They winced again, as, instead of the scissors, they had picked up a razor, and the trembling of their hands had slit a deep cut into their cheek. Shaving, after all, wasn't it?

"Lev." No, I couldn't just turn around and be a threat from afar. I couldn't once again leave for the night and pretend I had all just dreamt it, that it had once again been but a fever hallucination. I couldn't just shrug it off or mock it or even pay money to make it all better. I was the problem, and so I knew I was the solution as well.

"Lev, it's okay." They needed to know that.

Quietly but without doubt, I stepped into the bathroom and walked over to them. All this blood. All this fear. All that pain for a little bit of green. Gently reaching around their small frame, my hand moved to take hold of theirs. Underneath my palms ,I could feel the clover still growing, but also Lev's trembling, the panic that had taken a firmer hold of them than I had.

"I'm s—, I'm sorry."

"It's okay."

Through the mirror before us, they were staring at me, their eyes watering with big, veiling tears, but I looked at them directly, from the side, at their face so close to mine that I could smell the flowers within them, at their silently twitching lips until everything disappeared behind a forest of clover, and sobs so heart-breakingly violent left them that they almost doubled up over the sink. "I tried to stop it, I tried to keep them in, I tried to be n—, normal, but-..." Everything was drowned by soundful tears. Tears that fell as succulents. "I'm sorry. I'm so sorry."

"Is it dangerous?" I asked.

"No!"

"Does it hurt?"

"No!" Their free hand hammered against the sink. Two pots of plants fell to the ground, crashing. "No, that's not it, really, I'm—, I'm fine but–," They were shaking so heavily that I feared their knees would give in and cause them to fall. "I'm so stupid, I'm just so stupid, it's–, It wasn't supposed to happen today, you–, I–,"

"Stop apologising, then." I interrupted them, my voice just loud enough to drown out theirs, but quiet, nevertheless. I allowed myself to hold them by the waist, in the hope of being as much support as they had been for me. Underneath my palm I felt the plants finding their way out of their sweater, poking holes into the fabric. What a strange, wondrous thing. But, had I been amazed by them moments ago, I could only find sympathy in me now. And it was heavy, and it made me hold onto them tight. "There's nothing to apologise for. As long as you don't hurt–,"

"But you were supposed to like me!" Slowly they sank to the ground until their forehead was pressed against the sink and their hands clutching the rim of it.

Shaking my head, I had lowered myself down with them, my eyes on this marvel before me. "It's okay," I whispered again. "It's good. If this is you, how can I like you without it?" Their whole body was as soft as a field of grass in a forest, the plants underneath their clothes still growing. Many had already made it out, especially around their sleeves and collar, and all that had once been black and dark was now green and alive, vibrant in its colour, dazzling in its meaning. Carefully, I tried to turn them towards me, to let go of the scissors and hold my hand instead, to make them look at me, even if I could not see them. They let me. "You look beautiful."

"No." They kept shaking their head. "No, you don't understand. This is inside of me, always."

"Then you're beautiful, always."

"No."

"You look alive. Nothing's more beautiful than life."

Some of this green was stained red. Fresh blood dripping down on it.

"Please don't hurt yourself because of it."

"I'm a monster."

"No." I shook my head, hearing my voice filling with confidence and reassurance. "You're not." Where were their eyes? I needed to see their eyes, needed to have them see mine. If all this came from inside, then it wasn't by cutting the stems that you could stop it, but by addressing their roots. "Lev, there are many, many monsters out there, but you aren't–, you aren't one of them. Trust me. This truly does not make you a monster."

"How do you know? I'm disgusting. I'm–, I'm scarcely even human."

"Apparently, you're much more than that. Lev, you–,"

"Show yourself out, please."

I fell silent. Neither of us moved; only the occasional soundless sobs drove tremors through Lev's body.

Lev.

Lev, who was so very alive that even flowers grew inside their veins and bloomed out of their pores. Lev thought there was no light at night. Lev, who had made me smile without ever truly smiling themself. Gently, my hand went to caress over their hair, through the strands of black that were still to be seen amid all this green. "Do you really want me to go?" I asked.

"I don't want to ruin your day any further."

"But do you want me to go?"

"It won't stop if you stay here."

"Lev," I almost would've laughed if it didn't hurt so much to see them so defeated. "Answer my question. Just this once. Just this one answer to a question, please: Do *you* want me to go?"

Their head moved, and I realised it was so they could look at me. Slowly, they were twisting their wrist out of my hold, I had forgotten to loosen the hold that had disappeared beneath thick layers of ever-growing clover. I let go, ready to hear the 'yes' and leave. But that wasn't how they answered. Instead, their fingers curled into mine, holding me.

My breath halted. For the first time since I had smelled Jasmine, I feared losing the new weight within me if I were to exhale now.

Their eyes were on me. I could feel it, even if I could not see it. And then there was a shrug. A tiny, slow shrug.

I nodded. "All right." I let out my breath, brushing my thumb over their fingers, then leaned in and pressed a kiss to the clover on their forehead. "Everything's okay." It was not difficult to wrap my head around the wonders of plants growing out of skin, but it was difficult to accept that tears had been falling because of me, because Lev thought I could reject them for such a vastly beautiful, yet hardly significant ... detail. I sighed once more and looked back up, looking at them with a smile now. "Can I ask some questions now?"

They nodded.

"Does all of this have a name?"

They shook their head.

I hummed. "How long has it been going?"

Another shake of the head, this time slower. "I-..." A breath. "Years. It just started one day. My heart had been broken, and I was sad. So I turned into a tree."

I fell silent. From a small apartment to a bigger apartment to a small apartment.

"I didn't notice it at first. There was too much pain. I think I was too full of it, so my body couldn't hold it in anymore, and, eventually, the pain turned into branches and the sadness into leaves." Their voice was softening, becoming hardly more than a whisper.

"Healing?" I asked.

Lev gave it a slow shrug of their shoulders. "Protection, perhaps."

I nodded. Perhaps, yes. For another long moment, I looked at them in silence. Eventually, our breathing ebbed into the same rhythm. The leaves rustled in unison with us.

I felt something soft brushing over my fingers. It was a purple flower caressing my skin as it grew. Everything else had come to a stillness. "You know, I've never met anyone before who can hear Door speak. You could've told me."

"I've never met anyone else either. That's exactly why I couldn't tell you."

My finger had curled into theirs.

"I didn't mean to lie to you. It's just... Acting indifferent helps feeling indifferent. Sometimes." Their fingers held mine back just as tightly. "But it's all right, you know. Everyone deals differently with sadness. Some make love, others make oxygen."

I smiled, from within, and wondered. Was this something that was always on the verge of happening? Something that needed to be controlled to prevent it from breaking out? Was there medication for that? Even if it was the most beautiful power I had ever heard of, I could only imagine how hard it had to be to live with it. "I guess taking you out on a date isn't really an option, then."

A leaf of fern unrolled on their neck. "No."

"Not even if I did only a tiny bit of flirting? Beginner-level flirting?"

Another two ferns. "Not even then."

I nodded. "What about just going out like this? Not staying in one place, like a restaurant. Just ... moving through the city. Walk by the river? Getting a hamburger to go? Or we could bring tea and find an empty spot in the park? Is that not an option either?"

They sounded flabbergasted: "But what if it happens again? In public!"

"And what if? I mean, this is London. If it happens, people will think it's a costume for a party, or something. Or that you're a performance artist and toss money your way. Or they won't notice at all. It's not like someone will come running after you like in a superhero movie and try to do tests on you or anything. I mean, hell," I laughed, "you could probably go on live TV with that, and most people would still think it's just an act."

Lev was quiet.

I frowned. "I'm not trying to convince you. You don't have to say yes. I'm just–, Learning about the options."

"You're still ill."

"A little walk and some sunlight will do me well."

"Would you not be embarrassed by me?"

"Embarrassed?!" Even if I hadn't been someone to dress in metallic plastic jackets and jorts so short they showed my ass, I doubted I'd ever be able to find anything embarrassing about the life that was blooming out of their veins right now. Maybe I didn't understand it, maybe I never would, maybe there was nothing to understand about it, maybe I was going soon, but no. I could never, ever, feel anything like shame for such a marvellous gift. To feel so openly... On the contrary, I envied it. For the first time in three years, I wanted to feel so truly, too. What I said then, after listening only to the new and unfamiliar beating of my heart, was the most urgent of my truths: "I'm not sure I'm capable of such a feeling just yet."

Their hand reached out, moved to my chest. Purple flowers tickled my collarbone. "You're like me, aren't you?"

"I hope to become."

In the end, it was them who rose to their feet, murmuring a soft: "I have an idea," taking me with them out of the bathroom, through the corridor, to the door. I followed, my eyes steadily on them. I couldn't avert them, even if I had wanted to. They led as though it were a waltz, and I followed as though I were a dancer.

· · · ·

Not down we went, but up. To the roof.

I had never been up here and initially it appeared to be nothing but a concrete wasteland. Then Lev tugged on my sleeve and shyly began showing me around. Here was a patch of thin wild grass, there was a brave dandelion piercing through the cracks in the ground. Residues of vines patterned the grey and on the stone chimney the green colouring of moss told stories of a rainy climate.

I followed Lev as though this square little surface was the whole world and every nook and cranny was worth discovering. I followed as the warm afternoon sun softened my skin and a thick layer of clover covered Lev's body. Summer still lay in the air. Not measurable by warmth but by light. It was the first time this year that I noticed it, that I existed within the realms of our seasons. The light was caught in the darkness of Lev's eyes, flashing back out whenever they turned around to me, and I fell into their blackness the way most people fall in love. I followed them when I told them this, and pink carnations grew on their cheeks. When panic arose within them because of it, I paused to pull them close, told them that it was just them and me, *just you and me,* and that there was nothing to fear. I followed them as they walked from priest to bishop to pope to cardinal direction and showed me all there was to see of the County of London from here, almost as if we were tourists, until my chest was heavier than it had ever been, and still grew heavier with each new set of flowers as vibrant as the sound of their laugh. Their laugh. A sound I heard from then on so often, so much, and never grew tired of. It wasn't of any particular quality, neither chiming nor enchanting, in a way it was even rough and crackled on its sides, kind of broken, kind of hoarse, but the mere fact that it existed, the mere fact that it was so bright and loud and free, made it the most beautiful sound I had ever witnessed. It would shake Lev's whole body, make it writhe, make it bloom like Spring despite the world around us having fallen to Autumn. And I'd be left dazzled, adoring and keeping my promise. I followed them when we danced by the water – a waltz – and I followed them when we sank into the dewy grass.

By the time we sank to watch the sun pass through the distant skyline, I understood that Lev had spent many, many hours here. Days, even. Maybe a whole life: They had drawn the entirety of our building's blueprints with pebbles on the parapet. They knew who lived where. Why. Since when.

Because I'm scared.

"Here," Lev murmured. "For you."

I tore my gaze from the skyline. "Oh. It's pretty." A red poppy. I took it. "Thank you." Twirled it between my fingers. "There were a lot of poppies on the fields behind my house, you know. Back at home. I always loved the way their red was so ... bold."

"The farmers who worked those fields must've been pretty annoyed by them."

"Why?"

"Poppies are considered a weed. They require a lot of water and dry out the fields they grow on, making the crops weaker."

"Oh." I kept my gaze on the twirling flower. When I went fast enough, it turned into a smooth whirl of red. "I guess that only makes them prettier, doesn't it? To be unwanted and yet so ... unapologetically beautiful."

From the corner of my eye, I saw a violet bloom.

"Is it not sad?"

"What is?"

"To pluck flowers? Humans are always so arrogant towards everything around them. They look at a flower and think, oh look, how pretty, I'm going to kill it to enjoy it for a few hours."

Lev chuckled. "Flowers aren't humans, Antoni. They don't exist but for the purpose of their own beauty. To pluck them and put them in a vase is not to kill them, but to give their life a meaning." Their voice was light and full of ease, confident and reassuring. "We all die eventually, don't we? So, shouldn't we use our time alive doing what we know best? What we love the most? There's no point in being stuck in a field between a thousand others like us and only to survive in an attempt to stick out as long as we can, when we could as well be picked and brought into the most beautiful home, admired by the most beautiful eyes, until our hearts beat their last beats and die knowing that we have been happy. At least for a while."

I brought the poppy to my face, as though to smell it. Twirled it against my lips. Felt its softness. "Does it hurt to cut them?" I then asked.

"It's like with hair. I can't feel it when I cut them, it only hurts when I pluck them out by the roots."

I tucked the poppy into my hair, folding a leg under myself as I turned to look at them. The flowers breathed with them. Up, down. In silence, I reached out and let my hand hover over their chest. Their leather jacket was open, and I understood the use of it now; its thick and sturdy material didn't let the flowers pierce through, unlike wool cardigans or cotton shirts, which too easily ripped when flowers tried to make their way out to the sun. Did now, underneath my hand hovering.

My almost-touch caused small white flowers to bloom along with their wild, spiky leaves.

"What are those?"

"Strawberries."

I hummed. "What do they mean?"

"Why would they mean something?"

I pursed my lips. "Isn't there this language of flowers?"

"Oh." Daisies appeared. "Flowers don't speak. It's humans who attribute ideas to them, but-... No. Flowers just exist."

Existing. Living. Was the difference really only found in the purpose?

The wind blew through us and had us shivering. I would've moved closer, but didn't dare. Lev was already so green. Was it suffocating? To feel so much?

"You smell good," Lev said.

I blinked, amused. "Is there a reason why this should come as a surprise?"

"No." Lev shook their head, softly. "No, of course not. I just ... noted. Because Minush left you because of how you smelled, and such, I wondered how you smelled without the perfume."

"That stupid perfume. If it hadn't nearly cost my life, I'd call Mr C. Baker to thank him for introducing me to you." My smile softened. Or maybe grew cheeky. Honestly, I no longer paid close attention. "So what do I smell like?"

Lev hummed. "I'm not good at identifying-... At naming what I smell." But they turned a bit to their side anyway and brought their face closer to my neck.

I drew in a breath and held very, very still, knowing that even the smallest movement on my part would have their lips meet my skin. I felt as if that would have me bloom into flowers as well. Only when they finally pulled back did I dare to exhale: "And? What's the final judgment?" I cleared my throat. "Ginger?"

More strawberries bloomed. "No, not ginger. Maybe rather something like ... Italian strawflower?"

What? "I have no idea what Italian strawflower smells like."

"Well. A bit like you."

I laughed out loud, and it freed me from the spell that had befallen me just now.

"Also, maybe, a tiny bit like frankincense."

To that, I said nothing. I knew what frankincense smelled like.

Another swirl of playful wind went through us, and for a moment, they closed their eyes, tilting their head back. It allowed me to see the crisp lines of their jaw and the elegance of their long neck past the flowers. Their voice was always so low and rough, but this was such a feminine throat which showed hardly any sign of an Adam's apple. For just a moment, I wanted to reach out and feel the softness of that throat, but because I was not used to this feeling of genuine desire, because I was not sure if this even was genuine desire and not just a force of habit telling me to reach out, I held back. "What's your favourite smell?"

"I'm not sure. What's yours?"

"I don't know, actually. I guess-..." Did I really not? Or was I scared? "I guess the best smell in the world is when you're sitting in your room, doing your homework, and you know dinner will be your salvation. And then the smell of your mother's cooking is spreading through the house, and you know freedom is close."

A fern rolled out, hiding more of their neck. "I remember. This really is one of the best scents in the world."

"I also always liked the smell of—, you know, when it's really, really cold and you come home and someone made you hot chocolate? Or—, Oh! I know! Going to school in the early morning and walking past the bakery with the fresh bread!"

A chuckle shook the flowers. "You truly love food, don't you? Your mother's cooking, hot chocolate, bread."

I blinked. "Oh." I had not realised that. "I–, I guess?" For a moment, I fell silent. None of those scents were something I had smelled since I came here, were they? Would I even know how to recognise them when I returned to Poland? *If* I returned? And would I ever grow memories like these from my time in London? Funny. Perhaps I had favourites after all. Perhaps strawberry flowers would be my favourite flowers from now on. Lev's laugh.

Looking at the white flowers, I thought about the questions for a while, feeling still a little heavier than before. A mere week ago, I would not have been busy breathing it all away. Performing in contrapoint. A hard, old habit. I was breathing now. How did I know I was not still trying to alleviate it all?

Apprehensively, curiously, I raised my hand again to Lev's chest, let the tips of my fingers travel through the green, caress over the white petals, then find a stem to follow to its roots.

Lev allowed me, saying no more, and tilted their head to give me access to their neck.

With the greatest care for them and going only as far as I wanted to, wanted to, I pushed the green aside until I saw skin. The stem I had followed disappeared into it, disappeared deep underneath it. "The roots," I murmured, aware how my breath was just a little shaky. "They're your veins." Like the branches of a tree, exactly like the branches of veins, the roots of the strawberry flowers shimmered green and blue underneath Lev's pale skin. "Or are they inside your veins? Do they go through your whole body? How deep do they go? What happens if-..." I looked at them, but they still had their head turned away from me. "If I were to pluck them, would that–, would that affect your ... heart?"

Their hand moved to meet mine, petalled fingers softly wrapping around my palm. "Please don't pluck them."

My lips parted to say that, of course, I wouldn't, but I was so scared of breathing now; A dark red rose arose from where our palms met.

We stared at it, lips parted, heart aching, full, open, honest.

"Paint," Lev eventually said.

I blinked. "Hmm?"

They kept their eyes on the far-distant London. How long had it been out of reach for them? "The smell of fresh paint. Acrylic paint and water colours, right when the potted paint meets the water, along with the sound of the brush mixing both together, going in circles in the pot. Like that." They raised their hand and began holding an imaginary brush, began imitating the quiet swooshing, scratching, turning sound they spoke of. "That. That is my favourite smell in the whole world." Their hand sank to their lap, and I knew they could not look at or reach for me right now. "I think-... I think that's what happiness feels like."

And yet I felt myself nodding and thought of Jasmine.

• • • •

Slurp.

Sluuurp, they countered.

Sluuuuurp, I tried some more.

Daisies, then they leaned over their teacup, let a deep breath out and: *Sluuuuuuuurp.*

I burst out laughing. "You and me, Lev. You and me, we're meant to tea."

Behind the daisies, I could see their eyes widen a bit as they took in the joke. "What was that?" they asked, dryly. "A pun or a bad hook-up line?"

Grinning, I shrugged. "I don't know, but I'm good at both."

"Is that so." *Slurp*.

"Yes. Are you daring me?"

"No."

I cleared my throat. "Is your father a gardener?" I wiggled my eyebrows. "'Cause you're a flower."

Lev tensed.

"Hey, Lev. You're so hot, I wonder," dramatic pause, "are you perhaps a sunflower?"

Strained silence.

I leaned a little closer. "Am I Donald Duck or what? Because, hell, you're cute as a daisy."

"Oh for f–..."

"You're as sexy as soil, you know. Because you make me want to plant my–,"

"Antoni!" Quickly – realising I was not done yet – they raised a finger: "I warn you."

I crossed my arms and pretended to sulk. "Did you sit on a cactus or what? Because you're really acting butthurt."

"Butthurt! Right!" They were shutting their eyes tighter and tighter now while their voice slipped higher and higher.

"Don't worry. I'm just pollen your leg."

No response.

"But it's true, you know. You're strawberry, berry cute."

A tiny, high sound.

A whisper: "Berry cute."

And that was it. Lev burst into laughter; in the split of a second, they were covered wholly by tiny specks of multicoloured flowers; the scent sweetened the rancid little playground dwarfed by our apartment building with the dogshit in the sand and the syringes in the slides; the sound gave it all magnitude, importance, as though we had conquered far distant lands and not just a 50 square metre radius. We were sitting on a wooden fence separating the car park from the playground and what had once been nothing but a small patch of sad grass in this forgotten corner of London, scrubby and unkempt like the wig of a Woolworth drag queen after a long night, suddenly became the centre of the world to me.

Delighted, I drummed my fingers against the teacup in applause, partly for Lev, partly for myself. "Bravo!"

"You're the worst, Antoni!" Lev exclaimed, but undeniably still laughing. "That's stupid. I'm gonna start looking like a failed wedding bouquet now. They're getting everywhere! Antoni! Stop laughing! I'm trying to be mad at you!" But of course, they weren't really mad, or else the colours would not have been as beautiful.

"Poor Lev. I'm so mean. Can you beleaf it?"

Staring at me, they moved a few flowers around their mouth away to bring their cup to their lips, and, without losing eye contact: *Sluuuuuuurp.*

· · · ·

"Did you just throw a chip at me?"

"No." I grinned.

"And what is that, then?" they asked, holding up the potato chip I had thrown at them. "Eat, I said. Not throw!" They laughed. "You were supposed to eat them!"

I shook my head. "Not where I'm from. Where I'm from, it's a way to express your feelings when the other person, the *thrown-at-er, or* as we call them, the potatee, doesn't allow you to come near them."

HOW TO GROW FEELINGS LIKE FLOWERS

White strawberry flowers. White strawberry flowers everywhere. While I had gone to get us food, they had shaved; it was difficult to believe that just an hour ago, they had looked almost human again. How quickly they all kept coming now. "And what kind of feelings are those usually? The feeling of potato?"

I grinned for a while, at least eight to ten chips' worth of seconds. Something gnawed on me. Lev had said that the flowers didn't mean anything, but did they all belong to specific emotions? The way mainly strawberry flowers came when they laughed? Were they capable of creating all flowers? The apartment made me believe that, yes. But what *were* all these emotions? Was 'laughing' not just one? How could it create daisies and strawberries and multicoloured wallflowers? Today, they had been scared in clovers and cried in succulents. If they were to be scared and cry tomorrow, would they bloom the same? And what about all the other emotions I had yet to witness? Anger, envy, exhaustion, and all those nuances and nameless feelings which fragranted a laugh?

As curious as I was, I refused to force them out. "I wonder what it's like."

"The feeling of potato?"

My chuckle was quiet. "The feeling of ... feeling."

They were looking at me from the side, I could feel their gaze.

I took another breath, deeply. "Something happened a few–... A while ago. I–, Imagine a bathtub, yes? You–, you want to take a bath, so you sit in this nice, full bathtub, and you're warm and comfortable, and all is good. Until–, until someone accidentally nudges against the plug. The water drains! Not–, not fast, not all at once, but it keeps draining. So you pour new water in. But no matter how much you pour, the plug is still undone, so the bathtub can never be as full again as it used to be, and you're–, It's always half-empty and always empty as soon as you stop pouring. And you? You're–... You're always a bit cold now." For a moment, I looked at the white tiles that weren't really there before me. It was such a long moment that eventually, they turned pink. "Love – or any other emotion, really, anger, sadness, happiness and all that jazz – they come, sure, but they never fill my chest enough for me to actually feel it. They just disappear, draining away and making me feel … light. Like a bathtub full of air."

Next to me, I could hear Lev breathing quietly. Neither of us was eating chips now. "Who did it?" they asked, eventually.

"Hmm?"

"The person who tore that hole into your chest. Who did it?"

"Oh." I had not expected this question. I doubt I had ever even asked it myself. "I–," Perhaps? "I think I did it to myself?"

Lev shifted but said nothing.

Thus, hesitantly, I went on. "Yes, maybe I pulled the plug myself. Maybe it was on purpose, maybe I kicked it loose by accident. Those damn plateau heels, you see." I shook my head. "Sometimes it felt like that plug was my heart." I had removed it and placed it into Minush. I brought my hand to my collarbone, felt for this strange new sensation waiting for me there. "I think it was necessary. For a while. It was cold, always, but at least I wasn't drowning in all that suffering anymore."

Lev nodded. "Protection."

I closed my eyes, listened to the heartbeat. "Healing."

It started raining.

• • • •

"Oh, your hair turned all dark, almost chestnut," Lev noted when we had reached the inside of our building and turned the lights on. They looked exhausted. We had run from our building all the way to the main road and back.

I was still a little out of breath, too. The adrenaline of the day had pushed me through the last six hours, but now it did feel a bit like my bronchitis was catching up with me. I wondered if it too had run to the main road and back. "And straight, I reckon. Shows you how long it really is, doesn't it?"

They nodded. "What about me?" Each of their step was accompanied by dozens of droplets falling off their leaves.

I chuckled. "Still very beautiful. Or—, I mean, handsome. Depends."

The doors of the elevator closed behind us, and Lev pressed the button for floor ten.

"I still don't know if you're a girl or a boy."

Lev shook their head - more droplets fell - and laughed - white blossoms bloomed. After looking at their hands, down their body, up their feet, contemplating themselves, they faced me once more. "Well." Their voice was full of mirth. "Well, right now, I'm a strawberry bush."

· · · ·

Minush had not moved from her spot on the couch. She was curled up and asleep, not even reacting when I came home. Only when I touched her, she looked up with a chirp that sounded as though she was saying: 'I'm awake! I wasn't asleep! I don't know what you're talking about!'.

"I'm here to feed you, milady," I explained, then watched how Minush's eyes fell close again as though she truly was a lady who expected no less of her servants. Only after a moment did she begin to stretch and perform her morning toilet. Slowly, peacefully, as though she had all the time in the world.

In a way, she had. Ah, cats.

Once her bowl was set on the ground, she came hopping over, her yellow eyes glistening with anticipation. I sat next to her as she ate, playing with her twitching tail. It was cold in my apartment, much colder than downstairs. And despite both our apartments having the same setup, my apartment felt so much smaller all of a sudden. Lev's apartment was stuffed with plants and flowers and pots and greenery, so wasn't theirs the one that should actually appear smaller? It didn't. Theirs was an entire world, mine was just a place where a couch and a bed stood, where the light in the bathroom didn't work, a corpse rotted somewhere in the walls, and where the limits of my life here felt far too palpable.

My gaze fell back to Minush. I adored watching her eat. Same as for watching her clean herself, watching her sleep, watching her watch birds. There was something incredibly grounding about following a cat go about her day. Sometimes, we'd sit together for hours, I just living my human life, she just living her cat life, appreciating each other's presence in mutual silence.

After taking a shower and replacing the sticky, London rain with the reassuring drizzle of water that could be controlled, I returned to her, bread in my hand and sleepiness engulfing me comfortably. She was satisfied and demanded me to sit down on the couch, so she curled up on my lap for a while. I obliged, gratefully letting her warmth permeate me.

• • • •

"Lev is waiting for me," I explained when my hair was almost dry again. *"Do you want to stay here or come with me? Have a second dinner? Maybe smoke some catnip?"*

Minush licked her snout.

"I don't think they'd mind, no. But let's just ask them. It's just a staircase away, right?"

Minush chirped in agreement and then rose to follow me. Together, we made our way to the tenth floor, where the door to Lev's apartment still stood ajar.

"I'm baaack!" I called, closing the door behind us. "And I brought company! It's gonna be a party..." I looked around. "Lev?"

But Lev was nowhere to be found. My first instinct was to check the tree branches above me. I believe that says a lot about what kind of person Lev was. My second instinct was to check the kitchen. And I believe that definitely says a lot about what kind of person I was.

However, they weren't there either; only Minush was. She sat on the counter, looking at me curiously as though waiting for the promised catnip. In the apartment's darkness, she almost disappeared, she and her dark fur. Upon reaching out to pet her, she meowed and jumped to the floor. She rubbed herself against my legs, then looked up at me before walking towards one of the many vine-covered walls. For just the split of a second, I wondered if Lev had now perhaps completely and fully turned into a potted plant, but then Minush paused, gave me a last glance and disappeared into all the greenery.

I patted the vined wall down. "Lev, I swear, if you're hiding and watching me right now, quietly laughing at me, I will tickle the fucking memory out of you so no one will ever hear about-..." My hand found something. I pushed the leaves aside and found what I had been looking for ever since the first time I had come here: The door to the extra room.

So I had kept right. On floor eleven, there were two apartments. On floor ten, there was only one, fused together by the bathroom and – which I discovered now as I pushed open the door – the bedroom.

Or sleeproom, really, because as I stepped into the relatively cool and definitely very, very big room, I realised that there was a giant wardrobe, a large old desk with an arm chair pushed to it, curtains to the windows, and many, many framed painting covering the walls – but no bed.

There, where one would've been placed, was instead a patch of ... dirt. Earth? Soil.

Due to the darkness, I was blind to all details but still easily found Lev curled up in said soil, alone but for a pillow and Minush, and covered in nothing but their flowers and a thin, simple tartan's blanket.

A flowerbed, wasn't it?

Motionless, I stood by the door. They had told me about the sun, how they rose and slept along to its times, and yet, actually finding them asleep so early in the evening? It was barely ten. I shook my head. What a strange, strange person Lev was. How had I found them? Had they found me? For a long moment, I hesitated, not wanting to wake them up just to tell them I'd leave again, but also not wanting to just leave and have them wake up with a sense of bad-host guilt. And anyway, did I *want* to leave? Did I *really*?

I sighed and walked over to the flowerbed, kneeling down in front of them. Their face was visible and visibly asleep, and I smiled. It was such a beautiful face. The dark brows and eyelashes gave such a clear contrast to their pale skin, even in the scarce light. They looked so elegant, so peaceful, so hurtless.

Minush had loafed up behind Lev's neck.

"*Come on, we've got to go.*" I reached out and scratched her behind her ear, and she bumped her head against my hand in response.

But her tiny paws remained tucked underneath herself, and her shimmering eyes stayed on me in something like defiance.

I chuckled. "*Yeah, me neither.*" I looked at Lev again. "*You can stay. But I can't.*" They had invited me, yes, but I was certain they had not meant to just fall asleep, and the last thing I wanted was to scare them with my presence in the middle of the night. Thus, with great hesitation and an even greater lack of control, my hand moved from Minush's fur to their hair. "Good night." My hand lingered. Then, slowly, my fingers disappeared into the black strands as though disappearing into the night sky itself. It was not as soft as Minush's but rather rough and of a thick, resistant kind, but the feeling of it between the pads of my fingers had my heart beat a little faster all the same. It felt the same way their laugh sounded.

Just like, in this moment, their fingers were as soft as their drowsy smile, when their touch was as ghostly as their gaze in the moonslight. "Hi," they murmured. "The sun set."

The touch of their fingers was so very soft. "I know. I was about to leave."

But they didn't let go of me. "I'm not tired."

I looked at them, at the way their eyes fell close, again and again, heavy-lidded by the sleep I had robbed them of, and smiled. "I'll come back tomorrow, yes?"

"Tell me more jokes."

"You need sleep."

And then, with the confidence of a sunset, their grasp loosened. "I need you."

Surprise washed over me. For a moment, I sat in silence. "What if I don't want to."

"Then I will cherish the memory we have made." Lev had closed their eyes, but from time to time, they'd open, find me, then close again. As though the doors that led to the realms of sleep refused to lock just yet.

"How about a bedtime story?" I therefore asked softly.

With a few seconds delay, Lev smiled, and it softened their already gentle features. "That would be lovely."

And so I nodded and did as Minush had suggested. Quietly, I moved to lean against the wall. With my arms crossed over my chest, I looked at the ceiling and hummed. A bedtime story. I knew so many, but which to tell? Which would my mother tell now? What would my sisters request? I thought back to the village I had grown up in, the stories that spoke of the three great acorn trees by the cemetery, of the river that passed behind the old tavern, and even of the poppies in the fields behind my house. All of them had a story, and all those stories were beautiful. But my favourite one was one that had nothing to do with nature, but was a story of the humans that had made the village what it was today. "There once was-..." I started, licked my lips, then tried again. "Once upon a time, there was a great war in the country, and attacks on the small villages in the region weren't seldom. People would die of sickness, of blades, and of grief. The attacks came in silence, and they were often over before anyone even knew what had happened. Constant fear devoured the inhabitants of those villages, and life had long stopped being beautiful."

Lev, their breath still as even as before, turned onto their back and for a while, it seemed as though their eyes were going to stay open. But oh, they were so tired and their eyelids so heavy. It would've been as though they were deep asleep already if their fingers were not laced with mine and holding on so tightly.

I smiled. "In one of those villages lived a blacksmith. He had once produced bells and small wind chimes, but now that the war had been raging for so long, he was forced to produce the swords for the village to defend themselves. But he was no warrior himself. He did not know how to use the blades he forged, and one night, during an attack, he was killed. Everyone in the village was devastated, as you can imagine. How were they going to defend themselves now? How were they supposed to survive? Fear settled on the village like thick snow in winter. But it was one person in particular who grieved the most, and it was the smith's daughter. She had loved her father, you see, and the love had been genuine and pure, more sincere and beautiful than any love had been in this country for a long, long time. As she cried over his corpse, she remembered all the wind chimes he used to make when she was little and war had not yet damned their lives. She remembered how much she had loved the delicate melody the chimes would sing, and longed to hear such beautiful sounds now, if just to bask in her father's memory in songs of reassurance and comfort one last time." I could picture her so well. Her hair falling into her eyes as she leaned over her father's body, crying him endless streams of a river. "It was then that she had an idea." I looked over at Lev, but their eyes remained closed, their lips parted, while their chest slowly lifted and fell to the rhythm of their breath. "She collected all the metal she could find, the jewellery, the spoons, the door handles, and started forging something. Something big." I smiled. "You know what she forged?"

Slowly, Lev shook their head. "What did she forge?"

"Bells. Two giant, magnificent bells. Day and night and night and day, she forged and forged and forged until her hands were red and raw and her body meagre from the hard work. And then she hung them up, hung them on the highest tower in town, attached a rope to them, and then she sat by them and waited. And when the attackers came, she chimed the bells, and because of all the love she had poured into the metal as she had worked it, it was the loudest and purest sound the entire region had ever heard. Everyone knew it was her bells singing to wake them up, to warn them in time for them to prepare themselves for battle. From that day on, no attack could surprise the villagers anymore. From that day on, they could sleep in peace through the night and grow strong, could focus on their work and families, and know that when the attackers came, they would always be prepared."

Lev was smiling.

"That's the story of how my village survived the war, many, many centuries ago, and why, once a week, we ring the bells to remind ourselves of the safety they brought us."

Lev sighed. It was a very drowsy, very quiet sound, but it was a content one, too, and thus, it did not fail to fill my chest with adoration and something like pride. "That's a beautiful story," they said. "Sad. But beautiful."

I nodded. "It's my favourite. My mother used to tell it to us when we were little. She tells it better than I do, though."

"Why?"

I tilted my head to the side. "Why what?"

"Why is it your favourite?"

I blinked. If I were honest, I didn't know. I had never asked myself this question. For a moment, I tried to find an answer, then I had to shrug. "Why do you ask?"

For a moment, Lev lay silent. Then they spoke, and there was no force or certitude in their voice, but also no doubt or meekness. "I wonder if maybe it's your favourite because you like the idea that sometimes, being protected means you don't have to fight as much. Don't have to fight as hard."

I looked at them through the darkness. My heart felt heavy. So, so heavy.

Their hand squeezed mine, reminding me to breathe anyway.

"Maybe."

We said nothing more for a long while but I knew they were awake, listening to the echoes of that Maybe. Eventually they moved. Turning to their side, they came so close that I could feel their breath meeting mine, and their warmth soothing my cold skin. But they did not touch me but for our interlaced fingers. Not with demand, not with shyness, not at all until they asked: "May I hold you?" and I nodded.

Their body was so small, so delicate, and yet they pulled me down into the earth with them easily, wrapped themselves around me as though they were a vine of which the sole purpose was to engulf, growing around me as though each curve of their body was meant to fit mine, leaving me feeling even smaller, leaving me feeling safe. Their free hand came to rest in the crook of my neck, eventually driving into the soil-caught strands of my humid hair, the other one, the one that was still holding mine, was pressed against their chest, tightly, as though to make me feel the growing of the plants underneath their sweater, and our foreheads met.

I held still. There was a scent of soil, of eucalyptus, and of something very brave, like happiness. I inhaled it deeply and closed my eyes, letting it fill every inch, every corner, every piece of me until I was rich with all those long-forgotten emotions.

"Don't worry, Antoni," Lev murmured, and their voice was so, so close. "I'll protect you."

· · · ·

There was a petal between my fingers.

I could feel it before I could see it. It was just a little wilted, but soft, as though covered in baby powder, and bigger than the pad of my thumb. In my half-asleep state, I caressed it, over its flat side then along its rounded corners, the wrinkles where it had been attached to the flower and where it was now left with a little bulk, one that my fingers pushed to make it stick out on the other side, then push again, and again, and again, busying myself without noticing it. I was awake long before I knew I was. When I became aware of it, my fingers stilled.

I didn't understand where I was at first.

There were paintings everywhere. On the white walls, dozens and dozens were hung up; on the surfaces of the minimalist furniture, they were scattered with no apparent order or purposeful arrangement, some pinned up with multi-coloured thumbtacks, some framed in dark wood. Large paintings, small paintings, some on paper, some on linen, some on carton. The motifs of those paintings were everyday objects, stills of fruit bowls, of richly decorated tables, of the red buses outside, of high, glass-faced buildings, of flowers, of people. There seemed to be no common thread, no overarching theme, and yet they were all connected by one thing: they were all painted with watercolours.

A washed-out, fading, pastel style that used no black lines, just splashes of big brushes and the energy of abundant love. Undoubtedly, they had all been painted by the same person. Something within me told me it hadn't been anyone I'd ever met, though.

And then, my gaze focused on what was right in front of my eyes, and I saw the petal in my hand now. Even lying so close that it was nothing but a blurred fleck of red in my vision, it was of such a bright, flashy red that it immediately gave away the type of flower it had once belonged to. And then I remembered. I remembered it all.

"Lev?"

A soft, soundful sigh came in response. Arms, which I had not noticed around me, pulled me a little closer, and I stifled a happy sigh myself.

"Hello, there," I whispered and looking over my shoulder, I saw a flowerless, entirely human-like looking Lev, hiding deeply in the crook between my shoulder blades.

They hadn't put on their leather jacket again after we had run through the rain, I remembered, but I didn't remember if they had already changed into this hideous sweater when I had found them in the flowerbed last night. It was a large, green thing, so bulky and holey that it was almost a parody of itself. Stems and dried flowers were still stuck inside of it, caught in their attempt to escape, but other than that, Lev's skin was visible again. Their hands, arms, neck, face, everything looked like their habitual self – or at least the self I considered their habitual self. But there was also no blood, no cuts like the last time they had tried to free themselves of their flowers. Instead, all the flowers had fallen from them the way leaves fall from trees in autumn, and they were now underneath us, down in the earth, scattered all over with some of them already buried deep inside the soil.

I smiled. "So that's how it works, hm?" My hand let go of the poppy petal and slid into theirs instead, carefully lifting it so I could turn into their protective hold. Then it travelled over their arm, over the softness of their skin, up to Lev's shoulder, then further to their back, letting my fingers trail down their spine.

Lev lay still. For a long moment, I just looked at their face, at those sharp features in the midst of so much softness, at the curve of their nose, the thin spider-veins underneath their jaws, and the rosy colour of their lips. Eventually, I pressed a kiss to their forehead, and a single, dark blue forget-me-not bloomed on that very spot, large and proud.

Letting out a chuckle, I nudged their nose with mine. "I know you're awake, Lev."

And indeed, as soon as I had said this, a smile curved their lips and, swoop, they went to hide in my arms' embrace.

• • • •

"Have you ever seen it?"

"What?"

"The sun."

With a raised eyebrow, Lev followed my gaze out the window, where thick, dark clouds were looming over the city. Then they looked back at me. "Only images of it in ancient script rolls and on the walls of prehistoric caves," they replied dryly and turned back to their coffee.

I grinned, broadly, and said nothing. It was already late in the morning, but the light inside the apartment had not changed once since we had woken up. Not even a little bit. It was pale and cold and stone-faced like the giants on the easter islands, and if the hands on Lev's radio clock hadn't moved round, round, round, I would have started to believe that we had gotten caught in a time-limbo where it was forever six o'clock in the morning.

Not that I would've minded.

I gave Lev's foot a nudge under the table.

Blinking with surprise, they looked at me, then tilted their head to the side curiously.

I grinned.

They shook their head and rolled their eyes, turning back to putting butter on their toast.

I nudged them again.

"What is it?"

"Nothing."

Now there was a smile on their lips too, but they had it turn into a smirk, then let it disappear.

Both of my feet reached out, catching one of theirs, pulling it towards me.

Their whole body jerked back. "Antoni!" A laugh broke forth, and immediately, I saw something moving underneath the bulky green shirt. With a click of their tongue, pretending to be annoyed, they reached underneath it and cut the flower free.

"A sunflower!" I exclaimed. A second later, the sunflower was thrown at me.

"Stop playing footsies with me," Lev said, unable to hide the mirth in their eyes, not even as they ducked their head and black hair fell into their eyes.

Only with great difficulty did I detach my gaze, directing it towards the sunflower instead. Seemed like there was a sun here after all. In silence, I tied the stem around my wrist, making a bracelet. When I looked up again, I noticed that Lev was watching me. The corners of my lips immediately tugged me back into a grin. "Yes?"

"Pass me the honey, yes?"

I nodded. "I thought we had established you were too sweet for–..." My eyes grew wide. "Shit."

"What is it?" they frowned.

"Shit, shit, shit, shit, *shit*." I got up so brusquely that the chair fell over in my attempt to push it back. "Shit!" I scrambled to pick it up, then hurried past Lev to the living room.

"Antoni?! What is going on?"

"Lenny!" I shouted back, picking up my socks and sweater from the floor, then hopped back into the living room while trying to put it all on. "I haven't heard from him since his birthday party, and I got him into so much trouble! I can't believe I forgot about this. I have to give him a–, fucking hell, wrong side..." I took the sweater off again, turned it around and put it back on. "I have to give him a call! Who knows what stupid lies his father is telling him right now." I looked around. Where had I put my wristwatch? In the middle of the night, I had realised I was still wearing it and had taken it off in ... the bathroom! I tapped the light switch – surprised to see the light turn on – and then paused. My eyes were caught by something.

On a small drying rack, next to a multitude of dark sweaters, I found a thin, blue little cotton robe with a checked pattern. It looked strangely familiar. I picked it up, and it unfolded before me.

A hospital gown.

I knew it was mine.

For a moment, I stood still, then I brought it to Lev in the kitchen.

They raised their gaze to it, confused.

"What's this?"

"Yours."

"It's a hospital gown."

"Yes."

I frowned. So that week George Langston had spoken of, the week in which I had been away... "I was in the hospital?" And as I spoke those words, I knew they were the truth. I remembered it then. The angels of death in the bright light, towering over me, piercing my skin with syringes and talking about me. About who I was. About how I had no papers, no insurance, only George Langston's name in my wallet. I remembered getting up in the middle of the night, in the middle of my fever and leaving the hospital. How I had dragged myself through the streets of London, north, north, north. *Minush*, I had said, over and over again. And so they brought me to this building, and so I had walked up the ten floors to Lev's apartment, my lungs collapsing first, then me, at their doorstep.

"They will have contacted the police by now." And then another realisation hit me. "That's why Georgie was here." He had come to see if I was at home. To inform the police about my whereabouts.

Lev frowned at me, the knife was trembling in their hands. This time their silence was not shy or comfortable. It was tense and pensive, hesitant.

Within me, white flashing panic arose. "And you knew. You know that I'm in this country illegally, you know that if I got registered at the hospital, the authorities will get hold of me, you know–, You know all that but you didn't tell me?!"

"Antoni, no, that's not–,"

"Are you sick?!"

They flinched away from my voice, shut their eyes and fists, trembled against my own raging panic.

"Or are you stupid? Did you not realise that is exactly how they get us? Or do you *want* me deported?! Are you on their side?! Do you want me to never come back?!"

"No!"

"Well, guess what?" I turned and threw the door close behind me, left before I could see Lev disappear behind a thick layer of rose thorns.

. . . .

The stench of rot hit me as soon as I opened the door to my apartment. I ripped the window open. The wet, pale air cooled down the place rapidly but the stench remained anyway, hanging low, hanging in the floor boards, the walls. I smelled it with every step I took. I was pacing. I dressed. I was pacing. I pulled my suitcase out from under my bed. I was pacing. I hovered over the phone. I was pacing.

They would be here soon.

There was so much left to do and so little time. Each passing second slowed me down, each moment of inaction added to the list I had avoided making for five years. I should have prepared, I should have. But how do you prepare for the What Ifs of your worst nightmare? When your whole life is but the attempt to evade this inevitable outcome?

None of this was fair. Had I not just taken a whiff of the first scent of happiness? Had I not just come back to life? Was this my punishment for daring to feel? Or was this, cruelly, the logical continuation of the journey I had begun without my consent? Without my consent? I had to pack. I had to call them. I was pacing. None of this was fair.

And then I halted.

If this was the end, then it needed to be on my own terms.

. . . .

The strange thing with these apartment buildings was that although every floor was absolutely identical to the ones below and above, you still somehow knew when you had reached yours. There was no real, visible difference to any of the others, and yet they didn't feel the same. As though the light was just a little brighter, or everything was moved a tiny inch to the left. Maybe it was the scents from the apartments or the way the silence echoed differently. I wasn't sure. Reaching the twelfth floor shouldn't have been as weird as it felt like, I knew that, but my steps were careful nevertheless. Apprehensive.

There were no signs that there had been a fire here. No dark stains on the wall, no yellow tape indicating where not to go, no doors unhinged or pieces of walls missing. Had they fixed it all already? Or had the fire only affected the inside of the apartment where it had started? Which apartment was it again? I looked around and then touched the doorbell labelled 'Özedem'.

I didn't ring.

I just kneeled and slipped an envelope underneath the door slit. It was Mr Hendrikson's. From that night. I didn't want it. She had been right, a little.

I turned and was already a flight of stairs down, when the door opened a smidge and: "Who's there?" a fine voice called from the other side.

"Pokorny, your neighbour," I replied, bracing myself for possible insults.

"A moment, please." The moment passed fast, and after the door opened, I was faced by a young woman, perhaps a few years older than me, with dark, round eyes and a headscarf that sat slightly awry on her head. She looked much like the woman whom I had met pressing and cradling the baby against herself, but less tired, less worn. "What is this?" she asked, anxiously, the open envelope in her hands.

I hesitated. "I just found it lying in front of your door. I assumed it's yours."

She glanced into the envelope. "I highly doubt that."

I shrugged. "Well. You know. Finders, keepers. Maybe you can use it, you know, to pay off any debt concerning this fire debacle. Or whatever." And I hurried to leave, but the woman called me back:

"Mister Pokorny?"

I scrunched up my nose. "Yes?"

A warm smile had appeared on her lips. "Please, come in."

Something about her smile reminded me of Katharina. It was gentle, yes, but you knew you couldn't win a fight against it. Thus, ducking my head, I walked the stairs back up and entered her apartment.

"Anthony, come here, please!" she called as she closed the door behind me and asked, "Would you like some tea?"

I gave it a meek nod. "But I really don't want you to–,"

"Anthony!" The woman shouted again, and because her Turkish accent affected the way she pronounced that name, it almost sounded as though she was calling mine.

Smiling, I was seated at a large, round table and soon joined by multiple plates of sweets and biscuits.

"I know who you are, Mister Pokorny. My sister told us everything about you."

And yet she placed another gigantic silver tray full of pink jelly bites before me.

"She was very upset. We don't accept charity, you must understand."

"I know! I don't mean to–,"

"But," she said, quietly but just loud enough for me to shut up, "if this ensures our Anthony can pursue his studies, we will not be prideful."

She placed the envelope on the table between us.

"Don't misunderstand us, Mister Pokorny. We will, of course, repay you. Our Anthony—, Anthony, *buraya gel!* Our Anthony will one day be a doctor and pay everything back."

My mouth opened but she gave me a warning look without losing her friendly smile. No charity, I understood. So instead I said: "There's no rush. I'll be ... out of the country for a while."

She nodded, understanding as well. She served me some tea, but I couldn't bring myself to lift it to my lips, smell its scent. So, instead, I reached out to take one of the many offered biscuits, and just as it was on my plate, a boy stepped into the living room. He was tall and lanky with dark kind of peach fuzz shading his face. Still in his school uniform, he had stuffed his hands into the pockets of his trousers, but as soon as he saw and recognised me, he drew them out. As they hovered in the air, his gaze jumped to his aunt, then back to me, before he ducked his head.

I recognised his innocence. Standing, I held out my hand. "Hello, Anthony. It's nice to meet you."

After giving his aunt another glance, he reached out, and over the table, our hands met in a shake. "Nice to meet you, too," he said, almost mumbled it, but even so, I noticed there was no accent to his voice. A new generation, wasn't it? One with a brighter future.

The apartment's ground plan was exactly the same as mine and Lev's, except that just like Lev's apartment was opened to the apartment to the right, this one was also opened to the apartment to the left. There was no doubt that this was a large family, and the mere reminder of how lonely I was made it hard to even look at the biscuit on my otherwise empty plate.

"Mr Pokorny here is here to hear your apologies and gratitude, Anthony."

I cringed. "No, no, no," I shook my head, "please, that's really not–,"

"So what do you say, Anthony?" Aunt Özedem continued, giving her nephew a stern look.

"Oh, you really don't have to," I tried again, but Anthony was apparently too willing to oblige. He'd caught sight of the envelope and understood. A scholar he was, wasn't he?

"Thank you, Mister Pokorny," he said, and it didn't even sound forced.

I paused.

The boy had put his hands on the table and ducked his head so much that I wondered if it was supposed to be a bow. "You are helping us greatly, and we stand deeply in your debt. The investigations are still ongoing, but if we're lucky, we'll get away with only a small note on my record, which, for a family like ours, as you surely can imagine, means a lot. Your life shall be blessed and protected, and if there is anything you need in the future, I vow my life to help you. Please accept this tea in the meantime." It was a bow.

I was rendered speechless. This was definitely the most dramatic family I had ever encountered.

The boy didn't move. He kept his servile demeanour while his aunt looked very pleased.

I looked back and forth between them until I realised I was expected to say something. But what was I to say? That he really, really didn't have to be so overdramatic? That I hadn't done it to receive anything back? Or that I admired their ability to show their feelings to a stranger? I cleared my throat and reached over the large table to touch the boy's wrists. "I accept your vows and promise in return that I won't use them for anything that could harm you. Thank you."

The boy looked up, briefly, then ducked his head again.

Aunt Özedem poured herself a cup of tea as well, and so I pulled back and sat down properly on my chair.

"I hope you know, though, that I didn't come here to bathe in your gratitude. I just-..." I just wanted all this pain to have been worth something. Selfishness is an emotion, too, I suppose.

Before Anthony could answer, Aunt Özedem clapped her hands and let out a gasp. It reminded me a lot of my mother, and it drew a smile from me. "Anthony! Go show Mr Pokorny that you're doing your exercises! Prove to him that his money and time won't be wasted and that you're actually doing something to make him proud."

In silent discipline, he rose to his feet and nodded for me to follow him.

His room was one of those on the left side of the apartment, and to be honest, there was not much to say about it. While the rest of the apartment smelled of spices and was furnished with earthy colours, his room looked like the most typical boys' room. The walls were white, the bedsheets were plain blue, and there was hardly any decoration at all. If there was something to be said about it, then it was the fact that it was very clean. Even I, who had never really been a typical 17-year-old boy and whose room had always been tidier than the ones of my sisters, was impressed by the cleanliness here.

And indeed, on his desk lay a few school books, one of them open on top of various notebooks which were all bewritten in by a small, neat penmanship with no drawings on the marges like mine used to look like. "Wow." I said. "You have no troubles listening in class, huh?"

"I just think that if I'm already stuck there, I might as well listen. Saves time on studying before tests." Anthony explained in a mumble, shrugging a bit.

"Clever." I walked closer to the desk and looked into the open book. "Chemistry?"

"Yeah."

"I was never taught chemistry, never made it that far. I always wondered what it was about."

"I can show you one day if you want?"

Smiling, I looked at him over my shoulder. "I'd love to. Is it difficult? I'm not exactly a smart brain." Even if I had learned many physics formulas just by looking at the blackboards in one of my clients' living rooms, I knew hardly anything about the world of numbers and mysterious graphs. That I had learnt anything at all was probably due to the boredom; I had not been able to sleep due to his snoring. Perhaps Anthony, too, tried to keep himself from being bored by actually studying in class. "It looks a bit like maths."

Anthony gave me another awkward shrug. "It's a bit like maths, yeah."

"I was never good at maths. Then again, I was never very good at school in general." I laughed. "And you are?"

Another shrug, and Anthony's hands disappeared back in the pockets of his trousers.

I returned the shrug with a smile. "It's okay if you're not. I'm not a scholarship-giver who wants to see that my 'time and money' went to the right people, really." I did the quotation mark with my fingers to make sure that I was quoting Aunt Özedem's words without actually meaning to mock or insult her, and Anthony gave me a little, shy chortle for it. "I'm just glad to know I could help ... at all." With money. Still, always, just with my cold, heartless money. "As long as you're given a chance to try your best to graduate, it was worth it."

Anthony gave me a tiny nod and an even tinier smile. There a shimmer in his eyes which spoke of many, many words, but even if they never came, I knew they were of affirmation and pride, and that was enough to tell me that it had been worth it all. There was no recklessness, no arrogance, no disrespect towards his own future in those eyes, and therefore I didn't press further.

"For the future, though: If you want to smoke, please don't do it in your room anymore."

Anthony's eyes shot up at me. "How do you know?"

I laughed. "Didn't until now."

His mouth closed, then he ducked his head again, embarrassed. "It was just a one-time thing. Friends of mine wanted to try it. It won't happen again."

I nodded. "Yeah, I know." How I knew that? Perhaps I didn't. Perhaps because I wanted to believe him. Perhaps it was that shimmer in his eyes that told me. It belonged to someone who wanted to be good. To succeed in a world trying to make him fail.

Give him at least some control over his own future. I held out my hand. "I'll go now."

"Is there anything else we can do for you?"

I laughed even louder. "I think the vows of serving me with your life are enough for now."

But Anthony seemed to hesitate and because he still hadn't taken my hand and it was awkwardly hovering in the air between us, I dropped it, and leaned in a little, whispering: "If you really, really want to do something for me, give me some of those biscuits to go."

Anthony's lips curled into a lopsided grin as he looked at me, at least for a moment, and then he seemed to remember something. I could see the idea flicker brightly in the dark brown of his eyes. He turned away and crossed the room, starting to rummage through a few drawers. It didn't take long before he turned back to me and told me to open my hand.

I did with wide eyes that grew even wider when I saw what it was that he placed into my palm. A necklace. I immediately recognised the shape of the silver piece, the symbols on it, the elegance of its meaning.

"Please take this," Anthony said with an urgency I didn't know how to respond to.

"B–, But isn't this–, isn't this meant to–, to protect you?"

Anthony nodded, looking at me with determination. "But you protected me, so it's you whom I want it to have, so you can be protected, too."

I couldn't take my gaze off the talisman, of the words in the language I didn't speak, of the meaning in a beauty I didn't deserve. As my fingers closed around it, I felt them tremble. "Thank you." I breathed.

Anthony nodded. "Thank you."

Both Aunt Özedem and Anthony brought me to the door, and because Anthony mentioned that I had liked the biscuits, they gave me another giant pile. "This is the least we can do for you. Anthony shall devote his valedictorian speech to you."

"Valedictorian speech?" I asked.

"Next Summer. He's the best in his class, did he tell you that? We're very proud of him."

I paused, then looked at Anthony, who had ducked his head and stood behind her in silence and awkwardness again. His aunt's words echoed loudly through my mind, my body, my soul, and I smiled. "Invite me to the party." I was smiling.

Hurting, but smiling. Feeling heavy, but good.

And then I jumped down the stairs and stood face to face with a police officer.

• • • •

I sat on the curb next to the piss-smelling telephone booth for at least two hours. I did not notice the drizzle of rain, but I did notice when it stopped. Someone was holding an umbrella over my head.

"I lied to them. Told them I didn't know a Mr Pokorny." It had no longer felt like a lie like it used to, but still far from the truth. "They said they'll be back before tonight."

"They told me the same."

So it was true. "Why did you do it, Georgie? Why did you tell them where I live?"

"What?" George Langston's confused face appeared under the umbrella. "I didn't tell them nothing!"

I huffed. "I was at the hospital. I remember that they could find nothing on me but your business card. Then you show up at my apartment, telling me you've been looking for me for a week, have finally found me, and a day later, the police show up. Come on now, Georgie."

For a moment, George Langston just stared at me. "You really are too smart for your own good. But–,"

"Just admit it and tell me why. Have I really become such a burden to you? Or is it because I have a heart again, so you can use me less easily?"

George Langston blinked. Then, at some point, he shook himself and tried to sit on the curb with me. "Antoni," he said, "I did and would never tell the police where you live. Your conclusion is a clever one, and I admire your deduction skills, but you are forgetting a very important detail?"

I raised my eyebrows.

"We, too, have a heart." Finally, his round buttocks hit the curb, and it looked like a dollop of orange paint plopping onto a palette. "It was Richard Leaflet. Apparently, he found you by the river and was worried, so he called an ambulance. When they asked him, he gave them all the details, everything he knew about you, including your immigration status. He didn't mean any harm; he was just trying to help. As soon as he realised what he had done, he called me. That's why I came to check on you yesterday."

Shame. Guilt. Embarrassment. I shut my eyes. "I'm sorry."

"You don't have to apologise to *me* for risking your life. Really, sleeping outside in the rain when you've got a cold..." George Langston scoffed. "Now we have to find you a whole new apartment and–,"

"That's not what I'm apologising for."

Our eyes met.

"I'm a coward, Georgie." I couldn't have been more grateful for the softness that grew in George Langston's chocolate brown iris then. Even if I didn't deserve it. "I'm sorry for the way I treated you. As if you had any more choice in the matter than any of us. I'm sorry for kicking you out after you tried to help. For accusing you of her death when you'd tried to help. For never saying thank you, not once, for having helped me for three years."

HOW TO GROW FEELINGS LIKE FLOWERS

The chocolate brown eyes were wide and I wondered if it was the way they lay on me that brought yet again a new kind of heaviness to my chest. Anchored. I felt as though I was, for once, truly rooted in this world. In the reality of it all.

"I think I was angry that I had to ask for help." I clutched my knees, nails dug into my skin. "I just wanted her to look after me."

I felt the thin fabric of the umbrella come to rest on my head and then it didn't matter that there were tears once again veiling my vision because suddenly there was nothing but the darkness of George Langston's embrace. "I know. She made me promise I would. And still I couldn't do it. Not myself, not you."

I buried myself deeper into him; there is a type of 'I cannot' I had come to know so well over the last few years.

"And for that, I am sorry, too."

Eventually, the umbrella toppled over, and we sat in the rain together for a while, crying.

• • • •

"Hey, bud," I said, breathless, just having come up the stairs, "how's it growing?"

Lev, in the door, stared and stared and stared – and then let out a laugh. Violets bloomed all over. "Antoni, can you forgive me? I was not aware of the consequences, I would have never lied if I'd known, and then when you got mad – You were right to! – I didn't know what to say, I just froze, I–, I'm sorry, I was a prick."

I clasped my hand over theirs. "Not rather a rose thorn?"

Another airy, anxious laugh.

So I added: "I'm sorry, too. I panicked. I wasn't thinking right."

And because I meant it, it worked. The breath they exhaled in response was so great, it seemed to deflate their legs as well.

I caught them. Gazed at them. At their patches-covered hands, their sharp-angled features in a frame of gentleness, their black-and-white appearance, which at the same time was the most colourful I had ever seen. On the way, there was a shimmer of hope, of regret, of apologies, of fondness in their eyes when they raised them back to me. Of eagerness. At the way they so beautifully existed. At how I felt all of this inside of myself as well now.

The new feeling that bloomed as their fingers shyly curled into the hem of my jacket then was not the same as the one for Loretta, but it was similar, and I took a deep breath, allowing it to stay.

"May I?" they asked.

"Please." I nodded, and so they kissed me.

Their lips were as delicate as they were pink, as warm as their laugh, and as soft as the petal of a poppy. They moved in a dance of never spoken words, and stilled for all the feelings that had yet not received a name. Underneath my palm, I could feel their heartbeat vividly, or so I thought because when I pulled back from the kiss and looked down, it was another rose blooming between our hands, resting over my heart.

"I think I'm blooming, too," I breathed, and a laugh bubbled up from their chest. The sound was all small and genuine, all accidental and delicate, filled with a thousand melodies that sang of joy and love and infinite happiness, and it took flowers with it, made them spring all over their neck and shoulders.

Slowly, my gaze climbed back up to their face. I was met by the perhaps most dazzling smile I had ever seen. It wasn't broad or bright, on the contrary, it looked shy and delicate, but it reached their eyes and glistened pink with excitement on their cheeks, and as my heart was beating so fearlessly, I realised Lev had kept right: we were alike.

"Come inside?" they asked.

I shook my head. "I want to, but I can't. I have to leave the country for a while. You see, the police know where I live now. If they find me, they'll deport me, and then I can't ever come back. I could just move," which was what George Langston had suggested, "but I think... I think I want to come back. On my own terms. Properly this time. Start a forever-life here. And for that..."

They understood. "You need to become whole first."

I blinked. It was not what I had meant to say, but I believe they were right. "Yes."

"When will you leave?"

"Very soon. If possible, tomorrow morning, early."

The grip of their hand on mine tightened. "Come inside? Just for a while?"

I brushed my thumb over theirs. "As soon as I'm ready. There's a couple of things I have to take care of."

They nodded, bit their lip.

"I'll be back." I moved to take a step back – and realised I couldn't. My legs didn't move. I looked down and couldn't help a smile. Vines. Twining, green vines had started growing up my legs and held me to where I stood, sprouting out from underneath Lev's bare feet, twining up and around our ankles, our calves, our knees, holding me in place, holding me close to them.

"Please don't be sad," I murmured, knowing I was speaking to myself.

It only had them tilt their head to the side. "Why not?"

I knew no answer.

They leaned in and brought their lips to mine once more, and like a tap slowly being turned open, each kiss allowed more and more flowers to grow and grow and grow until soon we were both totally, perfectly, entirely hidden inside a forest of feelings.

• • • •

I had never longed for a clean pair of trousers as much as I did that afternoon after the chaos of the last 24 hours. Who knew emotions had such a smell to them? The rain had thoroughly rinsed me, but had barely washed the apartment of its stench. Every second the wind didn't blow in through the window was a second in which my wet shirt seemed to cling to me tighter and tighter. My socks smelled awful, I did not doubt that; my fingers kept making tacky noises whenever they touched each other, and because I hadn't even had time to brush my teeth this morning, I felt gross on the inside, too. How Lev had found pleasure in kissing me was beyond me. Gruesome. With every step I took towards my apartment, the more vivid my fantasies about having a shower became. It was a real wet dream, I tell you.

I entered the bathroom and – found myself surprised at the broken lightbulb. How long had it been broken now? A year? If George Langston wanted to sublet this apartment, this needed to be fixed. I rummaged through some cupboards and drawers in the kitchen and eventually found one that didn't rattle, then screwed it in.

The light turned on. I saw my face in the mirror. "Well." I took a breath. "*Hello, you, long time no see.*"

I undressed and stepped into the shower, ready to be fully drenched.

Chapter Six – Let them go when the time has come (next spring, there will be more)

. . . .

I waited.

"*Katharina Pokorny speaking?*"

"*Kasia.*" I smiled. "*It's me, Antoni.*"

There was a loud gasp and an even louder squeak. "*My brother! That's my brother! My brother is calling on the phone, and I'm the one answering. Oh, by the good Lord, what a beautiful night it is! I knew something was in the air, but I never thought it was going to be such a magnificent surprise. What have I done to deserve this? Oh, I'm sure it was the extra candle I burnt in church today. I was praying extra hard for you, you know, and I'm sure you must've heard me somehow, haven't you, Tolek? Oh, I need to tell Maminka that you're doing okay. We haven't heard from you in such a long while, we were all starting to grow very worried, especially Pia. You know how she hates it when she doesn't know how–, Oh! She loved your present! She's been wearing the bracelet ever since she received it, and whenever someone asks her about it, she says it's from her brother, and you should see her eyes! Her eyes light up like the eyes of Koliada himself! Ah, Tolek, I'm so glad you called. I cannot wait to tell them you called, they will be so happy to hear that. Oh, but what should I tell them? Why have you not called earlier? How are you? Are you doing well? You are not in trouble, are you, my handsome brother, are you? You're doing well, yes? Tell me you're doing well, you know we cannot bear it if you weren't, you know we love you so much, and miss you even more, so please, tell me you're doing all right. Tolek? Tolek, are you there? Are you all right?*"

Tears had started running down my cheeks. They were hot and burned with joy. Who knew there were tears for so many emotions? I struggled to speak as I feared Katharina would be able to hear me crying through the phone, and I didn't want her to hear me crying. I had promised my mother not to be sad anymore, after all. Except that, well, I wasn't sad right now, was I? So perhaps it was okay if she heard my tears.

I wiped them away and took a shaky breath. "*I'm coming home, Kasia,*" I whispered, and then listened into the silence.

And there was so much silence.

Then, finally: "*Oh, by the wondrous Lord who aligned all planets...*" A scream pierced through the phone, and with a start, I jerked it away from my ear. "*Maaamaaa!*" Katharina yelled, and there was a knock before her yelling continued farther away from the speaker.

"*Kasia?*"

A moment later she was back. "*Tolek, I call you back, no, wait, but I got to wake up Mama, I–, When?! When are you coming home? For your birthday? How long are you staying, no, wait, who cares, when are you coming? How soon, Tolek?! How soon will you come?!*"

"*I—, I should be there by Wednesday morning.*"

Another scream, this time fuelled by a thunderous laugh.

"*Kasia..!*"

But it was too late, I could already hear voices coming from the background. "*Tolek! Tolek called me and he says he's coming home! He's coming home, he'll be here in three days, Mama, Maminka, Mama, here, take him, talk to him, you got to hear it for yourself!*"

"*Antoni?*" It was my mother's voice. She sounded sleepy, confused, and incredibly alerted all at the same time.

"*Hi, Mama.*"

"*Antoni, is–, is it true what Katharina says?*"

I nodded, and although there was no way she could see it, she knew anyway. Perhaps because she was my mother. Perhaps because she didn't want to imagine anything else.

"*When?*"

"*Wednesday.*"

And suddenly there were multiple voices, talking all at once, and while I couldn't understand a single word, it was their sound alone which brought a smile to my lips and had me shut my eyes, tight.

"*Tolek, are you still there?*" Katharina's voice eventually reached me again.

"*Yeah, of course.*"

"*Mama just fainted, she's okay though; will you call us later again?*"

"*What? Is she-,*"

"*Yes, she's okay.*" Katharina laughed. "*You know her. Please call us later again, yes?*"

I gripped the telephone tightly. "*I can't. I have to do some things now, but-, I'll call you when I arrive in Paris, okay?*"

"*Okay!*" My sister's voice was bright and chimed with excitement. "*Oh, Tolek. I'm so happy. I love you so much, you have no idea.*"

I pressed the speaker against my lips until the familiar empty tooting was to be heard again, and I could finally let the sobs caught in my chest burst through my throat and free this heaviness which had built up inside of me. A heaviness of happiness.

· · · ·

There was only one thought left in my mind when the tears had ebbed away, and as I got ready to go out, it circled and circled around my mind, over and over again:

I love you, too.

· · · ·

"Georgie? I will need their numbers."

He was in the middle of puzzling up a carton box. "Whose?" He perked up from inside the box, saw me. "And why are you dressed? Where are you going?"

"I have a hole to stuff."

He barked out a laugh, then sobered as he understood. "You know that that's against the rules–..." I really think he understood. "I'll write them down for you and leave them by the phone. Don't be out too long. I'll be back by 5, before sunrise."

I nodded. "Thank you."

. . . .

"Antoni!"

I startled and swirled back around.

Mrs Potter was running after me, waving excitedly while her gigantic breasts flopped in all sorts of directions.

I grinned and waited. "*Good afternoon,* Mrs Potter."

"Ah, boy, I'm so glad to finally catch you! How are you, you–..." She looked me over. "You look older."

I gasped and clasped my own cheek. "Don't say that or else I'll have to go straight to the shops for a facial cream!"

She laughed. "No, love, I mean, the way you–... Well, Antoni, look!" She handed me a piece of paper.

"A work contract?"

"Mine!" She was beaming, glowing. "My husband has finally signed me a work contract! I'll be teaching young girls how to write on typewriters! Isn't that exciting?!"

"That's marvellous, Mrs Potter," I said, and meant it. "Things are improving with Mr Potter, then?"

She nodded, and then there was a mischievous glint in her eyes as she leaned closer to me: "I might even go as far as to say that I won't need your services anymore."

I stared at her and then felt my smile grow only bigger. Truly, really felt it without crafting it.. "You have no idea how happy I am for you."

• • • •

He did not hit me this time.

Gently, the arms of the armchair wrapped around me, held me, and, letting out a shaky sigh, I gratefully leaned into its touch. Mr Hendrikson's maid had told me to take a seat in the library. Now, I knew that libraries are in the habit of carrying a lot of books, but upon entering, whoa, I was dazzled by the number of books I found. The shelves stood wall-to-wall and so high that they had actual ladders installed on them. Just sitting here, letting the fire warm my feet, and gazing up at those shelves, flooded me with the feeling of missing out. So many books. Even if I were to read one a day, it would take years to read all the books in this library, let alone all the books in the world. I could spend my whole life in these other people's stories and still not have learnt all the lives and manners to live that are out there. The feeling was awe-inspiring, and I wasn't even a bookworm. How was it for people who actually aspired to be well-read? Were they aware that they'd never be able to be best-read? Were they aware that a life spent reading a book a day was a life not lived?

I shook my head and tore my gaze back to the fireplace.

It was such a cold, rainy day. Reaching the whitewashed house beyond Regent's Park, and I had been granted entry, my shoulders had immediately relaxed into the long, longed-for warmth. Autumn was finally here, wasn't it? Between the fireplace and the armchair, keeping me safe, I was slowly unfreezing.

That was, until Mr Hendrikson entered the library, and the air quickly felt shiver-inducingly cold again.

"Antoni." He was holding himself straight and confident, but his hands were clenching and unclenching nervously. The way his eyes were ever so slightly widened spoke of the same. "What are you doing here?"

"Trying to understand." I didn't get to my feet. Not because I feared my knees would shake, not because I wanted to look up to him, but because I was comfortable in this armchair, and I didn't want to run anymore. "Join me?"

Mr Hendrikson looked at the second armchair, hesitating. "Would you mind coming up to my office instead?"

I nodded. "I would."

Mr Hendrikson's eyes closed for a moment, then he took a breath and nodded. "All right." He looked back to the door through which we had both come, up at a random shelf, down to the armchair before finally taking a seat on it. For a moment, we sat in silence. Palpable, hard, crawling silence. Then he shifted. "I don't know what to say."

"You could apologise."

His breath seemed calm, but his gaze failed to find me. "I don't know how. Nothing feels–, Nothing I can say feels like it's enough. I–, I thought about it. I–, I thought about you so much but I–, I can't–, It's just–, I–..." He sighed, and once more his eyes closed, his brows furrowed. "I'm so sorry. So disgusted. So humiliated. So repulsed. I don't-,"

"You didn't think you'd ever see me again, did you?"

He pursed his lips. "No." His jaws clenched, then unclenched, resigned. "I hoped I wouldn't. I–, I hoped you wouldn't have to."

Yes, that made sense. Why try and come up with an apology when you didn't think you'd ever have to say it? My tone remained neutral. "I learned that running away rarely ever solves things. Your guilt will always be with you."

He nodded. "No matter what I say."

I huffed out a tiny chuckle. "No. No matter what you say. But say it anyway."

Silence. Then, at last, he looked at me. "I'm sorry."

I held his gaze. Perhaps to give him the time to say more, perhaps to see if his sincerity would flicker into a proof of lies after all. But he fell silent, and I knew that he was being honest. "Will you tell me what is happening to you recently? I've known you for so long, but these last few months... What happened, in retrospect, I guess I should've seen it coming. Something is wrong but–..." I trailed off. "Tell me what is going on with you. Please."

Mr Hendrikson's gaze went to the fireplace. "It's my son," he murmured eventually. "He's going to die."

My eyebrows rose while something in my chest twinged. Sympathy and pity. Two more feelings I didn't think I had to reintroduce to myself, but did, in that moment.

"There's nothing the doctors can do. It's only a matter of time now, they say."

I thought of home, and my throat tightened. I pressed my hand against my chest and took a few breaths. Habit; no relief. Soon. I'd be with him soon. "He was supposed to take over the company, too, wasn't he?" I asked.

Mr Hendrikson let out a shaky, exhausted laugh. "Yes. That, too. And he would've done a great job, too. He's–, He's a smart boy, my Feliks." And the fire made his eyes glisten.

I tore my gaze away, telling my lungs to keep inhaling, exhaling, inhaling, exhaling. Sympathy and pity, sympathy and pity, for the both of us. My heart muscles were just strong enough to allow it.

"My wife–... She says we should sell it."

"Hmm?"

"The–, the company. My wife says we should sell it. That we should move to the south of France together. Her, Feliks and me.

That we should just move away and enjoy the sun until-, until it's time to ... part."

I sat still. What a loud, powerful thing to say. "But?" Because there was a 'but', wasn't there?

"But I can't. I'm scared. I'm scared that if I stop working now, I won't have anything to distract me. That I'll just be staring at the doors forever, waiting for death to knock and come in." His hands clutched the armrests of his seat. "I'll lose her, Antoni. I'll lose him, then I'll lose her, and then I'll lose everything. There's nothing I can do. I don't–, I have no control anymore."

I felt it all, wholly, truly. "Sell the company and go to France."

For only the second time today, Mr Hendrikson looked at me, really looked at me. Although the light outside was pale and grey, his face was red with pain and illuminated by the soft tones of orange from the fireplace, and that was how I knew that maybe things would be okay again. Eventually. Softness, in this world of cold, could always be found. If only you knew how to look.

I reached out and took his hand into mine, squeezed it. "I've recently learnt that regret is a heavy and ugly emotion, Radek. Don't let it in, or you'll never get it out again."

With a soft, soft smile curling his lips, he placed his other hand on ours. "I'm so sorry for what I did. Please believe me."

I nodded. "I do."

"But I won't ever see you again, will I?"

I shook my head. "You won't. There's no way to erase the past, not even with sincere apologies. I can't trust you anymore. I might never again. But I did once, and for that, I wanted to come see you and say goodbye. Because if we can't erase the ugliness of the past, we can't erase the beauty of it either, can we? And I want to say thank you for the beauty."

Mr Hendrikson nodded. "Thank you to you, too, Antoni. I will miss you."

"Don't worry. You'll be busy staring at doors in France."

He laughed. It sounded free. "I guess I will be."

For another moment, we sat together and listened to the fire. It had so many secrets to tell, we noticed, its whisper filling the silence with stories of long-forgotten legends and not-yet-happened legacies. It was so young, its death would come by nightfall, and yet its wisdom was fuelled by the universe's atoms, it nourished itself with. Perhaps, I thought then, perhaps I should occasionally pick up books anyway. Perhaps write one.

After I had thanked the armchair for keeping me warm and Mr Hendrikson had brought me to the door, I told him: "I'll be back in London by the start of next year. If you ever need anything, please send a letter. Other than that, I suppose this is an adieu?"

"Adieus are difficult to speak."

I chuckled. "Let's not speak, then." Instead, I went to my tiptoes and gently pressed a last kiss to the lips of Mr Hendrikson, my oldest client, who, I knew this then already, I would never forget. Holding his face in my hands, I looked him in the eyes and smiled.

"Where are you going now?"

"Home to see my family. It's time for me to ... be honest."

"I wish you luck then."

"And I wish you love."

· · · ·

Now. I sat in front of the telephone at home. Who else had to be notified of my departure?

I rang the first number. The sun was setting. He should be done with work now. It rang empty. No answering machine.

For a second, it felt like my lungs were pinching me from the inside out. What was that? Disappointment? Anxiety? I did not allow myself to dwell; old habits die hard.

My finger pressed on the telephone plunger, then dialled Mr C. Baker's number.

"Hello?" It was a young girl's voice. No number, no name, just this tiny voice on the other side of the line.

I blinked with surprise. "Hello? Who is there?"

"Jenny," the girl said.

I hummed. "Okay. Well, hello, Jenny, I'm Ant–,"

"Jenny Johnson," she added, the way children sometimes interrupt you because their thought hadn't been finished yet.

I smiled. "Hello, Jen-,"

"What's your name?"

I chuckled. She was probably even younger than I had first thought. Four, perhaps. "My name is Antoni Pokorny, and I am calling to speak with Mr-..." My eyes widened. Mr C. Baker wasn't his real name, though, was it? I held my breath. Of course. "Say, do you know someone called C-, Curtis Johnson?"

"Yes!" the girl exclaimed, delighted. "That's my papa! Do you want to talk to him?"

I closed my eyes. Of course. I thought of the hut by the beach. The seashells on the window sills. The postcards. The way I had been held when I thought Minush had died in the fire. Of course, of course, of course. "No, dear." I smiled. "It's fine. Can you just tell him: Thank you for the perfume? I'll call back when I want more."

"Okay!"

"Okay. Have a good evening!"

"Have a good-, have a good evening!"

And with that, she hung up.

I stood in the hallway for another small moment, smiling at the realisation of why I had never been allowed to know and use his real name. It had been all for her, hadn't it?

How willfully blind I had wanted to be towards the unconditional love of good fathers.

. . . .

Thus, I worked myself down the list. For five, I got the answering machine so I encrypted my messages according to the specificities of their lives – a task as simple and straightforward as a handjob itself when you've done it long enough, when you've paid attention – but even for the four who did pick up, I was brief and direct. Most were too stunned to say much anyway; only our Queen Virgin gave it an elegant, formidable chuckle and thanked me, perfectly unfazed.

Two, five, four, not counting Richard Leaflet, that was all of them. Only the first name on this list was left now.

I called. It rang empty. No answering machine. I hung up. I stared at Minush's empty food bowl. Then I called again. It rang empty again. No answering machine again.

My lungs were pinching me from the inside out again. After a third attempt at calling him, I closed my eyes and breathed, trying to figure it out. It wasn't disappointment, not just jealousy. And it wasn't anxiety. But I knew it from somewhere. It was an old feeling.

I saw the barn. I saw my younger self's girl friends sliding up to boys on the dance floor. I saw the electricity of teenage touches, ultimately innocent but inherently forbidden to me. Of course. Jealousy.

Jealousy, not for a specific person, but born out of exclusion. There was a life, and I was not asked to partake in it. I was pushed out, through my own faults.

What a surprisingly nagging feeling, too! All while I packed, it kept nibbling at my insides, making me monologue inside my head and handing me a knife, which I either turned towards me to cut me and my faults, self-accusing my unloved state, or outward to threaten the one who had dared to exclude me from his life. I understood now why some people were torn into insanity because of this feeling. As it were, newly reacquainted with it as I was, I found myself almost morbidly curious to explore it. And by the time my little life was in bags and carton boxes, I had concluded that this was a feeling of yearning for conversation.

So I took pen and paper and drafted a letter, titled: *Dear Honey*. It contained an apology, along with an explanation, yes, but also memories and compliments, a description of this emotion in my chest and why I thought it had appeared, a line about how he did mean a lot to me even if, perhaps, we would have never been friends or lovers had it not been for my job, even if, perhaps, we would never be. It contained puns. It contained my signature. Because even if his father found it, he would but find the wave of a white handkerchief, and whether he read it as an act of surrender or a gesture of departure, it was all the same now.

Perhaps that was why I ended it on the line I had removed from all my other goodbyes today: *Let us say goodbye properly one day.* Why? I had a feeling that it was the only way to not just pushed the jealousy onto him, but truly resolve it.

For a while after, I just stood in my apartment and breathed. Mr C. Baker's perfume on me might have displeased Minush, but it did freshen up the room quite nicely, I found. Citrussy.

I smiled.

• • • •

If jealousy yearns for conversation, love yearns for proximity.

• • • •

I wasn't surprised to find that sleeping with someone you loved and who didn't pay you was the same as its opposite. What did surprise me, however, was how fiercely I felt afterwards when Lev lay in my arms, only barely managing to keep their eyes open.

Caressing the pink carnations on their cheeks, I kissed them whenever the black disappeared, longing to look at it once more, just a little longer, longing for the almost exasperated chuckles they gave me with each peck.

"Don't fall asleep," I whispered, and pulled their barely naked body closer against mine.

"I'm not."

"You are."

We kissed again.

"How much longer?"

I glanced at the moons outside. They were rising in unison, steadily, unstoppable. "A few hours."

"And you promise you'll come back."

I thought of Minush, who would be living here until the start of the next year. "How could I not? You have my heart?"

But Lev shook their head. "Keep it. I only want it if it's inside of you."

And we kissed again.

· · · ·

"Okay, is that all?"

I stepped into the elevator, looked back into my apartment one last time and then nodded. "I think that's all, yes."

George Langston, too, gave my empty apartment, which was now rightfully his again, a last look, then closed the door. The light of the stairwell was flat and harsh, and yet I was filled with softness when he looked at me. "Are you ready?"

I shrugged. "No."

He smiled and put his heavy hand on my shoulder, guiding me back into the elevator. "You will be when it's time."

"*Goooood*," the door downstairs wheezed as I pushed it open, luggage in hand, and then: "*byyyeeeee*." when I let it fall close behind me.

I looked at it with surprise.

"There we are," George Langston's voice cut into my thoughts. "Car's parked over there. If you can still fit into it."

I turned away from the door and walked towards the car, my every step heavy with those incessantly growing feelings within me. I opened the doors to the backseats to throw the one bag inside that I was actually taking home with me, and found that I couldn't because someone was sitting there. Someone with big blue orbs as eyes.

"Lenny!" Funny how you can live years without a heartbeat, but how a single missed beat can give you vertigo. "What are you doing here?!"

"I might've accidentally told him you were leaving," George Langston grumbled as he took care of my bag. "C'mon, I left some space for the both of you back there. Scoot."

So, Lenny scooted inward, and with a single gesture of his hand, he invited me to join him. After I shut the door, I turned to him, but he was preoccupied with his fidgeting fingers. It was only when George Langston turned on the car radio to give us privacy that I became unnerved by Lenny's silence.

It felt inevitable, then; I procured the letter and handed it over.

Lenny opened and read it with neither flourish nor hesitation. In fact, it was as though, while reading it, he became calmer and calmer. I was the one with fidgeting hands now. At last, when he was done, he lowered the letter to his lap and nodded. "So that's how it is."

"That's how it is."

"I did think that if my father fired you…"

I nodded. "I know."

"But that's not how it is."

"No, that's never going to be."

Lenny hummed. "Then why bother?"

I blinked, surprised and confused alike, and when I found the courage to look over to him, I realised he had been watching me the entire time. Huh. "Why bother what?"

"Why bother writing all this?" He raised the letter. "Why did you not just tell Mr Langston or leave me a three-line note saying we'd never see each other again? Why all this?"

I hesitated. Even if I had known the definite answer, it was difficult to grasp it. And then there was that look in Lenny's eyes, distracting. "Why are you here?"

He raised his chin a little, quizzical.

"Did you come to pick me up with Georgie solely because you–..." Why was it so difficult to say it? 'Because you have feelings for me. 'Because you like me. ' Why couldn't I say it? Never before had I struggled with clients getting too attached. So what was it now? "Solely because you ... want to take me out?"

"I have no interest in killing you, Mr Pokorny."

Had we been standing, I would've stumbled backwards. Blood rushed to my head as I took in all that was this response. The clinical use of my last name, the brusque topic switch, the fact that it was a pun, the fact that he said it with a straight face, the fact that, oh, was that the glint of a smile in his eyes? "Lenny."

The corners of his lips followed suit now, and a second later, he huffed out a little chuckle.

I covered my mouth with a finger, amused. "You've got me there."

"You've taught me that." He took my hand, brought it to his chest, and tilted his head, almost bowed down a little to meet my eyes. I always did forget that he was so much taller than I. "You're the one to teach me that there's two sides to everything."

And that's when I realised.

"You're right. I'm not here just because I might've fallen in love with you. I'm here because you actually mean so much to me. I mean, for three years, really, you've been my only friend, Antoni. Even if I wasn't yours or–, or will never be again. I'm going to miss you. I wanted to say goodbye because we had a good time. Or... Or I had a good time thanks to you, and I feel like I owe it to you to say goodbye properly. To those times we had."

So he had also known that after his birthday party, things would never go back to how it was before. Yes, that's when I realised: Lenny had grown up. This was still Lenny, no doubt, his eyes still jumped from object to object as he talked, his voice was still ever so airy, but there was confidence in it now. Secureness. As though he had suddenly figured out how to take control of his wants.

Slowly, I nodded. "I think that is why I wrote this letter."

"Then let us say adieu and see if maybe one day we can get to meet each other as strangers again." He lowered his hands with mine in them, and I noticed he had held two fingers over my wrist the entire time, as though feeling for my pulse. He knew. "I can't wait to get to know you."

• • • •

"Half an hour early."

"Good."

"A coffee?"

"If you pay."

George Langston laughed. "I'm glad to see that even after all that time, Little Antoni has stayed just the same."

I smiled but didn't reply. So much had changed, hadn't it?

In silence, I shuffled after George Langston to the bus station's café, Lenny keeping close to me as every sound around us spooked him. Wasn't he brave for having left his apartment for me? Proud. I was so proud of him, and hadn't we been in public, I was sure I would've surrendered to the need to cry some more.

"So, who is this ... thing that helped you pack this morning?" George Langston asked as we sat down on a small round table with too many legs. I feared it was going to run away any minute.

"Lev ... is a person, Georgie." I had introduced the two of them, but after Lev had looked at me with wide eyes and the thought "But I thought he was dead!" written all over their face, George Langston had pointed at his watch, and I had not gone into details. "Boy or girl?"

I shrugged.

"They weren't very–... Uh..."

"Responsive?"

"Responsive, yeah. A bit strange, you have to admit."

"A little, yes." I glanced at Lenny, jittery and jumping at every person that passed us too closely, reached out for his hand so he could focus on that. Then I looked at George Langston, at his clean-shaven face even at six in the morning, at his white-orange hair that seemed as though it hadn't changed in the last twenty years, the white, propped-up collar of his jacket. At the death in his veins. "I might be in love, though."

Both their eyes jumped to me, full of surprise, and I ducked my head, letting out a chuckle.

"Well, by Christ almighty!" George Langston said. "A Christmas miracle."

"It's barely October." My spoon plunged into the white foam of my coffee, dug deep into the cup, then emerged and twirled the foam into a little hat of soft innocence, hiding the black beneath. "I'll miss you, old Georgie."

George Langston placed a hand over his chest, mock-hurt. "I'm not going to get any younger if you remind me of my age all the time."

I smirked. "You're not getting any younger, even if I don't remind you of it. You're alive and living, whether you want it or not. Accept your fate and tell me you'll miss me too."

George Langston laughed and his whole body shook under the sound of it – having Lenny startle. "Of course I'll miss you, you know I will. I always do." And he repeated it again when the bus had arrived and I had loaded up my luggage.

"Are you going to be okay?" I asked Lenny, holding onto him with my hands over his ears.

He nodded. "Antoni?"

"Yes, honey?"

He smiled at the pet name, but I sensed it might be the last time I would use it. "This Lev. They must be the most marvellous person who has ever existed on this planet. If you're in love with them."

I gave it a slow, uncertain shrug. "And if not, if they hurt me, then I'll hurt, and I'll heal, and I'll grow some more."

He nodded and moved my hands from his ears, gave it another nod, then took a step back, let me go.

My heart was fluttering but there was a meaning to each and every one of those hasty beats, and while I knew I had to appreciate and welcome them, they weren't easy to acknowledge, and so I made sure to search for the chocolate brown of George Langston's trustful eyes and find the familiar comfort within them.

"I'll miss you."

"Don't do anything stupid."

"I hope you'll have a safe trip and a good stay at home."

"Don't sleep with children, don't ruin Ismail's future, maybe give him a proper job at The Second's company, hm? And for fuck's sake, please don't do drugs."

"Tell your mother I said hi and have a great birthday."

"Don't die."

"Stay alive."

We looked at each other, and then I boarded.

When the bus started, suddenly, a palm smacked against the outside of my window.

Georgie was running after the bus, yelling.

Hastily, I got up on my seat and opened the tiny window at the top. "What?!" I called through it.

"The two dollars!" he shouted between wheezes. "I never gave you the two dollars for keeping Minush alive!"

I laughed out loud. "Keep them, you fat-hearted moron! I never did do it for the money!"

· · · ·

Three days later, on the train, I woke up from a dream. Or rather, a memory processed.

"I feel like crying all the time now," I had admitted to Lev, right before leaving, when their vines and ferns and violets had refused to let me go. They had replied: "It's okay. Crying is okay. All flowers need watering."

Their words still echoed through my mind as I grabbed my bags and stepped out of the train onto a Polish platform of a tiny train station that held all those memories close for me to revisit, and the small, fragile frame of the most powerful woman in the world came running towards me and I disappeared in her arms.

In tears, she took my face into her hands and told me how much I had grown, how much I had changed, how much I looked like a man now, and in tears still, she pulled me back into her motherly embrace until breathing almost became suffocating in her scent. "My son, my son, my son," she whispered over and over again, and still in tears, she helped me carry my luggage to the bus station and still in tears, she pressed me against her chest as we rode home through those villages that I had once called my present and future. Now they were my past, and the colours were flaking from the doors and window sills, and the walls were grey from pollution, and the people looked small as they passed the bus, and the air smelled raw and old when we got out at our stop, and we were still fighting tears.

Our house was a pale yellow, three-floor high little thing with a wide front yard on which nothing had ever bloomed and which hadn't aged well over the years. It was plain in all possible ways: no flowers on the window sills, no charming paintings over the door frames, not even furniture like cute shoe racks or benches standing around in front of it, and yet no less powerful in its effect on me.

I felt my legs shaking, my hands trembling, my breath hitching, as I followed my mother to the door. Was this my old house, my past, the life I had left behind when this village had felt too small and fatal to me, or was this my home after all?

My mother called into the house as she gently pushed me inside, and before I could ponder much more, a loud, loud scream pierced through the silence of this never-forgotten place.

"*Tolek!*" It was Katharina. Her voice had always been the first and loudest, just like her body had always been the fastest and heaviest, and in the span of a few seconds, I saw her running from the kitchen down the hallway, was tackled to the ground, and found myself devoured by her weight. "*Tolek! Our Tolek made it back!*"

An exuberant amount of kisses were planted onto my face, and this time, I thought I was going to suffocate from laughter.

"*Let him breathe! Oh my God, Kasia, let him breathe,*" the calmest and most mature of all voices said, coming to my help and pulling Katharina off me with an assertive but loving grip. I gasped with gratitude. As I sat up and looked around for my saviour, I heard Katharina and my mother's all-too-similar laugh echoing through the hallway. The smile on Laura's face was just as sonorous.

"*Laura.*" I breathed, taking the hand she offered me. Her hair had always been long and fine, but it had grown since the last time I had seen her, and with her fringe and the way she had braided it today, letting it hang down her shoulder, it framed her face in a golden gleam that reminded me all too much of the nickname I had given her all those years ago: Saint Laura. "Hi."

She held my face for a moment before placing a kiss on my forehead. "*Welcome back, baby brother.*"

A second later, Katharina was sticking to me again. Me and Laura and my mother and all the time that had passed with us being away from each other, squeezing it back together as though to catch up on all that we had missed. I wanted to disappear in this hug, in this idea of timeless love, with no worrying about regrets and guilt, and no worrying about aspirations and survival, in this warmth and heaviness.

But a voice drew me back into the present. "*So. Is it my turn now, or should I wait another five years?*" Five years. Five years had passed since I had last heard that voice, and while back then it had been the voice of a girl, and it was now the voice of a woman, I knew immediately who it belonged to. Pia. My youngest sister, whom I had promised to protect, vowed to live for, sworn to die for, the unwavering, gleaming moon of all night skies. My beautiful Pia.

I turned. And halted.

This was undeniably Pia, but what had once been a sweet, pink-adoring girl with pigtails and a large gap between her front teeth was now – and there was no other way to put it – a punk. She had chopped off her hair and dyed it black. Her clothes were dark, jeans, leather, ripped and worn; her ears, nose and eyebrows were adorned with various piercings, and her features were as sharp and defiant as the gaze of her bright blue, eyeliner-smeared eyes.

"Holy shit," I said. "*You look like you made it your mission to fuck every single policeman yourself.*"

"*Antoni,*" my mother gasped behind me.

Pia had crossed her arms, her eyes fiercely on me. "*And you look like you already fucked every single colour paint pot in a home deco shop.*"

"*Pia!*" This time it was Laura who was gasping. "*We told you to dress properly today.*"

I could but narrow my eyes in an expression of challenge. Taking a step closer to my baby sister, I crossed my arms too, looking down on her, even if the height difference between us had mostly disappeared by now. "*So you're telling me you didn't accidentally throw all your clothes into a mincer?*"

"*So you're telling me you didn't go colourblind overnight?*"

"*Rather colourblind than textureblind. Jeans on jeans and leather on fishnet? Really?*"

"*It's called* I eat Poppers for breakfast."

"*Oh yeah, is Robert Smith your new cook?*"

"*Is George Michael on the menu?*"

"*Pia, please.*" Laura sighed, and my mother was about to add something when Pia's lips finally cracked into a grin because she knew I had nothing else to retort. Because she knew she was right. One glance, and she had understood it all.

I opened my mouth, shut it, and grinned, letting her fall into my opening arms as she sighed out happily. "*I missed you*, Tonton."

"*I missed you*, Peanutbutter."

• • • •

Together, we ate. We drank tea. We told stories, laughed, loved. My mother, Laura, Katharina, Pia, they were all here. But one person was missing, the one person I had run away from, all those years ago.

How long since I had last heard his voice? Since I had last seen his red hair?

Laura's hand came to rest on my arm. I looked at her. She knew what I was thinking. "*He's upstairs*," she said. Her voice was quiet but heard by everyone.

I frowned, confused. "*I thought he was at the hospital?*"

Pia shifted in her corner. "*No one told him?*" she asked, her voice low and rough.

We all looked at our mother.

"*Oh my God, Mama!*" Katharina exclaimed, her mouth wide open in bafflement.

"*I wasn't sure how to,*" she admitted, quickly. "*I wanted Antoni to come home on his own terms, I didn't want to guilt-trip him into coming home.*"

Katharina straightened up, looking from my mother to Laura, then back again. "*Do you think he's awake now?*"

"*He might be–,*"

"*Oh, for fuck's sake, who cares?!*" Pia interrupted with a frown. "*If he isn't, we'll wake him up.*" She pushed herself off the wall and stomped upstairs. "*Come, Tolek, I show you to him.*"

More than confused now – fearful, thinking about every dark scenario possible before even noticing that I was, before even taking the time to gather myself and what was about to happen—I got up too and hurried to follow her. "*Since when?! Why did no one tell me? I thought he was doing badly?!*"

"*You know Mama.*" Pia shrugged. "*She was probably just waiting for the right moment to tell you.*"

The last step of the staircase winced underneath me. It had always done that. "*Tell me what, though?*"

Pia looked at me over her shoulder, a small smile on her black lips. "*You'll see.*"

And I saw.

As soon as I had opened the door to my parents' bedroom, my eyes were on the man in the bed. He was covered by a thick comforter and sleeping quietly in his wedding bed, his olive-toned skin was pale, and his usually fire-red, wild hair was balding from his forehead to the crown of his head – but it was him. It was my Papa. Thin and weak but more alive than I had ever allowed myself to hope for. "Papa." I heard myself whisper.

My heart dropped, and then it began racing. It came back to me now, everything came back to me now: the hospital, the coughing, the strikes, the helplessness, the beatings, the bus and the bus and the train and the train and then the streets of London. Five years. Guilt. Regrets. And so much helplessness with every new message from home, telling me that he was still not better, that it was still not time for me to come home.

"*Should I wake him up?*" Pia asked roughly.

I shook my head, incapable of taking my eyes off the face that people had always said looked so much like mine.

The door closed quietly as I carefully crossed the room, memories and colours blending together, fading away, making space for the only thing I wanted to think about, the only face I wanted to look at, to forever look at, never not look at, ever again. He was alive. He had survived. All the operations and all the relapses, all the additional illnesses and weakening nights, he had survived all of it and was now here, back at home, lying in his own bed. Pale and muted, but alive.

I took his hand into mine and pressed it against my forehead. In gratitude. In relief. In hope.

Slowly, the fingers of the hand twitched and freed themselves from my grip to move to the top of my head instead.

When I looked up, I found the eyes of my childhood. Dark green like a bead, gleaming with life, and with a steady glint of mischievousness within them. Even now. "*Tolek. My Tolek?*" His voice was hoarse, broken, hardly more than a whisper. "*Am I dead after all?*"

A shaky laugh escaped me, and I shook my head. "*No, Papa. We're both alive.*"

My father let out a sigh, and his eyes closed again.

Glancing over my shoulder, I wanted to see if Pia had stayed with me for guidance. But she had left the room, and so I turned back to my father with as much hesitation as eagerness. There was but me, my past and my future now. My mistakes and the consequences.

"They didn't tell me you were out of the hospital."

His hand was still on my head, and indeed, he had not gone back to sleep. He smiled. *"Your mother tried keeping me to herself, it seems. Thief."*

Another laugh fled my lungs as the trinity of gratitude, relief, and hope took more and more space up inside my chest. *"Papa-thieves, all of them, yes. How dare they."* A moment passed, and when my father still hadn't said anything, I summoned all my courage to ask the question I feared the most. *"So, are you back for good? Are you-... Are you okay?"*

"I was going to ask you the same question, my son."

My lips parted, then closed again. *"I-... I'm-,"*

A very hoarse chuckle interrupted me. *"Don't you dare apologise."* A breath was taken, and then my father moved to sit up. It was obvious that it wasn't easy for him; he grunted and wheezed, but eventually, and after batting my helping hands away, he managed to find himself in an upright position. He was holding his side, pressing down on some very young scars to ease the pain, but his free hand had fallen to clasp mine anyway. *"Don't you ever dare apologise, Antoni."* He was smiling again, and now that his heart had been woken up and was pumping more blood, his face regained colour. He looked so terribly alive. *"If it hadn't been for you, I wouldn't be here today."* He glanced towards the window, then back at me. *"Tonight."* I had almost forgotten about that smile. This unkillable playfulness of his.

"But I abandoned you without a word! All of you."

"Did you?"

The day we had gotten the confirmation of his illness, the day I had tried to tell my family the truth. After weeks and weeks of coughing blood, after weeks of kissing boys in secret. No, no, no, I wasn't ready. I wasn't ready to face all my past mistakes, my selfishness, all that guilt that had been the last to leave my chest two years ago. No, I wasn't ready. And yet I could not stop pouring it all out for my father. *"I did. I was so scared that without you working, I'd have to support Maminka and work in the mines, and I–, I can't ever work there, Papa, I can't. I'm so scared of the dark, and there's no life down there, nothing grows, and I–, I wanted to travel and see the world, and I thought if you'd die, I'd never be able to again, and so I–, I just ran away. I'm sorry! I should've helped, but instead, I just abandoned you."*

"Tolek..."

"If only I had told you! If only I had said goodbye. And instead, not one day passed where I wasn't feeling guilty for having left you all behind to deal with your illness yourself, and feeling even worse that as long as you weren't healthy again or–, or dead, *I'd never be able to come back. I couldn't come back because how am I supposed to look you in the eye after what I did?"*

"Tolek." My father had tilted his head to the side. There was patience in his gaze. *"Did you?"* There was more emphasis on those words now. *"Did you really leave?"*

I stared at him, helpless, not understanding. *"I don't-..."* I trailed off.

My father's smile softened. *"I am getting better every day."*

I shut my eyes, continued to press his hand to my head.

"My body needed and took its time to recover, yes, but this was time I had because my son never forgot about us."

"Papa..."

I was shushed quiet. *"Of course I missed you, Tolek. But we live in a world where the warmth of your hugs wouldn't have been enough to save me. And honestly, neither would've had the money from the job Adasiek would've given you at the mine. So yes, perhaps you left for selfish reasons, to see the world and dress like some royal jester, but Antoni, my son, whatever reason made you stay, whatever reason allowed you to stay, with every letter you wrote to us, you proved to us that you cared about us, cared for us, and with every phone call, you proved you weren't ever really gone."*

"But-,"

"Antoni." He reached for my chin, lifted it clumsily so I could look at him, look at the green eyes that were mine also. *"You've always felt so much. Even as a child, your heart was always too heavy for any of us to help you carry it. But I am your father, I should've tried to help you better. I didn't. Instead, you had to leave and be strong for us, grow strong enough to protect us all, and you did. You grew so strong. So please. What is that feeling that you cannot carry alone? Let me help you, just this once?"*

My throat closed up.

"Is it regret? Is it forgiveness that you seek?"

Tears rolled down my cheek.

"You're forgiven, Antoni."

• • • •

George Langston had kept right. The time had come, and I was ready.

Finally, this one last feeling spread, like petals, in my chest, and I was, after all, at last, human again.

About the Author

"I write so that I can one day quote myself."
    --Jey Withane.